those
who
come
after

For absent friends

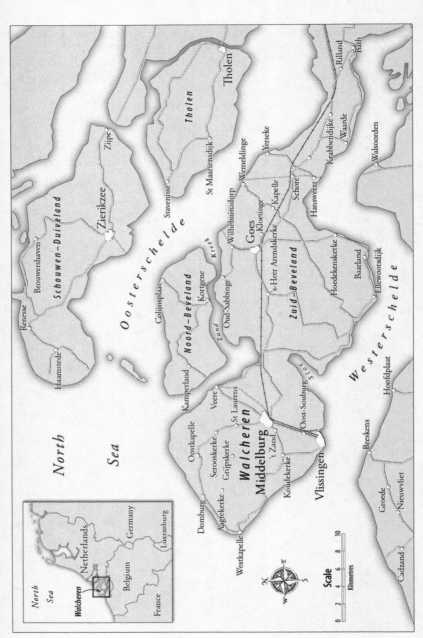

THE PROVINCE OF ZEELAND

Only the last one hundred years or so need to be mentioned.
Lady Katrien Stolburg

1

Land of the Sea

Trains. Efficient Dutch trains hurtling above aquamarine marshes. Past Rotterdam, a phoenix of modernity, risen out of war, and into Zeeland, land of the sea.

At the bottom of Zeeland lies a heart-shaped island called Walcheren. At the centre of that green and sceptred place is a city: Middelburg. The mediaeval battlements coming into view through the first-class carriage window are the stuff of my dreams, the shape of my nightmares.

'*Mevrouw*. Are you crying?' An elderly woman is peering at me through round, gold-rimmed glasses. Her skin is a creamy parchment, her eyes vivid as clouds.

'I haven't been home for a long time.'

'*Ach zo*,' the woman says. 'What is your name, dear? Perhaps I know your family.'

'Stolburg,' I whisper. 'I am Juliana Stolburg.'

'*Ach*. Lady Katrien is dead, then.'

The train crawls into the station along one of two tracks leading in and out of Middelburg.

'See, dear?' The woman's glasses twinkle. 'The flags are at half-mast.'

I watch as she unshackles her bike from the rack and rides over the bridge and across the great canal that bisects the island. She waves to me from the other side then disappears into the city.

I have returned to Middelburg, in the south-west Netherlands, on a Sunday. Church bells are ringing. Carillons for the Catholics, dour notes for the Calvinists and, beyond those, a single mourning bell sounding at one-minute intervals.

★

Two nights ago I was leaning out the window of our apartment in the Kirchberg, overlooking Luxemburg. The air was so electric with possibilities I heard the conversations on the concourse fourteen storeys below. I thought I heard Mama's voice.

'Truly I have lived through dark times.'

She was so close I could smell her lavender scent, Boldoot, the only perfume considered suitable for women of our Calvinist sect. I heard the impatient tap-tapping of her high heels on the parquetry floor and a door closing . . .

My husband Oscar is in the next room, swearing

as he trips over hurriedly packed boxes. I should be getting dressed. But I want a final look at Luxemburg's fiery autumn colours.

'Come on, Jules. We'll be late for the opening. You're still in your dressing gown.' He turns to the stereo and places Mahler's Fifth on the turntable. Smiles. 'One last time.'

One last time, the opening chords of Mahler's funeral march echo round our apartment. Across the gorge and below the citadel, where the palace, casino and government buildings are, the sunset touches the treetops.

'Look, Oscar. The tips of the trees. It's as if the citadel's burning.'

'For God's sake, Jules. Get dressed.'

The cathedral bells of Our Lady of Luxemburg have begun their summons to the faithful. A boy's voice of purity and youthful vigour – *Hear us, O Lord! Hear us* – is about to have a dialogue with a mighty organ.

But not for our ears.

With a harsh scrape Oscar tapes the lid of a box shut and writes AUSTRALIA on the address bar.

'My father never called Australia home,' I say.

'What?'

'I wish we weren't going to this exhibition. I'd rather be at the cathedral to hear *the voice*.'

'Everybody who is anybody will be at the exhibition.' He sighs. 'I'd rather be at the cathedral, too. I doubt we'll ever hear the likes of *the voice* again. Now come on, Jules. Show them you don't give a damn.'

In the lift on the way down Oscar checks my make-up and dress. I've put on weight recently and hate putting stress on the seams. Mama knew all about seams. 'At the seams,' she said, 'is where everything falls apart.' When I buy clothes I always test the strength of the seams.

Outside, the concourse throngs with Eurocrats headed for the exhibition opening. 'Juliana! Just heard. The Skippies have recalled you. Will there be another European posting?'

'I'm retiring. We are going back.'

The evening has turned crackling, humid. Soft drizzle casts a damp spell over everything. Oscar holds an umbrella over my head.

'Good grief,' he says. In front of us, squashed and demented and just completed, is the Musée d'Art Moderne. 'A pyramid. In Luxemburg. What was the architect thinking? That thing's going to slide into the gorge.' He looks longingly at the building next door, the Philharmonie, whose whirlpool shape provides almost perfect acoustics, despite initial predictions. 'I'll miss the whirlpool.'

Everybody, it's true, is at the MUDAM. Everybody from the diplomatic corps, the government, the banks, the insurance industry, the European Union. And my lot, the intelligence arm of the North Atlantic Treaty Organisation, NATO. The frantic exchange of kisses turns the air moister still.

'Juliana! Bloody Skippies. Are you devastated? The MUDAM is to be all installations, you know. Hung paintings are so last year.'

The habits of a profession are not shed within the life of one short sentence. Once inside, and without appearing to do so, I study the exits. I note the positioning of the security staff. I keep an eye on people of interest, although ever since East Germany reunited with the west and the Russian bear caught a capitalist fever, those of us who were once of interest to each other are now no longer interesting to anyone except ourselves.

In the centre of the Grand Hall is a steam train. Poised precariously on its roof is a washing machine. Other odd contraptions hang from the engine, making grinding and gurgling sounds. Oscar takes one look, raises both eyebrows, utters another *good grief* and stalks off. When he meets someone he likes, his head bobs down. Otherwise he stares at people along the length of his broad nose. From time to time he circles back. 'Do you think we could leave, Jules? Catch *the voice*, after all?'

'The grand duke hasn't arrived yet.'

A white spotlight flips onto a famous Luxemburg chef. She is climbing a ladder fixed to the side of the steam train. Plates of food are passed up to her. She takes the plates and hurls them into the washing machine.

'I wonder,' murmurs a man's voice in my ear, 'how she was persuaded to do this for the sake of art?' The voice is light and familiar, part Belgian, part Dutch. It belongs to the only person in the room taller than Oscar.

'If you say, Monsieur, that you've heard the Skippies have recalled me, I will kill you,' I say to the grand duke.

He laughs and gives me the three times kiss of the Dutch. A sickly, suspiciously sweet smell rises out of the train's rear end. Black sausage-like shapes plop onto the white marble floor.

'Turds!'

The stench builds and builds. The famous chef, still mounted on the train's roof, manages a stoic smile while loading one exquisitely presented dish after another into the washing machine.

'How ever,' the grand duke asks, 'will we eat at her restaurant again?'

From up high, a sail is unfurled: *Cloaca by Wim D*. Wim D, the Belgian artist responsible, is standing before us with a microphone. 'It has to do with shit,' he bellows. 'Shit.'

People scurry for the exits. Wim D's shouting words chase them across the plateau. '*Shit. Shit. Shit.*'

The grand duke taps me on the arm. 'Sorry about your aunt.'

'My aunt?'

'Haven't you read today's *Volkskrant*?'

'Good evening, Monsieur.' Oscar emerges from the scattering crowd, his head bobbing. They shake hands. Police on motorbikes are waiting to usher Monsieur into his Mercedes and back to his chateau.

'Let me know, Juliana, if there is anything I can do . . .' With that, the grand duke disappears in a shower of flashing blue lights.

'My aunt is dying,' I say to Oscar.

On the walk back to our apartment, and then on the ride up in the lift, Oscar does not look at me. My job has often required me to be absent, sometimes for months. I never have any trouble recalling the difficult angles of his long body, his sexy nose, the upside-down smile that boomerangs down his chin, all the permutations of his penis. But I can never quite recall the colour of his eyes.

'Too late to catch *the voice*,' he says, opening the door.

Three issues of the *Volkskrant*, the Dutch daily newspaper, are sitting on a taped-down box. I had planned to read them on the plane to Australia. I pick up today's and turn to page three.

Lady Katrien Stolburg dying

The press office at Paleis Noordeinde, The Hague, announced today that the Lady Katrien Stolburg, who has served the royal household since 1920 as lady-in-waiting to Queen Emma, Queen Wilhelmina, Queen Juliana and Queen Beatrix, is dying in a hospice at Wassenaar.

Katrien, born at Middelburg in 1900, is the only daughter of Count Siegfried Stolburg, known as the 'Lord of the Islands', and Françoise, Lady Stolburg. Katrien has two brothers. The eldest, Justien, was murdered in 1945. The youngest, Jack, was the famous wartime Resistance leader known as 'Spanish Jack'.

Jack Stolburg, his wife Janna and their daughter Juliana left the Netherlands for Australia in 1959 . . .

I ring The Hague. Katrien's alive. The comptroller of Queen Beatrix's household tells me the name of the hospice and urges me to hurry.

Oscar is cradling a cup of cocoa. 'I suppose you'll have to go. I'll cancel your flight. I could come with you, if you want.' His legs are spread wide. Tie pulled to one side. The apartment is packed. Emotionally, he is already on the plane.

'Better if I do this alone.'

Oscar accompanies me to the train station next morning. He organises the ticket. 'You won't want a return.' He takes a couple of shallow breaths. 'I'll give the key to the concierge. The food in the fridge . . .?'

'Leave the food for the maid.'

'Yes. Good. You'll ring of course, Jules?' Oscar dislikes hugging and kissing in public. He bends down from his great height, lands a smacking kiss near my ear and strides off before the train has left the station.

There's a discarded *Volkskrant* on one of the seats. The crowd stampeding out of the Cloaca exhibition has made page one. A few pages on, the grand duke expresses regret at the imminent death of his distant cousin, Lady Katrien Stolburg. 'Like me,' says the grand duke, 'Katrien can trace a direct descent from the emperor Charlemagne.'

A small paragraph in the diplomatic section of the paper makes mention of an Australian Department of Defence attaché, Juliana Stolburg, being recalled after eight years' service in Europe. No connection is made between one Stolburg and the other.

Luxemburg's velvet-green wealth fades fast the moment you reach Belgium and the province of Wallonia. Ramshackle, unattended stations front deserted towns. I catch a Dutch train at Brussels. '*Bonjour, goeden middag, good afternoon,*' says a ticket inspector at the border crossing, sliding the merest glance at my piece of paper.

'What about a German greeting?' a German tourist pipes up.

'*Heil Hitler,*' mutters the inspector.

At The Hague, armed policemen and women patrol the station in pairs. A skinhead barks in the face of a heavily veiled woman but the police officers don't seem to notice as he trots straight past them, eyes to the ground.

Driving through manicured, upper-class Wassenaar, the taxi driver points out the mansion behind a high fence where the Prince of Orange and his family live, shunning the many palaces at their disposal.

A desk clerk guides me down the wooden-floored halls of the hospice. Some of the doors have nameplates for long-term residents. Katrien is behind a blank door. 'She is not often conscious,' the desk clerk says. 'And has refused all medication. A hundred and five, you know.'

My aunt is a skeleton. Bones and sinews poke out of her hands. Her body barely makes an impression on the mattress. The long, thin face is as I remember: high cheekbones, bloodless lips, sparse white hair drawn away from a domed forehead. She is asleep, perhaps unconscious. A television murmurs nonsense in the background. In the bathroom are fluffy towels and spicy soaps, a bottle of Boldoot on the shelf. I unscrew the cap and smell all the women of my childhood.

Katrien's jewellery is in a bowl. I recognise a diamond bracelet, a gold watch. Her bible, presented to one of our ancestors by John Calvin, lies open at Ecclesiastes. I ease it shut and stroke the Stolburg coat of arms: a gold lion wearing a crown studded with rubies. From between bared fangs the lion's curling, purple tongue warns potential enemies that here is a creature who leads a fearsome dynasty.

Katrien stirs. She is mumbling something.

'*Tante*,' I say. 'It's me, Juliana.'

Cold blue eyes register my presence. A corner of her mouth lifts.

'*Hoe is't in't vreemde land? Nog steeds vreemd?*'
What is it like in that strange land? Still strange?
'Yes.'

'Jack was never happy in that country.'
'No.'

'Nice of you to come from such a long way away.'

I wonder if she means Luxemburg or Australia. Her mouth moves silently. Afraid she will fall back into unconsciousness, I reach for the bible. Forty-five years since I heard Ecclesiastes in Dutch, yet I slip into the rhythms I learnt as a child.

We will fall into the hands of the Lord, and not into the hands of men . . .

'You read well.' Katrien's voice is strong. 'Your mother spoke beautifully, but you have the same timbre as your father. *Ach, lieve Jack.*' Tears half a century late trickle down her cheeks. She sleeps.

I doze as well, in an armchair beside the bed. When I wake a woman is thrusting a tray of soup and bread at me. The red–gold branches of a pin oak tap on the window. The afternoon is closing in. A nurse puts a stethoscope to Katrien's barely moving chest. There are no drips, just a catheter depositing the occasional drop of urine into a bottle. My aunt is starving and dehydrating to her death.

'I hear you do some writing now.'

Her voice is straining. I wet her lips.

'Little stories,' I say. 'Some poetry. Government reports.'

'*Ach*, you should write the Stolburg story.'

'The whole thousand years?'

Katrien's eyes focus on mine. 'Only the last one hundred years or so need to be mentioned. Tell them about your mother and Jack.'

She's struggling for breath.

'Australia . . .'

She's rummaging in the attic of her mind for the final crumbs of our family history. In the bottle beneath her bed, the catheter deposits another drop of urine.

'The Japanese connection need not be dwelt on,' she says, imperious to the end.

Outside, there is movement in the pin oak: a pair of jackdaws, squabbling, their antics throwing dying leaves to the ground. When I look back my aunt has gone. Only her corpse remains.

★

The wheels of the hospice bureaucracy move quickly. With Katrien's dead body still in the room, I pack her belongings, leaving her nightclothes for the staff to dispose of. There are no day clothes.

A knock at the door: a distinguished-looking man, a courtier, in an expensive suit. As the body is wheeled out he gives the trolley a half-bow.

'One understands she has left you everything. There are complications. Death duties and so on. You may be quite well off. I will drive you to your aunt's lodgings and give you some moments to, ah, collect some items that may be of interest.'

He has not introduced himself and does not speak as we glide past signs pointing to the beach resort at Scheveningen. We enter Paleis Noordeinde from the rear, through gates of black and gold, which he opens with a remote control. 'I thought the, ah, stables entrance.'

The Queen's flag is not flying. Beatrix must have gone to one of her other homes for the weekend. The car purrs through woodland, past stables and garages.

'All palaces are the same, aren't they?' says the courtier. 'Magnificent at the front, a mess at the back.'

We negotiate a series of rubbish bins to reach a courtyard surrounded by small cottages. In front of each cottage is a square of lawn and a garden seat. 'The old ones sit out here for the sun.' The courtier nods towards one cottage, as nondescript as all the others, and produces a key. Opens the door. Switches on a light. 'Your aunt had other quarters at Paleis Het Loo, but as that's a museum now, it might be, ah, difficult. I will return for you later, yes?'

This is Katrien's grace-and-favour cottage. Peeling plaster. Fading carpet. Two rooms up, two rooms down, and one of the upstairs rooms is empty. Her bed has been moved downstairs. Furniture has been pushed to the walls to accommodate it. I switch off the harsh overhead light and turn on a lamp. A cloud of dust rises when I sit on the couch. I try to imagine the room without the bed.

The Dutch word that uncoils in my mind from half a century ago is *kachel*: stove. In the winters of my childhood every room had a coal-burning kachel with small windows. Behind the windows flames danced and created fiery dreams. The kachels I grew up with had long brass handles, so brightly polished I believed they were made of gold. The brass handle on Katrien's kachel is dull, and greasy to the touch. Inside are two boxes. The first is a document box containing a will leaving 'everything' to me but not detailing what everything consists of. The other box is a dome-topped coffer. I rub my hand across the mane of the sprawling gold lion. This lion has lost the tip of his purple tongue.

Poor old fellow; there's only me now.

I hesitate. I know without looking what's inside the coffer: a five-strand choker of black pearls. Clipped onto the necklace is a single gold rose, and in the middle of that a blood ruby. Underneath is a separate compartment, and I know what that holds, too: a three-metre string of black pearls, to be wound around the neck and draped down the bosom. I have never put it on before. In front of a dusty mirror I slip the long strand over my shoulders. I have to wind it around my neck several times to avoid tripping. Katrien was taller than me. When she stood erect the necklace did not reach the ground.

How I longed as a child to touch the pearls, to feel if they were as silky as they looked. Sometimes, my hands, as if of their own volition, would edge stealthily toward the necks of my grandmother and aunt. 'Look, don't touch!' they'd cry, and just as my hands got close they'd be wrenched away. My grandmother wore the choker, while my aunt wore the long string. Mama loathed both. She preferred cheerful jewellery, diamond brooches and multicoloured bracelets that sang silly songs.

Once there was also a ring, a cornelian set into a coronet, which the emperor of Japan gave my grandmother when she married my grandfather in Nagoya in 1899. The ring was stolen in Australia in 1975. Irrationally, I feel for it among my dead aunt's belongings, knowing it cannot possibly be there.

The courtier does not return. I lie on Katrien's bed, thinking I'll rest for an hour. When I wake it's dawn. I don all the parts of the black pearl suite over my jumper, and slip diamonds and emeralds on my fingers. Wearing a fortune in jewellery under my coat and gloves, I walk through the palace courtyard and back past the rubbish bins. I don't know what I'll do if the gates are locked.

As I approach they swing open for a carriage and four horses. One of the groomsmen hops down and

holds open a side entrance for me. My mobile rings
– Oscar, no doubt.

'Ah, Lady Juliana.'

It is the courtier. To hear myself called Lady is a
shock.

'The matter of your aunt's last wishes could take
some time to sort out. Perhaps, ah, years. One hopes
you found what you were looking for. *Tot siens.*'

The rear of the palace is adjacent to a poor Muslim
area. Women in headscarves emerge from rundown
apartment buildings, clutching their robes close to
their bodies to avoid the mouldering rubbish. They
keep their eyes fixed on pavements made treacherous
by the bulging roots of English plane trees.

In the *binnenstad*, or inner city, Middelburg's narrow
streets of tall houses feel as claustrophobic as I
remember. The doors to the Oostkerk – the Calvinist
church where my family once worshipped – are
about to close. The church has a central area where
ordinary congregation members sit, and tiers for
those who can afford to buy family pews. For three
hundred years my ancestors perched in the most
prominent pew, convinced of their piety, assured of
their superior social status.

Instinctively I head for our pew. Sitting there is a
woman and a little boy. How vain, to suppose that after
half a century's absence there is a place for me in this
house of worship. The little boy's feet kick out with
boredom. His mother's hand rests across his legs.

From the lectern, the *predikant* thunders, 'The Lady Katrien Stolburg is dead. Pray for her soul.'

Hear us, O Lord! Hear us.

'Katrien,' he continues, 'was the last Stolburg.'

A verger whispers in his ear. The predikant buries his chin in the stiff white ruff around his neck.

'*Neem mij niet kwalijk.*'

The phrase he has uttered is almost untranslatable; it means, roughly, *Don't hold this against me.*

He coughs. 'It seems the niece, Juliana Stolburg, is with us. Welcome Juliana.'

'Welcome Juliana,' the congregation intones without passion. The boy in our pew plays with his tongue behind his lips, as if he would like to point it at me.

When the service is over I thank the predikant for mentioning my aunt before God, but hurry away before he can engage me in conversation. Tubs of flowering geraniums and orange cotoneaster clutter the ancient streets near the church. The front doors of the towering houses are painted a uniform black. Where curtains are pulled aside, gleaming windows reveal prosperous interiors.

The Stolburgs lived within walking distance of the Oostkerk on a street called the Heerengracht, the gentleman's neighbourhood. Around a bend in the road are my parents' and grandparents' houses. I had forgotten how big my grandparents' home was: four storeys high, and extending to the street behind, with a mountain of marble steps leading up to the black front door. Below street level is a basement area where the servants lived. Under the roofline, the date of construction, 1743, has been picked out in gold.

The much plainer house across the street, built in the 1690s, belonged to my parents. Both homes bear plaques declaring them to be of historical interest. The plaques do not mention that they are resewn versions of the originals, approximations of what they looked like before the war.

A short walk from the Heerengracht is the *markt*, the great town square, and facing onto that is the Stadhuis, the gothic palace from which the rulers of Zeeland governed the province for six hundred years. On Sundays after church my parents and I would dine at the café opposite the Stadhuis. Food and alcohol could not be served until the Protestant God allowed. As it was then, so it is now. A waiter takes my order. But my lunch cannot come until the church bells ring.

The November day is warm enough for me to sit outside. In the Novembers of my childhood, I waded to school through snow and ice, in winds so fierce they whistled through the holes once occupied by my baby teeth. My parents chose this café, perhaps this very table, so that Papa could check the rebuilding of the Stadhuis. 'See here, Janna! Here, Juliana! There used to be an extra course of bricks below that third window on the eastern side. *Ach*, these builders don't know what they're doing.' Propped against his glass of gin would be a pile of pre-war photographs. He'd compare them with the reconstruction taking place before his eyes.

Two photos he referred to again and again. One, taken in 1939, shows the Stadhuis looming over a bustling market. The chaotically cheerful bunting and canvas provide a perfect counterpoint to the building's gothic symmetry. On the back of this snap Papa wrote:

Zo was het voor de oorlog. Nu is alles verwoest.

This is how it was before the war. Now everything is destroyed.

Verwoest, however, means something more than mere destruction: the sense that a page in a dark night of history has been turned in a book that can never be reopened.

The other photograph Papa cherished was one of Mama standing in front of the Stadhuis ruins. It was taken the morning of 18 May 1940, the day after the German Luftwaffe reduced the city of Middelburg to a wasteland. Mama is looking not directly at the camera but into a distance she was yet to experience. A place called Dachau.

Without fanfare or witnesses, my aunt Katrien is cremated. Instructions regarding the disposal of her ashes have been left with her *advocaat*. Advocaat is the Dutch word for lawyer and the name of a popular liqueur made from egg yolk and gin. The women of my mother's generation drank this potent drink, convinced that the alcohol content was not so great.

A *notaris*, or notary, shares rooms with the advocaat. This place of business was once a family home. I remember when these streets thrummed with the noise of children playing games and bicycle bells ordering pedestrians out of the way. The notaris shows me pictures in a lifestyle magazine of his renovated house. 'An old place the wife and I bought cheap. Barn makes a great garage. See that leather couch? Scandinavian.'

He wants me to sign some documents pertaining to my inheritance.

'Can't I sign these after I've met with the advocaat?'

'You can do, I suppose.'

The advocaat's office is glass and steel, the chair to which I am assigned unforgiving.

'*Zo*, diplomat, eh? No doubt the reason you didn't sign the papers the notaris wanted you to sign.' He turns away from me. '*Zo*, come in, *meneer*.'

The courtier I met at The Hague enters the room. He bows. 'Lady Juliana.'

'The Lady Juliana has not signed the papers,' the advocaat says. 'Diplomat. What exactly was it you did in Luxemburg?'

'I slipped between the languages spoken within the NATO sphere of influence.'

'The Skippies, um, Australians, interested in NATO, are they?'

'We have been a signatory to various agreements since the 1950s. Australian soldiers are presently serving alongside the Dutch in Iraq.'

'Ah,' the advocaat and the courtier say in unison.

'*Zo* . . . Iraq . . . She will want to know what she has inherited. And, ah, the death duties.'

'You know, of course,' the advocaat says to the courtier, 'that no death duties were paid when the father died in Australia in 1962?'

'Really?' The courtier feigns surprise. 'They wouldn't be backdated to that time, would they?'

'They could be.'

I look at the courtier. 'Why are you interested in this matter?'

'Instructed, ah, to be helpful.'

'Also,' the advocaat continues, 'there is the question of citizenship should you wish to accede to the titles and properties.'

'As a diplomat I could not serve two masters. I do not have dual Dutch–Australian citizenship. But I was born prior to 1949, to a Jewish mother, therefore the special considerations of the Dutch Nationality Act apply to me.'

'Ah.' The men shake their heads. 'She's checked it all out.'

'Please give me the documents relating to my inheritance.'

The advocaat splutters. 'You must understand. Ancient properties. History has to be respected.'

'The documents, please.'

A call is put through to the notaris. He is waiting outside. A small packet of papers is handed over.

The courtier has been silent for a few moments. 'The Japanese connection. Ah, delicate matter.'

'Your aunt's ashes,' says the advocaat. 'Where do you want those?'

'I will let you know.'

'Will you sign the papers now?'

'Not until I know what I am signing.'

'You must make a will. Decide who is to succeed you, Lady Juliana.'

'I am the last.'

The windows of the Rue du Commerce, the hotel at which I am staying, have been done up with red canopies to suggest a Parisian frisson. Wood panelling and cheap chandeliers adorn the bar and dining room. Nothing that's left gives any hint of the hotel's wartime connections.

Before we left for Australia, Papa showed me all over this hotel. He wanted me to see the basement rooms where the Zeeuws Resistance lodged during the war. He laughed as he told me that by the time the Luftwaffe was finished with Middelburg, the German high command hadn't left themselves a building grand enough from which to govern. For two years the Germans ruled the land of the sea from the top two floors of the Rue du Commerce, unaware that members of the Resistance were hiding in the basement, using the waterway in front of the hotel to enter and exit Middelburg.

My top-floor room has walls so thin I can hear the pounding of the man next door's laptop keys. The packet of documents from the notaris lies untouched on the bed. Oscar will want to know if there is any money when he rings.

'Nothing so far,' I tell him. 'Whispers of death duties to come and death duties unpaid in the past.'

'Never mind. That's not what it's about.'

'What is it about, Oscar?'

'Well, Mum's great. The horses are getting a bit much for her, though. Joanie is, well, Joanie. Mum's knitted me a jumper. Doesn't fit, of course. They never do.' Oscar is back on his mother's farm outside Goulburn, in the Southern Tablelands of New South Wales. 'She's feeding me as if I haven't eaten for a year. Irish stew. Spotted dick. Jam roly-poly. Shanks. Roast parsnip.' He sounds content, tight within the skin of his family. 'Listen, Jules, Mum's given us five acres at the front of the property. We can build a house there.'

He misinterprets my silence for agreement.

'Good. We'll discuss everything when you get here. God it's dry. This drought; you should see the garden.'

The first of Katrien's documents consists of a list of properties from which she collected rent. The amounts are ridiculously low and seem never to have been adjusted. The same families have lived in the two houses in the Heerengracht for decades.

Then there is Buitenrust: *buiten* outside, *rust* rest, a place for relaxing outside the city. Buitenrust was our country estate, where my grandfather Siegfried bred horses. The family would gather there in the summer months. I remember it being a world away from our life in the city. Yet the stroll from my hotel room takes less than fifteen minutes. Where once there were ornate gates, a rough wooden beam now greets me. Either side of the driveway are two gatehouses. When I was a child you entered the manor house at Buitenrust through a grand front door, a Stolburg lion in the middle panel. The new door is blank and made of plywood.

On the ground floor, the reception rooms are bare except for some boxes belonging to the last tenants, an organisation concerned with saving the wildlife of Zeeland. The floor of the pretty ballroom is covered in bird shit. In the basement kitchen, where huge ovens once prepared bread, game and whole sides of beef, the oak and pine tables are no more. In their place are metal benches for treating animals. The bedrooms upstairs are empty, intricate fireplaces removed, floors littered with strips of curled-back wallpaper peeling off the walls. Everywhere I look, single bulbs have replaced chandeliers.

Rising from the ground floor to the tower is a staircase. It decreases in grandeur with each level, until just below the top it becomes a ladder. I ascend slowly, testing each rung before putting my weight on it. An oak panel. A trapdoor. One push – and my eyes are dazzled by sunshine. I am inside the cupola, at the top of the tower, surrounded by dust motes and the glorious, pellucid light of Zeeland.

'Look up, look up,' I hear my grandfather say to my six-year-old self. 'Look up, Juliana!'

★

It is 1953 – a week, a month perhaps, after the great flood that swept over our island at midnight on 31 January. My grandfather Siegfried, close to death, although I do not realise it then, is pointing to a cupboard no one else knows exists, as if he senses some day I will need this knowledge.

'Child, press the corner so. Then the other corner so.'

The panel trips backwards, revealing layers of gold and blue.

'The Germans tortured your grandmother and me to find out where the standard was hidden. We never told them.' He chuckles and wheezes. 'Ah, the Japanese never tell anybody anything if they don't want to.' Siegfried's voice quavers. I hope he will not cry. There has been so much weeping since the night of the flood. 'I never thought,' he says, 'we would have to sacrifice our island twice in eight years. *Ach*. Extract the flag carefully, Juliana. We don't want it unfurling here. Think of it as a parcel that must not be opened until the right moment. Now, attach it so. Twirl the rope. Help me, Juliana. My, how strong you are.'

The standard pauses for a moment at the bottom of the spire, waiting for a breeze. Then it whips up into the sky: the crown of Charlemagne, the gold Stolburg lion, a blue background. Siegfried lifts me up in his arms, high enough to touch our standard. Body trembling, he lets me slip back down.

*

Standing here now, behind the railing, I can see across Walcheren all the way to the North Sea. The park below is green and tranquil. Stick figures walk their dogs beside ponds that look like puddles. I avoid, for as long as possible, bringing my eyes closer, hoping that time has removed the things.

They exist. Ten concrete bunkers: part of the Third Reich's Atlantic Wall. A group of schoolchildren is being led past them, no doubt learning how in 1942 the German high command moved out of their headquarters at the Rue du Commerce and requisitioned Buitenrust. My father Jack Stolburg, head of the south-western Resistance, and his brother Justien were on the run. Mama was in hiding on another island. My grandparents, Siegfried and Françoise, were put under house arrest and tortured in the hope they would give up their sons to the Nazis.

The children are too far away for me to catch their expressions. One child points in my direction, to the tower, and shouts something at the others. All the children turn and wave. In deference to my dead aunt I should lower the standard to half-mast.

Instead I wave back.

There's a gust of wind. It catches the flag. It's as if the lion is struggling against the forces that would pull him down. Cheering, the children rush closer. They have lost all interest in the rubbish the Germans left behind.

2

I Was Born

'What are you going to do now, Juliana? Oscar's all right. He can teach. But what about you?' Oscar's mother, Pearl, is staring at me. Iron-grey curls stand up from her bony skull like question marks. She is at one end of the massive dining table, Oscar at the other. Oscar's sister Joanie and I occupy the lonely middle lengths. Acres of polished Australian cedar separate the four of us.

In honour of my arrival, we are eating in the formal dining room instead of the kitchen. Pearl has brought out the Royal Doulton dinner set Oscar and Joanie gave her in the 1960s. The pattern is of autumn leaves. It must be the dreariest ever produced by that factory.

'What I like about these plates,' says Joanie, 'is there's no gold. You can fling them in the dishwasher.'

'I don't think they're unbreakable,' Oscar says and smiles.

'Only three plates broken in forty years,' says Pearl. She pulls her mouth sideways. When I first met her, thirty years ago, she'd do this at odd times when she was annoyed. Now, at eighty, it's become a habit. Joanie is beginning to develop the same tic. Although he is the older child, Oscar's unlined face makes him seem years younger.

'The government has given me a handsome retirement package,' I say. 'I don't have to *do* anything.' Once out, the words cannot be smoothed. 'I might do some writing – about my family.'

'I'm that pleased,' Pearl says to her son, with a sideways tug of her mouth, 'that you and Juliana have decided on those five acres.'

Joanie nods. 'That land's on the road. Damn valuable, once this bloody drought's over.'

Oscar gazes at a lithograph of horses hanging above Joanie's head and adjusts his length in his chair. 'That land's rocky, if I remember right.'

Pearl has made a will and has split the farm: half to Oscar, half to Joanie.

'When you cark it,' says Joanie, 'I'm going to sell my half and take a world trip. See all those places where Oscar and Juliana lived.'

'Some places we didn't enjoy as much as others,' says Oscar. 'The only parts of Asia I ever need to see again are the airports. And I won't miss teaching the brats at the international schools wherever Jules was posted.'

Pearl leans for a moment towards my section

of the dining table. 'Did you mean a little memoir, Juliana love? How will you begin it?'

I decide to take Pearl's black labrador for a walk. Dog – he does not have a name – has taken to following me everywhere. He races up the drive to meet me, tail wagging, as though he has been imprisoned for weeks. We climb to a rise high above the farmhouse and he nibbles playfully at my feet.

The sandstone farmhouse has shadowy verandas on all sides. It was built in the early years of the twentieth century. The garden has succumbed to the drought and is now little more than a collection of skeletal trees and desiccated bushes. Tough old-species roses cling to life along tanks and birdbaths. In threadbare paddocks, the Australian and Welsh ponies that Pearl and Joanie breed pull listlessly at bales of straw.

New, raw-looking housing estates are creeping towards the property from Goulburn's edges. When Oscar first brought me here in the 1970s the countryside was green. The Wollondilly River had broken her banks three years in a row. There was a view of emerald hills clotted with merino sheep, and no new houses at all. Walking back to the farmhouse, I stumble over crusty ground. Crows scream overhead, poised to suck the lifeblood out of any dying thing.

'Hey, Jules. Do you like this fellow?'

Joanie is a walking quilt of triangles and squares. From a flat plane, her hair plummets to her shoulders and is sawn off, a style that suited her in her late twenties. She's close to sixty now, with a neck that disappears into her shoulders and no waist. Her legs propel the squares of her body; she does not turn so much as pivot.

By her side is a stallion. His muzzle is a purplish velvet, covered in soft bristles. Big dreamy eyes are fixed on the horizon.

'He's beautiful.'

'Bought this boy to liven up the fillies. The last lot of foals weren't up to much. Blame the drought.'

'How long has it been?'

'Ten years officially. Poor rains four years before that. Fourteen years, I reckon.'

She fusses for a while with the stallion's harness. Then in one balletic movement she is on his back.

'Sorry about your career, Jules. And that aunt dying and everything. Oscar! Open the bloody gate, will you?'

She grins affectionately at her brother. He wobbles the gate back and forth, teasing her, then runs a hand down the stallion's flank as the animal walks past.

'Here's his shirts. Ironed as himself likes them.' Pearl clumps upstairs and enters our bedroom without knocking. 'What's this, then?' She touches the coffer lying open on the bed. 'Jeepers creepers. Black beads. And this red stone – my mum had a garnet like that. Only smaller.'

'Ruby. The stone is a ruby. And the beads are black pearls.'

'Yeah? Didn't know I came in black.' Pearl beams, pleased with herself. 'From your family in Holland, I suppose.'

Pointless to remind Pearl that Holland, the name of two northern provinces in the Netherlands, is not where I come from.

'Well,' she says, 'things to do. No rest for the wicked.'

Minutes later she's back.

'Here's his jeans – European, I bet. You and Oscar will have to cut back on luxuries if neither of you is going to work. Ah, there's a grand view.' She gestures out the window, to paddocks rolling all the way to smoke-hazed hills. 'Makes me cry to see the land that filthy yellow. I could tell you stories about this farm, Juliana. I was born right here, see. Halfway between the first and second world wars. My dad was ruined by the war – the first one. He was at Gallipoli. Never talked about it. Not like them now. Everybody talks about everything.'

Pearl sticks her head out the window.

'You bloody nong, Oscar. Don't swing on that gate. You'd think that boy was twelve not going on sixty. Long thing he is. Gets that from my dad. Died in 1940. Couldn't take the thought of another war is what I reckon. Particularly heading into another drought. There's nothing as heartbreaking as lambs blinded by crows. And the army requisitioned all our guns. Couldn't even put the lambkins out of their misery. Moved into horses after that. Horses for the hobby farmers. Crikey, the number of ponies I must have sold.'

She steps back from the window.

'You haven't put those shirts away, Juliana. You don't want them getting creased. He was always fussy about his shirts, Oscar was. Couldn't stand going to school without his shirt being ironed.'

'Do you like this brooch, Pearl?'

She holds the bluebird in her big hands, twirling it around so that the sapphires and diamonds catch the light.

'That's lovely, Juliana. From your aunt?'

'My father gave me the bluebird when I was a child. I haven't worn it for a long time.'

For hours I sit at the desk where Oscar used to sit as a high-school student. Snatches of conversation and animal noises drift up from outside. A climbing rose – crepuscule, I think – has curled round the window frame and an early bloom sprays a cinnamon perfume throughout the room.

A hesitant knock. 'Only me – Joanie. Mum thought you might like to have her office chair. It belonged to her father and grandfather.'

The leather on the seat is worn. But the timber of the armrest and splat-back gleam with age.

Oscar follows Joanie in with some paintings and prints. He starts hanging them up. 'This room is dreary. I remember thinking so when I was fifteen.'

At last, they leave. The paper before me is white, unlined, and on it I write the words *I was born* . . .

★

I was born to everyone's surprise, especially Mama's, as she hadn't realised she was pregnant. She hadn't had a period since the war and had grown used to the idea that at thirty-seven she'd negotiated an early menopause. In the months before my arrival she complained bitterly that she was developing a potbelly yet the rest of her still had the shapelessness of a concentration camp survivor.

When the birth pains came, Mama crossed the road from our bombed house to my grandparents' less damaged home. Despite her frailness, it did not occur to the family that she should go to a hospital to give birth. Stolburg children were delivered at home and that was that. I was underweight, less than five pounds, and no one, least of all Mama, could say whether I was undersized yet full term, or premature.

I was born on a bitterly cold January morning into a watery world trying to recover from the Allied bombing of the *dijkes* protecting our island. In a final push to flood the Germans out of the Low Countries, the Royal Air Force, with the help of the Resistance, sank the island of Walcheren on 18 November 1944. The sinking of our island was called 'liberation'. Large trees that had graced Walcheren for centuries, a source of timber for heating, were killed off by the North Sea saltwater. Oaks, beeches and chestnuts that had seen conquerors come and go were bulldozed to shore up the breaches in the dijkes. All that was available to keep me warm on the day I was born was a reeking, poor-quality coke that gave off little heat. So my grandfather, Siegfried, burnt a set of seventeenth-century oak dining chairs. He liked to joke that I was the most expensive baby born in Europe that year.

The doctor declared me fragile and advised the family to have me baptised as soon as possible. That afternoon, Siegfried went down to the Nissen hut serving as a temporary town hall and had my birth registered. In the space for name, occupation and titles, if any, he wrote: *Count Siegfried Stolburg*. Next to my name is a hole his fountain pen made.

Siegfried and Françoise, his half-Japanese wife, led the procession walking to the Oostkerk to witness my baptism into the Calvinist faith. Following them were my mother's Jewish parents, who lived across the water in the Dutch part of Flanders, and behind them was Aunt Katrien, released from royal service for the day. She travelled to Middelburg in the company of Prince Bernhard, son-in-law of Queen Wilhelmina. The prince was my godfather.

My christening dress was more than a century old, far too big, lacy and flimsy to keep out the stinging cold. Just as the party was about to leave the house, Prince Bernhard removed his army greatcoat and wound it around me. I was carried to my baptism wrapped in the same coat that the handsome warrior prince had worn when he accepted the German surrender.

The predikant sounded out my first name – Juliana – thinking perhaps that I was named after the crown princess of the Netherlands. But I owed my name to a distant ancestor, the first Juliana Stolburg. A gasp went up as my other names were made known.

Miriam.

Esther.

Jewish names.

Names of women Mama had known in Dachau, women who died there. Mama, overcome by nerves, left the church before the formalities were completed.

Before the war, Papa photographed Mama wearing the latest fashions adorned with fabulous jewels, positioning her in front of historic landmarks in Switzerland, Austria, Italy. After the war, he took endless shots of the reconstruction and fewer shots of Mama. Then from the moment I was born he turned his lens on me. Never has a child been so obsessively photographed going about the minutiae of everyday baby life.

There's me, in hundreds of photos, an almost bald baby peering at the camera: curious in one, smiling in the next, distracted in another by something out of frame. And there's me approaching my second birthday, an earnest toddler seated under a window at a child-size table. On the windowsill is an old porcelain-headed doll, looking out at the world below. On the table is a pile of blocks, carefully arranged, with a metal bucket on top. On the floor is my favourite toy: a tiny tin stove complete with saucepans.

For my second birthday Papa commissioned a studio portrait. Black eyes, with the hint of an oriental slant, stare back at the camera. Bright curls that will darken in a few years encircle a heart-shaped face.

Confounding the doctor's predictions, I thrived.

'Come to my party,' I am supposed to have said to everyone I met in the weeks before I turned two.

Papa fetched Oma and Opa, as I called my mother's parents, from their village on his motorbike and sidecar. Katrien descended on Middelburg from whichever palace she was living in. The events of that day have been told and retold, and flashes of memory and confused meanings ... a bluebird brooch ... convince me that I do remember, sort of, what happened.

I woke with a slight cough. I practised coughing a few times. I used to collect sounds and mimic them: the growl of Papa's motorbike, the hollow clip-clop of horses' hooves on the cobblestones below my window. This particular morning, I stacked up my dolls and teddy bears in a corner of the cot. And we all jumped out.

'You monkey!' said Papa, upon finding me sitting on the floor surrounded by toys. He wrapped me in a blanket, lifted me onto his shoulders, and carried me downstairs and across the road to his parents' house, where the women of the family were waiting to dress me.

'Look Jack,' Françoise said to my father, 'how marvellously Janna has altered this frock of Katrien's for the child.'

They'd found a note in the box the dress came in: *Worn by Katrien Stolburg for her fifth birthday, 1905.*

'Oma loves the little dress. Don't you, Oma?'

Oma nodded, as though she understood everything Françoise said. She didn't really. Oma and Opa only knew their Yiddish–Flemish dialect. They didn't understand Dutch at all. Françoise and Siegfried always called them Oma and Opa, my pet names for them, as though that was their only identity.

'When do you think rationing will end, Jack?'

'Soon, Mother. Good times are just around the corner according to the government.'

Papa tied a red bow around my waist and popped my arms into a bolero jacket that Mama had converted from a mink stole.

'Stand still, monkey.' He pinned his present, a bluebird brooch, to the collar of my dress. 'Look, diamonds in the tail and sapphires for the eyes. Can you say that, monkey?'

'Diamonds in the tail and sapphires for the eyes.'

'Perfect. Who's my clever monkey?'

'I am, Papa. I am.'

I put on white woollen tights that Katrien had worn a long, long time ago. They were too big. I danced on tippy toes and they fell around my knees. Mama and Oma laughed and spoke some soft words in their language. The tights were scratchy, and when I thought the adults weren't watching I stepped out of them. *Het kind*, the child, is in bare legs, said Katrien. But no one took any notice.

The two grandfathers, Siegfried and Opa, waited for us in the black and white receiving hall. Opa was smiling, a cigar stuck in the middle of his face, his cheeks a wonderful crimson. Fires blazed in the fireplace and inside the little kachels in each corner of the room.

'I found some timber out at Buitenrust,' Siegfried said and winked.

We sat in a row of high-backed chairs, facing the front door, as the invited adults and children streamed in. The ladies, in their long black skirts, gave deep curtsies to Siegfried and Françoise and bowed their heads at Katrien and Papa. To Mama and her parents, they nodded. The men bowed to Siegfried and ignored everybody else. I ached to undo the ribbons and rip away the shiny paper of the presents piling up for me on a nearby table.

The adults and little girls gave me the three times kiss. The boys shook my hands awkwardly. My cheeks were wet from being kissed and my hands hurt from being squeezed.

Whirling, whirling.

Head spinning.

Husky and huskier.

The adults laughed at the funny sounds coming out of my throat. My stomach crumpled, an awful taste filled my mouth. I bent over and vomited on the floor. I couldn't stop vomiting, even though I couldn't remember eating anything.

'Too much excitement and black market cake,' Katrien said with a sniff.

I might have been two but I knew all about the black market. The black market dominated the conversations I overheard. The black market was where nylons, zippers, buttons, fruit and butter came from. In the black market, money was unacceptable. The fairies and goblins who in my head ran the black market dealt only in gold. Mama visited this place every second week, returning with glowing cheeks and excited eyes.

Papa grabbed me. 'Time for this monkey to have a rest.'

Oma sat next to my bed. I heard laughter in the distance. The adults were drinking gin. Papa drank a lot of gin. Oma pinned the bluebird brooch to a ribbon and tied it to a railing in the cot. The diamond tail glittered in the moonlight and the sapphire eyes twinkled like stars. The sapphire eyes saw everything.

Jack Stolburg woke slowly, thinking he heard a noise. He was often disturbed by the creaking of the old house. Just as he was falling back to sleep, he heard the noise again. He slipped quietly out of bed, so as not to rouse Janna, and found his dressing gown. The pre-war woollen fabric was as new. 'God bless the English and their manufacturers,' he said to himself. The only decent clothes any of them had were those they'd bought before the war.

He crept down the icy hall leading to his daughter's room. Must, he thought, install some sort of heating in this passage. If I can find fuel.

He opened the bedroom door carefully.

Lying spreadeagled on the wooden floor, naked and red all over, was the child.

He put his hand out to her body. His hand recoiled from the heat. He heard a gargling deep in her throat. He flipped the child over and watched in horror as her eyes rolled back, revealing the whites.

'Katrien! Katrien!'

Katrien's room was on the floor above. She stumbled downstairs, grumbling that she needed sleep.

Her greying hair hung loose down her back. Usually it was wound into a tight chignon.

'The doctor, Jack! Quick.' She lifted the child back into the cot and found wet cloths to cool the terrible fire racking her body.

Jack grabbed his helmet and leather coat. He put them on over his pyjamas. His motorbike was in the stables at the back of his parents' house. 'Have the Nazis come again?' Françoise murmured, half-asleep, as Jack's bike roared up the Heerengracht.

The family doctor, who lived on the other side of town, had served with Jack in the Resistance. During the war Jack would throw stones at the doctor's upstairs window whenever he needed him. He did so again now – and the window shattered.

'*Mejn dochter*,' he said to the angry face above him. He kneeled on the cobblestones, next to his motorbike. 'My daughter is dying.'

The doctor flung his coat over his pyjamas and grabbed his bag. He climbed aboard, clutching Jack's coat, and they screeched down the narrow streets of the mediaeval town. The Stolburg houses were blazing with light. A knot of curious neighbours had gathered near Siegfried's front door.

'Not Count Siegfried, Jack?'

'My daughter. Pray for her.'

Hear us, O Lord! Hear us.

Janna was hysterical. Screaming. She had returned from Dachau carrying an empty cardboard suitcase given to her by the Americans, unable to speak of what had happened. The Nazis had handed Jack back a wraith, someone who looked like Janna but was not the woman he married. Oma and Opa clung to Jack, hoping he might tell them something. Rapid Dutch hurtled around them and they could not understand.

'*Heilige Got, acute gewrichtsreumatiek.*'

'Holy God, acute rheumatic fever,' the doctor said.

For the next hour Jack and the doctor placed the child in cold baths. As soon as the fever warmed the water, they'd immerse her in another. The doctor had thought to bring a new miracle drug: penicillin. He injected massive doses into the child's thin arms and thighs. 'To prevent infection of the heart muscle,' he said.

'Shouldn't she be crying? Those needles are so big.'

'She's not conscious.'

The child, at last, was still. Sleeping, the doctor said. Jack lifted her from the cot and carried her to his and Janna's bedroom. Siegfried had lit a fire in there. 'Another seventeenth-century chair for Juliana.'

Katrien made tea in the kitchen, three floors below. She brought a bottle of gin for the men. Jack and the doctor settled in armchairs in front of the fire. 'That was some ride, eh, Jack? Across Middelburg in our pyjamas. Is Janna any better?'

Jack shook his head.

'She needs a psychiatrist,' the doctor said. 'A sanatorium.'

Siegfried and Françoise went back to their own house. Katrien sat listening to Jack and the doctor's wartime reminiscences. The three of them dozed. Katrien stirred after a while, feeling chilled, and went over to the big bed to look in on the child.

She shrieked.

'Juliana is turning blue.'

The child's throat was swollen to double its normal size. She was struggling to breathe.

'*Nee, nee.* She's allergic to penicillin.'

The doctor inserted a thin blade into the trachea to release pent-up air. Then he inserted a tube into the hole, letting the child breathe through that.

'I don't know what else to do. They say adrenalin, but I don't have any.'

Downstairs there was banging on the door. Someone looking for the doctor. Another child had presented with the same symptoms.

'I'll send a nurse to insert an IV to replace fluids. Her heart is fluttering. I'll be back in the morning. Keep her warm. That's all you can do. God bless you, Jack.'

Katrien showed the doctor out. Only after she'd closed the door did it occur to her that he'd have to visit the next child on foot and in pyjamas. She put on her slippers and crossed the street to wake Siegfried and Françoise. To tell them the child was going to die, after all.

A hard-faced nurse, the red cross of mercy embroidered on her cape, arrived with a drip suspended from a grey metal tripod. Jack had seen these contraptions in field hospitals during the war. The nurse roughly inserted the intravenous needle. 'This is a waste of time. There are other children in the hospital who are going to survive. A rheumatic fever epidemic is hitting the Low Countries.' She swept one hand across the vast bedroom. 'This frail generation, the first ones born after the war, are all at risk.'

I woke in Mama and Papa's big bed. Thirsty, thirsty. The adults were sleeping by the fire. Why hadn't they gone to bed?

'Drink, please.'

I sat up and blood poured out the hole in my throat. A strange tube fell on the sheets. I spoke again and more blood bubbled, and I laughed at the sight of it.

'Monkey.' Papa was awake, and smiling.

Mama came in. Looked at me. Turned whiter than any sheet. Fell down on the floor.

'Oh, Janna, Janna, she's going to be all right,' Papa cried.

The doctor returned and put a bandage on my throat so there wouldn't be any more blood. 'I came back to write a death certificate, Jack.'

Oma and Opa were weeping.

'Everybody's crying,' I said to the bluebird pinned to my nightdress.

I was not out of danger. A week later I got pneumonia, followed by diarrhoea so fierce I was afraid to eat. As soon as I swallowed a drop of water or a teaspoon of porridge, cramps would rack my stomach. Often I didn't have time to say I needed to go to the toilet. Better not to eat at all. Every second day the nurse with the blood-red cross on her cape came and stuck a needle into me so that I would have some nourishment. The needles were awful, but better than the cramping diarrhoea I thought might tear my body apart. Better than the look on Mama's face when she saw I had soiled the bed again.

By my third birthday I weighed half what I had weighed twelve months earlier. I couldn't walk unsupported. Papa made little crutches for me and painted them bright red. My curly hair was all gone and I wore a woollen bonnet to keep my head warm. My face was scabby, my eyes too big. I was no longer a pretty child.

And my mother couldn't bear the sight of me.

*

Opa is looking for driftwood. Sometimes he finds other things, bits of metal from ships sunk during the war. My red crutches are difficult to manoeuvre in the sand. I cannot go far, only to the edge of the water. Oma is looking for winkles, her legs spread wide, her bottom poking up in the air. I want to touch the lovely mound of Oma's bottom.

Opa returns with a bundle of wood and lights a fire. Oma boils water in a tin then adds the winkles she's found. They taste like the sea. She lathers the bread she made in the early morning with butter as white and soft as cream. After we have eaten all the winkles and bread, the three of us walk single file through the dunes. The beach has tired me out and for the rest of the day I lie in a hammock under the chestnut tree, watching Opa work in his orchard. If Oma and Opa need to communicate with me, they mime. They are not allowed to teach me their language. People like us speak high Dutch, Aunt Katrien says.

Oma and Opa sleep in a cupboard in their living room. The cupboard has double doors, and when you open them there's a bed inside. Every night, even in summer, I sleep in front of the kitchen stove, in a bed Opa made for me out of the boxes he uses for his fruit. When Papa came to visit I told him that sleeping in that bed made me dream fruity dreams. Papa put his head in his hands. I think he was crying.

Sometimes Papa collects me on his motorbike. If I haven't seen him for a long time, I wait for him on the road in front of the cottage. I can hear his motorbike coming from far away. Oma doesn't want me playing on the road, but I like to sit near the little gate and watch the army trucks go by. I can tell by the signs on their sides whether they are American or British. Papa says the trucks are going to Antwerp to help rebuild the port. When he arrives, he kisses Oma and shakes hands with Opa, then he places me and my red crutches in the sidecar. Oma shoves cakes, bread, eggs and butter in with me, to give to my other grandparents in Middelburg. Siegfried and Françoise love Oma's food.

Papa has an important job looking after the dijkes for the whole of Zeeland. He is away all the time. I cannot stay with Siegfried and Françoise for long; they're too old. Siegfried limps and walks with a cane, and Françoise has sore shoulders and trouble with her eyes. Françoise likes it when I brush her hair. She can't lift her arms anymore.

'Why is your hair white at the front and dark all the way down your back?'

'The white is my Japanese blood coming out.'

'Blood came out of my throat when I was sick.'

'Yes, child.'

'What's Japanese blood?'

'Japan is the country where I was born.'

Shortly before my fourth birthday I got rid of one crutch. But my left leg was still weak. On the morning of my birthday, Papa announced he was going to fetch someone as a special surprise. I thought he meant Oma and Opa. Françoise fussed over my skirt and jumper. She wanted me to wear a little string of pearls. I wanted to wear the bluebird brooch. 'The bluebird was with me all the time I was sick.'

'Let her wear what she likes,' said Siegfried.

We assembled in the black and white hall. It was January again and the fireplace was crackling. The door opened and Papa came in with a woman whose skin looked like my porcelain doll's. Her curly hair was auburn like the chestnuts Opa roasted all through winter. The lady's eyes were blue, like heaven.

'Kiss your mother, child.'

I burst into tears. 'I don't have a mother.'

The beautiful woman turned around. Her high heels tap-tapped on the marble floor. She slammed the door. Papa went after her.

'Let's cut the cake, shall we?' said Siegfried.

Oscar is reading, his long legs outstretched. Dog looks up at him adoringly. Oscar's hand fondles the animal's ears. The space of the farm is dizzying.

'This island is so big,' I say.

'Mm?'

'That's what my father said: *Everything about Australia is too big, or too small.*'

Oscar hates shaving, but he hates facial stubble even more. Rubbing a smooth chin against my cheek is his signal that he wants sex.

'Not on your mother's living-room floor. Not with Dog watching. They could come in at any time. Anyway, why aren't you out helping round up horses or whatever it is people do on a horse stud?'

'They don't need me. Joanie will tell me I'm in the way and Pearl will call me a great gangling something or other. Let's go upstairs and fuck. It's been a while.'

While Oscar showers, I watch the late afternoon light play across the walls. The door to the bathroom has jammed open. Oscar is visible behind the pink shower curtain. There isn't one part of him that isn't long. He comes into the bedroom naked. Pauses in front of the mirror to examine a spot on his thigh.

'Even your dick is long.'

'Thanks. Only just noticed after thirty years?'

He sprawls across the bed, half on top of me. We are mismatched, anatomical opposites. The first time we had sex, he said he loved the small bits of me. I have always worn high heels – my back held straight, chin out — in an attempt to complement his height.

'Oscar?' Pearl is yelling up the stairs. 'Was that you having a shower?'

Oscar nuzzles my neck. 'Bugger, bugger, bugger.'

'Only one three-minute shower a day. We don't want to be having to buy water.'

3

A Carriage and Four

Drought winds have blown away the fine gravel of the driveway and left deep ruts. Oscar negotiates the lumpy track with care. Ponies stick their noses over the fence to inspect us as we pass.

'Don't speed will you, Jules, if you have to go into Goulburn for anything.'

'I think I've forgotten how to drive.'

'Yeah.' Oscar chuckles. 'Chauffeured everywhere. Helicopters. Planes. How will you cope back in the real world?'

He hits the brakes hard as we round a bend. The stallion with the dreamy eyes is standing in the middle of the drive, pawing at a rock.

Oscar whispers, 'Stay back, Jules. Call Pearl on the mobile.'

'I don't know the number.'

'Press 1.'

He walks slowly up to the stallion, hands at his sides, palms open. 'Come on, boy. Come on. There's nothing in my hands. Poor boy, that's a nasty cut. Did you get that jumping a fence? What scared you, boy?' The quivering horse lets Oscar touch his neck. 'Poor you.' He places a hand in the horse's mane. The animal flinches. 'Jules, go round by the paddock and close the gate. If he should get onto the road . . .'

The paddock nearest the road is the land Pearl has given to Oscar. It's littered with rocks. At the bottom of a burnt-out tree is something brown, with eyes, and a forked tongue that flicks out, then in.

'There's a snake, Oscar,' I say softly.

He does not hear me. I have been an Australian citizen since 1965 but other than in a zoo I have never encountered a snake. For all I know this snake might be a species capable of chasing me around a paddock. I edge backwards, away from the creature. It's been so long since anyone closed the gate that it has warped in the middle. It's heavy. I can hardly budge it. Behind me, the stallion is deliberating whether or not to bolt.

Suddenly the gate jerks across the cattle grid and clangs shut. The stallion takes a few hesitant steps towards me. Stops. Tosses his head.

A mare comes trotting down the drive. Pearl is riding her, a spare bridle in one hand. Joanie follows, carrying a rifle, Dog behind her. I am afraid Joanie will shoot the beautiful stallion. I want to shout out that I don't think the injury is so bad. But before anyone can say or do anything the animal sinks to his knees. Foam dashes out the corners of his mouth.

'Snakebite!' I yell. 'I saw a snake.'

Pearl turns and gallops back up the drive.

'Where's she going?'

'She'll be getting antivenene,' says Joanie. 'And ringing the vet. Where was the snake?'

I point to the blackened tree.

'Christ. Not again. Snake there last year. Should have blasted that stump.' Joanie bounds over the fence and with one economical shot dispatches the snake. 'Back broken. The stallion must have stomped on him. The bite will be low down. Near the hoof. If the bastard hit a vein . . .'

Pearl returns on the mare. She dismounts swiftly, fluidly, belying her eighty years, and throws the antivenene at Joanie.

Joanie rubs the vial between her large hands. 'Cold and hard – been in the fridge since last year.' She stabs a needle into the top of the vial. The fluid refuses to be drawn down.

'No. No.' Pearl is crying. 'He's my last stallion. I'm too old to start with another one. He's that beautiful.'

Oscar holds his mother close. Joanie manages to half-fill a syringe and tries to inject a vein. A horse's skin is tough. The needle is sharp enough to pierce the skin but the fluid refuses to trickle down the cylinder.

Pearl moans. 'I knew that fridge was set too cold. I meant to adjust it.'

A car horn sounds: the vet. But now the heavy gate is stuck shut. Before Oscar can run to help him, the vet clambers over the top and yanks the syringe out of the horse's leg. 'If this is from last year it won't be any good.' He tosses it away and injects a huge vial into the horse's neck. Then he sits back.

'Don't you have to find the bite? Cut out the poison or something?'

The vet looks at me as though I'm stupid.

'I think this fella is going to be all right. Mightn't have copped that much venom.'

He pushes his hat back and rubs tired eyes. Oscar grabs my hand and tucks it under his arm. We two stand well back from the horse and the three people gathered round him. After a while Oscar suggests we may as well return to the house. 'I'll sort out my records.'

Oscar's vinyl collection and elaborate sound system occupied all of one wall in our apartment in Luxemburg. I lost count of the number of times we moved from country to country. Cambodia. Malaysia. Singapore. America. England. Belgium. Ireland. America again. Oscar's records accompanied us on all my postings.

Pearl has allowed him to erect shelves in the living room. 'I can put the records the way we had them in Luxemburg,' he says. He is particular about where everything must go. He does not need me, and in truth the whole process of setting up speakers, pre-amplifiers and all the other paraphernalia bores me witless. I should sort out Katrien's jewellery jumbled in boxes under the bed. My jewellery – the modest pieces Oscar bought me over the years, and the pieces Papa gave me as a child – are in a drawer of the dressing table. With jeans and a white shirt, the bluebird is fashionable all over again.

There'll be bluebirds over the white cliffs of Dover,
Tomorrow, just you wait and see.

Long before we ever learnt to speak English, Mama and I used to sing that song. Mama hummed and sang when she was happy. After she came back from the sanatorium I lived in fear of being struck down by diarrhoea again. It was not until I was much older that I realised that, to Mama, the smell of shit mixed with fear was the stench of the death camps.

Papa was still away often, sometimes for weeks at a time, rebuilding the dijkes destroyed in the liberation flood of 1944. I avoided Mama and instead haunted Siegfried's library, with its desk and its little kachel. The library sprawled over two wooden floors, and there were gaps in the shelves where books had been sent to antiquarian booksellers to raise money. Children's books were not wanted by anyone and so long as I was careful, I could play with these, pretending I could read. Siegfried's legs and hips were getting worse and he could no longer climb the ladders to reach the highest parts of the library.

'How are your legs today, Juliana?'

'Fine, Grandfather.'

'Good. Carry this book up the ladder and put it on those shelves near the window. You'll soon be rid of that crutch.'

I always said my legs were fine, whether they were trembling that day or not. If Siegfried had visitors I hid under his desk.

'When do you think rationing will end, Count Siegfried?'

'Soon.'

'*Ach*, the black market will beggar all of us.'

On one such occasion, when the visitor happened to be a black-clad churchman, I couldn't contain myself. I popped up from under the desk. 'We're very poor, you know. Françoise says she's given as much gold to black market as she gave to the Nazis. Mama has to go there all the time. Françoise says we won't have any gold left by the time rationing ends.'

The black-clad churchman turned red then purple. Siegfried had trouble keeping a smile in check. He roared with laughter the moment the churchman left.

'What's so funny, Grandfather?'

'You are, monkey.'

In the summer after my fourth birthday I began walking without crutches, and Siegfried was able to take me with him when he inspected his properties. We went to Buitenrust, and to a mediaeval keep on a neighbouring island, and to the many farms he owned. The land was becoming productive again after the salty invasion of the liberation flood.

We had no use for cars. Siegfried preferred horseback. He'd wear jodhpurs and an English tweed jacket, and if the weather was cool a woollen waistcoat. He was meticulous about his leather riding boots, polishing them with lard until they shone. His cane was always tucked into the saddle; because of the arthritis in his legs and hips, he couldn't mount or dismount without the cane's help. 'You should have seen me when I was young, Juliana. I could sit on a horse all day and half the night if I had to. Cold, rain, snow – none of it bothered me.'

I rode side-saddle on a leather pillow in front of Siegfried. When I grew tired, I'd tuck my head into Siegfried's jacket and drink in the scent of grass, horses and the salted liquorice drops he adored. At the farms we visited, I played with the children while he chatted to the farmer. I looked around the modest farmhouses. Then I'd return to our house in the Heerengracht and see rooms of furniture covered with crimson brocade, rooms where timber panelling climbed walls dotted with paintings that had been in the family for centuries. Françoise had pearls around her neck, gold rings and bracelets on her hands. The women I met when I accompanied Siegfried wore simple wedding bands. I realised then that we weren't poor.

Shoes were a problem, though. They were simply unobtainable. I asked for clogs once, as these could be bought at the market in front of the Stadhuis. 'Peasants, farmers and Catholics wear clogs,' said Françoise. 'Not people like us.'

In the closets of my grandparents' house were dresses and coats, men's suits and shirts; all sorts of things that hadn't been worn for fifty years and more. Papa had given Mama a Singer treadle sewing machine before the war. Materials were becoming more readily available, but they were of such poor quality that Mama asked Françoise for permission to make new clothes out of the old clothes. Françoise said yes, and soon Mama's Singer sewing machine was transforming silk, satin and lace into summer dresses for Mama and me, and providing Françoise with new bodices. The material was ancient and fragile so our new clothes didn't last long. 'Doesn't matter,' Mama said briskly. 'The cupboards are full of old stuff.'

Sometimes Mama would find a bolt of material that had been stuffed in a trunk and forgotten. She subscribed to women's magazines, worthy weekly publications such as *Libelle* and *Margriet*, where interminable articles about the royal family were interspersed with fashion pages. Mama would study them until she was confident she could make a pattern out of brown paper or newspaper. She'd pin the pattern onto the fabric and cut carefully around it, so as not to waste any material.

Then it was the turn of the sewing machine. The throb of the needle, the movement of the treadle – backward, forward, backward, forward – soothed Mama's nerves. She'd concentrate so intently on maintaining a steady motion on the pedal that she couldn't possibly tear her eyes away. For a long time after she came home from the sanatorium, she avoided looking at me.

It was from behind the Singer sewing machine that she told me the story of her early life, as though she were reciting a poem, rocking to the cadences of the stanzas of the seasons, tuned to the Singer's soporific rhythm.

Backward, forward. Backward, forward.

'I remember the guns of the Great War,' Mama began in a singsong voice, her eyes half-closed. 'The battlefield closest to us was Ypres. We saw soldiers creeping through our village trying to get to the Schelde. If they made it to the coast and could get across the Schelde, then they were in the neutral Netherlands and free.'

'Couldn't they catch the ferry like we do, Mama?'

'Don't be silly. This was wartime. Not the Second World War. This war happened when I was a little girl. Now be quiet. Otherwise I won't continue.

'One day we heard guns booming from ships in the Schelde, and other guns from the battlefield at Ypres. Missiles were flying above our house. Oma and Opa said we had to hide in the cemetery. The four of us crouched down among the headstones of family from a long time before who came from Salzburg. My brother Piet and I sneaked away to the back of the cemetery, to a place where there were tall stones. We climbed to the top of one of them. And what do you think we saw? A British ship exchanging fire with a whole group of smaller German ships. The British ship was on fire and had turned on her side. Sailors were swimming for their lives, trying to get away from the Germans, who were firing at them. The next day Opa went down to the beach. He found all sorts of things. Crates of food. Bodies.'

'Did you see the bodies, Mama?'

'Opa wouldn't let us look at dead sailors. But he told us about them. The guns stopped, just like that. We couldn't get used to the silence at first. Queen Wilhelmina of the Netherlands came through our village on an inspection tour. She was in a big open carriage and the horses were throwing up dust all over Flanders. The Queen kept one hand on her ugly hat to stop it blowing away. With her other hand she waved to us. You've never seen anything so funny as Wilhelmina's wave. She rolled her arm from the shoulder. Piet and I walked around for the next few days rolling our arms, we thought it was so hilarious.

'The Dutch officials wanted us to forget about being Flemish. They made us change our names and learn their language. An old lady in the village school tried to teach us to speak proper Dutch, but we had to help at home and in the orchard. I wanted to learn to read. But there wasn't much time for school. Oma and Opa couldn't read or write and neither could any of our neighbours. No one in our village had much use for reading.

'We were told not to mention being Jewish to any Dutch officials who came snooping. The Dutch didn't really like Jews. But we weren't *very* Jewish. There was no synagogue, no rabbi. Oma and Opa had been married in a registry office. Opa even kept a pig – although he sold all the meat to the Lutherans. They had their own church in the village and a pastor. We didn't mix with them and we never ate any part of the pig. Most of the Lutherans couldn't read or write either. I liked playing on the road. We didn't have many toys.'

'Did you have shoes, Mama?'

'We had clogs. Opa carved them from beech-wood.' She stopped sewing for a moment and looked out the window.

'It was all right for you to wear clogs?'

'If we didn't wear clogs we went barefoot.' She laughed. 'Oma and Opa had one pair of leather shoes each for weddings and funerals. That's how it was. Sometimes a man came and asked Opa what his name was. If Opa forgot to give his Dutch name, the man charged him a florin. The florins had the face of the Queen on one side. Oma said the Queen was taking the food from her children's mouths. You know that large chestnut tree, Juliana, the one you love to sit under when you visit Oma and Opa? That tree is twice as tall now, but it was big even in 1920. I used to hide in the branches. If I stayed up there long enough, Oma and Opa would forget where I was. I could see over the fields to the Breskens Road. I used to watch for carriages and automobiles. I knew when a carriage was coming because carriages stirred up more dust. Most carriages had one horse, sometimes two. The Queen's carriage had four. One day I saw a huge dust cloud and I knew it had to be a carriage with four horses. I climbed down from the chestnut tree, yelling for Piet.

'Opa and Oma brought a little table out and sat it next to the road, with jars of preserved fruit, and vegetables that they'd pulled out of the ground. I was right. There were four horses, and they had black plumes on their heads. On the carriage doors was a gold lion. These visitors weren't royal but we could tell they were highborn. The carriage came on fast. For a moment we thought the visitors weren't going to stop. Sometimes I wonder what would have happened if they had never stopped . . . *Ach zo.* Oma put a clean apron on. Opa wore a jacket on top of his work pants. We didn't have much. We were peasants, that's the truth. We children played on the road, climbed trees, went barefoot in summer. But we washed every night before bed, not like some. The Lutherans, well, never mind.

'Jack was the one I noticed first. Such dark eyes. And black hair. We never saw that colouring in our village. The Lutherans were blond or light brown, and we Jews had reddish hair. There were two other children in that carriage. You know who they were, don't you? Katrien of course, the oldest, no colouring at all. Like a sparrow she is.'

At this, Mama paused once more in her sewing and touched her own lovely auburn hair.

'And Jack and Katrien's brother, Justien, the Stolburg heir. Justien was pale, like sand. His eyes were cold and grey like the North Sea in winter. He was quite handsome, mind. And he carried a whip with a fancy gold tip. Your father once told me that Justien used his whip like other people used a gun, in the war, the second war . . . no, no. The mother, Françoise, she was all in black. Her eyes were like coal. Whoever these fine people were, they looked as if they had come from a funeral.'

Mama paused again, then resumed, softly.

'Your grandmother, Françoise, she studied me

with those eyes. *Jee oh Jee.* I had never seen eyes like them. You have her eyes, Juliana.'

'But I have Papa's eyes. Everyone says so.'

'Françoise gave your father her eyes and he gave his to you. Anyway, Justien, he never got out of the driver's seat. Just sat there, looking ahead, not interested in anything. I stared and stared at the gold buttons on Jack's coat. Each button had a lion and a crown on it. I had never seen such a thing. The grand people spoke to us, but we barely understood one word. I hadn't been to enough school to remember any Dutch.

'Jack spoke slowly, pointing to himself. Jack, he said. The Lady Stolburg, he said, pointing at his mother. Then he pointed to me – Janna, I said.

'Françoise and Katrien looked at the vegetables and the fruit and bought everything Opa showed them. Then they were asking for something else. Opa nodded as though he understood. I knew he couldn't possibly understand. *Nee, Mama,* Jack said. Jack looked like he was about to cry. I couldn't see how a beautiful boy like that with gold buttons on his coat could have anything to cry about. Katrien got back in the carriage and stared out the window, away from us. Françoise gave Jack her purse, the same one she still uses. You know, Juliana, the one with the gold clasp on top? Jack counted out a pile of florins. We had never seen so much money. What could they want from us that was worth all that money?

'Then Justien whistled through his teeth. Françoise climbed back in the carriage. Jack had to help her lift all those black skirts. Justien jumped down from the driver's seat and stood looking at me. Then he grabbed me. He was pale, it's true, but he was strong. Before I knew it I was wedged between Katrien and Jack. These people are going to give me a treat, I thought, maybe a short ride to the end of the village.

'But then Justien turned the horses so fast that one of the horses stumbled.

'He made the carriage fly out of the village.

'And then Oma was screaming.

'I begged to go home. And that's when I started crying. Katrien pinched me on the arm to make me stop. Jack stroked my other arm. He was nearly crying, too, I think. We drove through Breskens at a gallop, right onto the ferry. I had never been to the other side of the Schelde. How would I ever get home? There was an argument between Jack and his mother. I think it was about me. She was so angry I thought she might strike him. Jack made signs at me, holding up both hands and pointing to himself. I understood he was ten, the same age as me. I held up all my fingers. I could count to ten. Françoise held up ten fingers and three more. She had persuaded herself I was thirteen.

'I fell asleep and must have slept for a while. Next thing I knew we were travelling past a magnificent palace, lights in every window. *Ach*, Juliana, you should have seen the Stadhuis in those days. We got to the Heerengracht and I had never seen such a big house. Françoise walked quickly into the black and white hall, holding me by the arm. A man with gold hair, he had a kind smile, came slowly down the stairs. Who is that child? he said. What have you done, Françoise?'

At this point I had to interrupt.

'Mama, how do you know what the man said if you didn't speak Dutch?'

'I just know,' Mama said. 'Now shush or I won't go on.'

She went on with the story.

'The man with the kind smile was Siegfried. Françoise said to him: We need servants. Everybody is getting them from Flanders. And this child seems bright.

'Then a fat woman came to take me away. She was the cook and her name was Saartje. *Ach*, you should have seen the kitchens before the German bombing. All done out in blue and white. They were like a world beneath the ground. There was a room for cooking, with a big table where the cook and her husband ate, and behind the stove were more rooms. These were divided into bedrooms. Families had lived for generations down there. Probably the people upstairs never even knew the names of all the ones living below.

'The cook's husband was called Huib. He was the groomsman. Huib brought in a tin bath and poured hot water into it. Saartje undressed me. She looked very hard at the little gold necklace I always wore. The water was hot, much hotter than at home, and when I was finished Huib took away the bath and threw the water over the cobbles in the yard. I was amazed. At home we all used the same bathwater. Saartje wrapped me in a big warm nightgown. She put me to bed in an alcove behind the stove.

'A little later I could hear laughter, high up in the house. I knew it was the boy, Jack. I wondered what he thought was so funny. I heard Saartje talking to her husband. I heard the word *Jood*.'

'But Mama,' I was aching to know, 'what did Oma and Opa do when you didn't come home?'

'Opa went to Breskens on his old horse to see the Dutch police. His daughter had been taken away in a grand carriage, he said. He described the gold lion on the carriage door. The police said he was slandering a powerful family. They knew all about rich Middelburgers coming over to Flanders to steal servants. They told Opa that he'd better stop talking if he knew what was good for him. Then they pushed him down the stairs.

'*Is dat niet zielig?*'

Isn't that pitiful?

I said nothing.

Neither did Mama.

'That first morning,' she continued at last, 'horses' hooves woke me up. They were mad about horses, the Stolburgs. The windows in the basement were high up. I got on a chair and there were all these hooves in front of my eyes. I nearly fell off; I thought they were going to kick the window in. Then I saw the bars and I knew I was safe. I could see black boots, and a whip. That had to be the one they called Justien. His boots were polished so brightly I could see my face in them. You know why the kitchen windows were so high up, Juliana?'

'Because the kitchens were three-quarters under-ground, Mama?'

'No. Because Calvinists wanted their servants to work. To not be distracted. I was looking out that window when I heard a faint rustling behind me. Someone was coming. It was Françoise, and she was wearing something I had never seen in my life. A silk coat over a white nightdress. I wondered why such a grand lady would wear such an ordinary nightdress, one that did up at the neck and the wrists, and then put a coat on top. I didn't know that this coat was called a kimono. Your grandmother had black hair then. It streamed down both her cheeks and all the way down her back. I stood on the chair. I didn't dare move. She reached for the David star on my neck. I thought she was going to rip it off. But she didn't. She just touched it. Her hands were beautiful. She never did any work, except embroidery. She was wearing her rings, of course, the wedding ring on the right and the other one, the Japanese ring, on the left.'

'Did she say anything, Mama?'

'She just turned and went away.'

When Mama stopped talking I stepped outside, looked right and left, and walked across the road to Siegfried and Françoise's house. I slid across the black and white hall, past seventeenth-century Dutch master paintings, and through a narrow doorway to the dining room. The Allies had borrowed our table for their discussions late in 1944, as it was the only table in Middelburg able to seat twenty-four. Whenever we ate at that table Siegfried grumbled about how General Eisenhower had accidentally scratched his signature into the oak surface.

Beyond the dining room was the conservatory, where Françoise liked to sit and catch the last of the afternoon sun. The glass had been blown out of the window frames and never replaced. She said she didn't mind. 'I like to feel the breezes,' she'd say. Her eyes had a gentle cloudiness about them. On a little table next to her were silver-framed photographs of her children.

'Juliana. How is your mother today?'

'Talking.'

'*Ach*, good for her to talk. We must watch out for the silences, *nee*?'

I sat on a stool by Françoise's feet, close to the black silk of her skirts.

'Papa is away fixing the dijkes,' I said. That was the way I began every conversation. I was tremendously proud of my father's name appearing in newspapers I couldn't yet read. 'May I see your ring?'

Françoise's hand was unmarked by time. The ring, the Japanese one, consisted of a heavy gold band, branching into a coronet, and in the coronet was a cornelian, as cunningly faceted as the blood-red ruby she wore on her neck. She took off the ring and allowed me to hold it in my hands.

'Where did you get the ring, Grandmother?'

'A great Japanese emperor by the name of Meiji gave the ring to me when I married your grandfather.' Her voice never sounded old. She had the full-throated strength of a much younger woman.

'Why?' I asked.

'As a mark of respect to my father, a Dutchman, his trusted friend, his secretary of state, a *waterbouwkundige*, a manipulator of water, a builder of dijkes. Like your father, Juliana.'

'Why was the Meiji emperor in the Netherlands when you got married?'

'He wasn't. He came from Kyoto to Nagoya, where I lived with my father. I married your grandfather in a Calvinist church in Nagoya. The two places are quite close. The emperor didn't have to travel far.'

Until that moment, I had thought of Françoise as being like all the other black-clad women of our religion. Now, in my fifth year, I realised she was someone quite different.

★

The next day, Mama resumed her place at the Singer sewing machine.

'After a few weeks at the Stolburgs',' she said, 'I was allowed home to visit my parents. I walked seven kilometres to Vlissingen to catch the ferry across the Schelde. Then three kilometres to our village. Oma fed me. We all cried. I had a little nap. Then Opa put me on his horse and took me back to the ferry. It was dark by the time I reached the other side of the river, so to get back to the house I had to follow the road by the canal, using the lights of Middelburg as a beacon.'

'But Mama, why didn't Oma and Opa keep you with them?'

'They were afraid.'

Mama turned away and fiddled with a pattern, which she then very carefully pinned to some colourful material. I waited quietly for her to finish.

'First thing I did every morning,' she said, 'was stand on the stool in my bedroom and look out the window. The horses were kept at Buitenrust, and if they were needed for one of the carriages they were brought into the city. I liked to hear the hooves on the cobblestones. Sometimes a horse would bend low enough, outside my window, for me to feel its warm breath on my face.

'One morning Huib came into the kitchen, grumbling that Justien was bringing the black filly to the Heerengracht to be serviced. Makes no sense, said Huib, the filly belongs at Buitenrust, she won't like the high walls of the courtyard here. I don't think Count Siegfried approves.

'*Ach*, said Saartje, it's not for us to question the higher-ups. Then Huib turned to me. Janna, he said, if you're a good girl, you can come into the yard and watch. Saartje reckoned a horse being serviced was no sight for a young girl, but Huib said Janna's from the land, like us.

'The next morning I followed Huib into the stable yard. He lifted me up and sat me on a ledge. Don't move, he said. Justien led the black filly into the yard. She was tall, with a deep chest. She hadn't been broken in properly, and she whinnied and kicked, desperate to be back in the fields. Huib was right. She didn't like the courtyard. Huib brought out a stallion, much smaller than the filly, a nice fellow. The stallion looked at the filly. He seemed scared of her.

'Justien and Huib went to position the filly. They tried and tried but she refused to stand still. Justien stood in front of the filly, attempting to look into her eyes, saying shush, shush. The whites of her eyes were red. She snorted a little, not sure whether to trust him. Slowly, slowly Justien lifted his arm. Then whack! He lashed the filly across her nose and eyes. *Ach*, that poor animal, I can still hear her, sobbing like a woman. I had to stuff my apron in my mouth to stop myself from wailing. I didn't want to stay on that ledge but there was no way of getting down by myself.

'The filly was bleeding from the face. Yet she started dancing around Justien, as if she wanted to please him. Huib was sweating, his shirt wet and hanging off his back. The stallion tried once more to enter the filly. Huib lifted the penis for him. But the stallion was too short in the legs. Justien whipped the filly across the back, to make her kneel. He must have released his grip on the halter for a moment. She reared up. Screaming. When she came down one of her hooves landed on the stallion's shoulder. A great gash opened up. He cried from the pain. Now both horses were screaming. And Justien was furious. He bared his teeth and he kicked the filly and he tried whipping her again. She reared up at him again, wanting to get away.

'I saw Siegfried and Jack come running out of the house. What's going on here? Siegfried shouted. The filly reared up one last time. Up, up. She slipped on the cobblestones and landed across a water trough. I heard her spine snap. I held my hands over my ears. She lay panting across the trough.

'You idiot, Siegfried said to Justien. He went inside. Came back with a rifle. Shot the filly through the ear. Then he examined the stallion's wound. The wound wasn't deep. It would heal in time.

'Siegfried looked at Justien for a moment. Then he shot the stallion. Justien was crying: Papa, Papa, I'm sorry, so sorry. Siegfried went back inside the house.

'They forgot about me, sitting up on that ledge. It was Jack who helped me down.'

★

Oscar repeats his warning about negotiating the drive carefully. He stops the car to inspect the snakebitten stallion. The horse's head is bowed. He ignores Oscar.

'That animal's depressed,' Oscar says. 'He should be overjoyed that he survived.'

'Darling, while you're busy here, would you mind if I returned to the Netherlands? For research? There are things I need to check.'

'Won't the internet do?'

'I won't be gone long. Six weeks.'

The intake of his breath is sharp and shallow.

'A month, Jules.'

'All right. A month.'

I look away from him, determined not to record the hurt on his face.

4

The Company of Men

In the last of the autumn light, the palace of Het Loo gleams red and gold. Soon, in winter, it will turn a pearly grey. Het Loo was built in the golden age of the Dutch republic by Willem of Oranje-Nassau and his wife, Mary, daughter of King James II. William of Orange, as the English knew him, preferred the company of men. For much of their early married life he was away fighting battles. In his absence Mary created extravagant gardens — box hedges, artificial lakes — in imitation of those at Versailles. She is supposed to have said these were the happiest times of her life, before she and her husband, who was also her cousin, became joint monarchs of Great Britain.

When my aunt Katrien reported for duty at Het Loo in 1920, Mary's back garden lay obliterated, planted over with meadows and trees. That was the summer Mama was brought to live with the Stolburgs, and the family was caught up in the preparations for Katrien's new life in the royal household. Floor-length skirts, white coifs and bodices of grey silk accumulated in Katrien's bedroom. Françoise wanted her daughter fitted out as a pious Calvinist yet in a manner befitting her aristocratic rank. She taught Mama how to starch white headdresses, how to embroider delicate, feathery stitches on all sorts of materials.

Katrien spent as much time as she could that summer at Buitenrust. She liked riding with her brothers. The stud bred Zeeuws horses, stolid beasts that had carried knights into battle. Arab thoroughbreds were introduced from England in the nineteenth century to refine the heavy look of the breed, and the result of this crossbreeding was a highly strung animal that was exciting to ride yet retained the stamina of the ancient Zeeuws breed.

On fine days the Stolburg siblings would set out for Buitenrust in a landau, an open carriage, with Justien driving out front and Katrien and Jack facing each other inside. Janna, the servant girl, sat on a dicky seat at the back: never looking forward, never seeing a place emerge from out of the distance.

As soon as they arrived, the three Stolburgs would run upstairs and throw off their dark garb in exchange for more cheerful clothes. On her last visit to Buitenrust, Katrien tossed her black clothes over the banister. They landed four floors below. 'Pick them up, Janna,' she said. 'Put them in my room.'

'That's not fair, Kat,' Jack said, coming out of his bedroom, a red handkerchief round his neck. 'She has to go all the way downstairs to bring those things back to you.'

Katrien grimaced. Earlier that morning, she'd modelled for her parents a new outfit she'd ordered from an English catalogue: a split riding skirt, a top hat and a bright yellow veil. 'Makes your complexion sallow,' Françoise said. Katrien stalked out of the breakfast room, determined not to let her disappointment show. Some time later Françoise brought fresh flowers into the hall and noticed the yellow veil wrapped around a vase.

Janna enjoyed the outings to Buitenrust. While the Stolburgs rode she'd wander the gardens, catching glimpses between the trees of the others galloping after one another, jumping over creeks.

'Race! Race!' Jack shouted, and Katrien followed close behind, bending low beneath branches, lying flat on the horse's back as it glided over impossible jumps. Justien kept up for a while before turning off in a different direction.

Janna was in the apple orchard when Jack rode up. 'Hey. Want to learn how to ride?'

She glanced at Jack's prancing horse. She shook her head.

'You could sit behind me.'

'You wouldn't let me fall?'

'Here, grab my hand.' He heaved her up effortlessly and manoeuvred her behind him. '*Hup-la. Hup-la.*'

They met Justien riding towards them.

'Are you mad, Jack? What is the servant girl, the *Jood*, doing on your horse?'

'I thought she might like some fun.'

'Get her off. Remember who you are.'

'What business is it of yours if I give Janna a treat?'

Justien hissed. 'How dare you. I am the heir.'

'And not likely to produce any more heirs.'

With that, Jack gave his horse a little kick and it set off on a wild gallop, through orchards and meadows. 'Hold on tight,' he yelled at Janna as they sailed over a wide ditch. 'Put your arms around me.'

Back at the stables, Justien was waiting for them. As Jack dismounted, Justien raised his whip. 'I'll teach you.'

'You've just killed two horses,' Jack said calmly. 'You are not Papa's favourite. I am. If you hit me, Papa will send you to the Household Cavalry.'

'I want to go there anyway.'

'No you don't,' said Katrien. 'The Household Cavalry would not suit you at all. Jack, get that child off your horse. She hears too much.'

'She doesn't speak much Dutch yet, Kat,' said Jack.

Katrien peered at Janna, sizing her up. 'I know you've been teaching her to read, Jack.'

'I'm trying to make a Christian of her.'

Katrien's usual expression was stern, unbending. She flashed Jack a smile filled with satirical understanding.

'*Lieve Jack*, don't be ridiculous.'

Jack was clever at school, an athlete, and he made friends readily. He'd charm the most dour of the

Calvinist women in his mother's circle by looking into their eyes from beneath long black lashes while offering them cups of tea or a small glass of advocaat. Janna had seen grim Calvinist ladies blush under the scrutiny of ten-year-old Jack. Justien, at seventeen, was handsome, but he lacked his brother's easy charm. There was whispered gossip among the servants that Justien did not like women.

One day Janna said to Saartje, the cook, 'Jack says Justien won't produce an heir. What does that mean?'

'Some men are not meant to marry, that's all.' Saartje lifted her huge bosoms so that they rested on the kitchen table.

'All the men I know are married,' said Janna, 'once they're old enough.'

'It's different with the higher-ups. All that refined blood. And who knows what sort of blood Françoise brought into the family. This is not a matter for us to wonder about.'

'If Justien doesn't get married, does that mean Jack . . .?'

'Enough!' Saartje snapped.

It was unusual for people to speak harshly to Janna. She had learnt quickly when to question and when to leave something alone.

★

The day of Katrien's departure came. Her brothers and the servants lined the black and white hall in readiness for the farewell ceremony. Siegfried emerged from his study, dressed in travelling tweeds. Knowing the weather might be cooler in the north, he draped a green cloak over his shoulders. Françoise was fussing with a spray of flowers under the hall mirror when Katrien came down the stairs. She saw Katrien's reflection in the glass and had time to compose her own expression before turning around. Katrien, without consulting her mother, had ordered outfits from a store on Bond Street, London. Her reddish–brown travelling skirt exposed – shockingly – trim ankles. Her shoes had small heels.

Françoise did not acknowledge what Katrien was wearing. She gave her daughter the three times kiss and withdrew to the conservatory.

Three long days the journey took, across the islands, through the former duchy of Brabant, past the old Roman town of Nijmegen and into the city of Arnhem. Huib had never driven the big carriage such a distance. By the time they reached Arnhem the four horses were exhausted and Huib was afraid his arms would drop off. 'I can't fold my elbows,' he moaned.

The party rested for two days at an hotel on the outskirts of Arnhem before undertaking the short final leg to Apeldoorn and Het Loo. From the terrace they could see the mighty Rhine weave through some of the richest farmland in the Netherlands. Summer crops had been harvested and the ground prepared for autumn. Barges flying the Dutch tricolour puffed downstream, laden with goods from Germany. Few barges went the other way; the First World War had impoverished Germany.

On the second night Siegfried asked Katrien to join him on the terrace after dinner.

'The Queen's daughter is a precious child,' said Siegfried, puffing on a cigar. He poured himself another measure of gin and popped a liquorice drop in his mouth. 'There have been five miscarriages and a stillborn son. There will be no further pregnancies.'

'No, Father.'

'I have set aside a significant dowry for you. The Indonesian estates are producing handsomely. The rest is up to you.'

'Yes, Father.'

In the morning Huib polished the brass on the carriage. He paid close attention to the coat of arms on the carriage doors. A group of young men hung about, watching, admiring the plush velvet upholstery and the cunning cupboards set into the backs of the doors where brandy and glasses were kept. 'Hey, *Jochie*, are those gold tops or just gilt? Oh, excuse me, Count ...' The lads took off their hats and gave the half-bow due to a senior aristocrat as Siegfried climbed into the carriage.

Not far from Apeldoorn, a detachment from the Household Cavalry waited to accompany the Stolburgs to the palace. The troop insisted on trotting, an uncomfortable pace halfway between walking and cantering, and the carriage horses got their legs all in a muddle. After a couple of miles of this, Siegfried roared out the window, 'Either canter or walk, damn you. My horses will break their legs if you insist on trotting.'

They arrived at the gates of Het Loo at a canter, nearly colliding with a gypsy wagon pulled by a Shetland pony. Siegfried removed his hat quickly.

'Your Majesty,' he said to the lady driving the gypsy wagon.

'Ah, Siegfried,' said Queen Wilhelmina. 'And Lady Katrien. Forgot you were coming. Such a glorious day. Thought I'd go out and do some sketching. Hendrik will look after you. He's going to see Willy after lunch. Why don't you go with him, Siegfried? Poor old Willy gets lonely.'

In the back of the gypsy wagon sat a glum lady-in-waiting, an upright lit stove between her legs. 'Never ever,' said Siegfried to his daughter, as they pulled away, 'place a lit stove between your legs. If Wilhelmina gets cold while sketching or watercolouring, you tell her from me that she can put the damn stove between her own royal legs.'

'Yes, Father.'

Siegfried reported to Wilhelmina's husband, Prince Hendrik of Mecklenburg-Schwerin. The tartan walls of the prince's study were covered in antlers of all sizes. The two men drank a toast to celebrate Katrien joining the royal household, while a maid escorted Katrien to her rooms on the top floor.

'Where are the bathrooms and toilets?'

'You can use a chamber pot, Lady Katrien. We will bring a bath to you every second day.'

'In our house in Middelburg the bathrooms have been connected to running water and sewerage since the 1880s.'

'Yes, Lady Katrien.'

She asked the maid to unpack her clothes. 'Are you any good at dressing hair?'

'I am, Lady Katrien.'

She instructed the girl to roll her hair into a chignon. She stuck a diamond pin through the middle and took the three-metre string of black pearls out of the leather coffer. She wound them around her neck and went down to lunch.

Siegfried and Hendrik sat at one end of the table, drinking and swapping hunting stories. 'The boar in the Black Forest, Siegfried. Monsters. They charge at the horses – no fear at all. Emptied my guns into one of those beasts before he dropped. Unattractive tusks. No good for mounting. Next summer I'll take your boy Jack with me.'

'The red pheasant have been magnificent at Buitenrust this year. But Jack is tiring of that sport. I brought a brace of pheasant, by the way.'

At the other end of the table was Queen Emma, mother of Wilhelmina. She asked Katrien to sit beside her. She complimented Katrien on her dress, admiring the intricate cross-stitching around the jet buttons on the cuffs.

'Tell me, Lady Katrien,' she said in her thick German accent, 'where do you have your clothes made?'

'In London, *Majesteit*.'

'Lon-don?' Queen Emma touched the black pearls. 'One has heard of the black pearls. Part of the treasure of Zeeland. Such a pity to deprive the province of the pleasure.'

'My mother has retained the choker with the great ruby,' said Katrien.

After lunch Queen Emma invited Katrien to escort her around the gardens. Siegfried and Hendrik rode out of Het Loo to pay a call on the deposed German emperor, Kaiser Wilhelm II – Willy to his family and friends – who'd recently retired to the Netherlands and lived in the nearby castle of Doorn. Willy had quite endeared himself to the village locals, inventing a new persona as a country squire who hunted and fished and was assiduous in his politeness to any ladies he encountered.

The next morning Katrien accompanied her father as he called on Wilhelmina and Emma to bid them farewell and formally hand his daughter over into their care. Queen Emma wished him a pleasant journey. She asked if he was taking the black pearls back to Zeeland. 'Where they belong.'

'The black pearls are exactly where I want them to be, *Majesteit*.'

As Siegfried and Katrien left the royal presence, they overheard Queen Emma say to Queen Wilhelmina, 'I don't think the girl *looks* particularly Japanese.'

Nowadays at Het Loo only the public rooms – the stage sets of any palace – and Queen Wilhelmina's study are open for viewing. Wilhelmina's oak desk is battered and modest. For nearly half a century she ruled the Netherlands from this desk, much to the chagrin of her government's ministers, who hated making the two-hour journey from The Hague. Inside the palace stables is an exhibition of Wilhelmina's paintings. Most are watercolours of the forest and nearby heath. A photograph shows Wilhelmina on the roof of Amsterdam's Dam Palace, an old lady wrapped in coat and scarf, hunched over an easel, painting the gilded city skyline.

There is nothing for me at Het Loo, nothing to show that my aunt spent eighty years of her long life here. Despite her magnificent dowry and aristocratic forebears, Katrien never married. As far as anyone in the family knew, she never received a marriage offer. In the last handful of photographs taken of Katrien her Japanese heritage is obvious. She outlived all the Stolburgs. Except me. And until the time of her death we had not spoken to each other for forty years.

I should go back and sort out her affairs. But standing on the platform at Arnhem, waiting for a train that will take me to Middelburg, I am beset by depression.

I am the last.

I have known for many years that it would end this way.

I ought to have prepared myself.

No, I won't go to Middelburg, not yet. I give in to an impulse and decide to head north instead. But first there is a pilgrimage I must make.

The war cemetery at Oosterbeek is located just out of Arnhem. I walk along peaceful forest paths that saw some of the bloodiest fighting of the Second World War. There are azalea and rhododendron bushes, and acres of neatly aligned crosses. Often the ages of the dead are not given. Where they are given, the average age seems to be about twenty.

I seek out the Australian graves, young men, many of them from farms ravaged by drought in the 1940s. One of these has a notification from the Commonwealth War Graves Commission.

Australian soldier. Known only unto God.

Above me, a flock of swallows heading south for winter darkens the sky.

Leeuwarden is in the deep north. *Leeuwarden*: the keep of the lion. A solitary tower on the edge of town is all that remains of the keep. Amid the masonry rubble I find a Stolburg lion, his crown in pieces around him, a pile of unidentified stones in the knacker's yard of history.

A short train ride away is Harlingen, a bleak town straddling canals. Police at the ferry terminal check disembarking passengers, telling a huddle of Dutch louts singing football songs to move on. I venture into an eatery and retreat at the sight of the proprietor picking his nose. With my suitcase-on-wheels purring behind me, I search for an hotel instead. Only one has vacancies. It's perched picturesquely above a canal. Inside, cigarette smoke and grease have coloured the walls a grey yellow. The owner offers me a 'welcome' cup of tea at the bar. I peer into the smoke-filled hole and decline.

The only working channel on the hotel television is the Christian station. Hours of worthy documentaries cataloguing every misery to be found on the planet that day.

Oscar's voice when he answers the phone is light, casual. 'Are you in Middelburg?'

'Harlingen.'

'Harlingen?'

I hear him rustling, looking for a map. 'You're up the top, Juliana. You couldn't be any further from Middelburg.'

'I wanted to find evidence of the Stolburgs in the north.'

Silence.

'Oh, well. Guess what, darling? I went into the Wesley Mission in Goulburn and found six Haydn symphonies. I now have all the London and Paris symphonies.'

'How many Haydn symphonies are there?'

'One hundred and four. Still missing a few in the twenties and sixties. I met an interesting man there. He's a collector, like me. Grew up in Melbourne, like you. Lives in the old part of Goulburn, behind the cathedral, works in Sydney as a répétiteur for Opera Australia. He's invited me to his house for dinner. I don't think his sound system will be as good as mine but I'll be interested to see what he's got. You must meet him when you get back.'

'What is the name of the man you've just met?'

'Frederick.'

'Is there a Mrs Frederick?'

'No.'

'How old is this Frederick?'

'Fiftyish. Are you all right, Jules? You sound a bit flat.'

'Tired. Isn't Goulburn rather a long way from Sydney?'

A pain has developed in my stomach. In the bathroom I discover I have a period, the first in nearly a year. I had assumed this part of life was over and no longer travel with tampons or sanitary pads. I stuff wads of toilet paper between my legs and cower under the blankets. At least Oscar doesn't have to put up with this event.

I wake at half past two in the morning to shouting and shattering glass. Light disappears from the room. Through the curtains I see a group of men swaying by the canal's edge, rejoicing at the destruction of a street lamp. They cross the road to the hotel. I call reception and the phone rings and rings. The doors to the lobby are made of sturdy nineteenth-century glass.

Surely there are bars. Please let there be bars.

'*Hoi! Hoi!* Break the doors down.'

The downstairs doors shatter and my room shakes. Running, booted feet thump up the stairs. A heavy kick to my door. The flimsy timber buckles. I throw on jeans and a jumper and stuff more toilet paper into my undies.

'*Vrouwen! Vrouwen!* Women! Women!'

From the room above me there are sounds of violent sex. I am afraid they might tumble through the ceiling. A young man is weeping, begging to be left alone.

What's the Dutch emergency number? I try triple

zero. Nothing. I saw the Dutch number somewhere. Think. 112!

'*Commissaris van politie*,' an annoyed voice answers.

'I am . . . I am . . .'

For a moment I cannot think who I should say I am.

'I am Lady Juliana Stolburg. I am an Australian citizen. A drunken gang has invaded my hotel. I think someone upstairs has been assaulted.'

The phone is slammed down. I don't know if the police are coming or if the commissaris decided my call was a hoax. I scan the room. Nothing to defend myself with. I make the bed and hide behind the dusty curtains and hope they'll think the room is empty. Another kick to the door. Leaning against the glass windows, I feel the vibrations of the sea as it pounds into the dijkes.

I watch six police cars glide silently into the street below. Men and women in uniforms, hands ready at holsters, enter the hotel.

'Police! Police!'

They thud up the stairs. Angry conversation erupts in the room above. The young man is crying again. I listen to the sounds. Try to make sense of them. The police, it seems, outnumber the louts.

'Look out, pig. I nearly fell down the stairs.'

Outside, I see men loaded without fuss into police vans. When all but one of the vans has driven off, an ambulance arrives. A figure covered in blankets – the young man from upstairs, I assume – staggers out of the hotel, two policemen propping him up.

He is having trouble climbing into the back of the ambulance. The policemen lift up his legs.

There is a polite knock on the door.

My voice croaks. 'Who's there?'

'Commissaris.'

The commissaris is middle-aged, and handsome, in a pale Dutch sort of way that coarsens with age. His uniform, even though I woke him up, is immaculate.

'*Zo*, Lady Juliana Stolburg, an ancient Dutch name. But Australian? We will speak English. Passport please.' He notes down my details. 'May one ask why you are staying in this hotel, Lady Juliana?'

'I'm on a budget. The young man upstairs . . .?'

'No need to concern yourself, Madam. A drug business gone wrong. Problems in Harlingen recently. A drugs war. Do you want me to call the Australian embassy? Or Queen Beatrix perhaps? No? Well, try to sleep. Do you want a man outside your door? No? Very good, *Mevrouw*. Sleep well.'

I regret using my title. A little more than a month ago I was a diplomat specialising in matters to do with intelligence in the NATO sphere of influence. I knew how to behave in every situation.

I expect to lie awake, listening to the booming of the sea, yet I plunge into a deep sleep. During the night the wads of toilet paper dislodge themselves. The bottom bed sheet is stained red. My shower is a bloody affair.

The breakfast room is filled with men smoking.

Bastards. Where were you last night?

Breakfast consists of white packaged bread, sweaty cheese and brown ham. A thermos that I cannot open contains hot water for tea. A fat girl who appears to be in charge grunts when I ask her to open it.

'Can you speak properly, please?' I say. 'I can't understand you.'

Fixing me with a furious stare, she unscrews the thermos.

'Why was there no one in reception last night?'

No answer.

'Milk for my tea, *als je blieft*.'

A jug of milk is banged down, splashing the front of my jumper. Suppressed snorts come from the other diners. Carefully, I pick up the jug and pour it over the table. A beautiful white stream trickles to the floor, slowly turning brown as it absorbs the filth.

I pack my bag and change into another jumper. The girl is waiting for me at reception.

'Pay please.'

'I am not paying you. The desk should have been attended last night.'

'I will call the police if you refuse to pay.'

'Call the police. I will wait here.'

The girl chews her lip. 'If you pay there would be no further unpleasantness.'

'Call the police. I insist.'

The handsome commissaris pulls up in an unmarked Mercedes. As he enters the lobby he salutes me. A shiver of pleasure runs up my spine. He asks if I managed to sleep.

'She won't pay her bill,' the girl interrupts, 'and she threw milk everywhere.'

The commissaris starts yelling in rapid-fire Dutch. Several times he uses the word *samenspanning*. It takes me a few minutes to recall what this means. Collusion. He is accusing the hotel owners of collusion.

'I will take you to the station, Lady Juliana. You are not required to pay.'

'They have my credit card details. What if they charge my account?'

'This will not happen.'

His Mercedes smells of scrupulously tended leather. And mints. 'We Dutch are addicted to mints,' I say. The ride over wooden-bridged canals takes less than five minutes. I would have liked it to last longer.

The men carrying the various components of my bed groan and struggle up four flights of stairs to the top storey of Buitenrust. I have been unable to buy, anywhere in Middelburg, an Australian-style queen-size bed. The Dutch prefer separate beds locked together, each half with its own set of sheets. The men dump the parts down in the middle of the room I have chosen as my bedroom. Papa used this corner room before the war. The uncurtained windows face east and south and on bright days they catch the sun. All electricity to Buitenrust has been disconnected. I scurry from room to room, hoping for a flicker of power. I am queen of a cold, unlit castle.

At first light, tired and hungry, I explore my

demesne. First I crawl up the tower to raise the standard. The last time I was here I didn't fold it properly, and as a result it rides the ropes awkwardly. Sea mist wafts across just as the flag clicks into place, reducing it to a limp, unreadable rag. I must hope for sun and wind to dry it, otherwise the delicate eighteenth-century linen will rot.

When my mobile rings I nearly drop it.

'Where are you, Jules?'

'Middelburg. On top of the tower at Buitenrust. You?'

'I'm with Frederick. We've been listening to Mahler's Fifth. Frederick has the most marvellous house, views all over Goulburn.'

The mobile crackles. I hear unfamiliar background sounds.

'Hello, Juliana. Frederick here. Can't wait to meet you. Oscar has told me so much about you. Don't you think he has hilarious legs? Like a stork. He's so thin and tall.'

'Yes. My husband has hilarious legs.'

'I'll give you back to Oscar.'

'When are you coming home, Jules?' my husband asks.

'Soon. A few things to arrange.'

'Is the weather awful, darling?'

'Gosh no. This is Zeeland. Crisp days, blue sky, sunshine.'

'Lovely. Frederick is calling me for dessert. Got to go.'

The mist creeps through the bottom of my jeans. But in Zeeland the weather never stands still for long. By the time I walk to the edge of the estate, the sun has come up and the lie I told Oscar has come true.

At the advocaat's office, all semblance of niceties has evaporated.

'This is the statement of death duties owing.'

'There are six zeros. I do not have enough money to satisfy three of them.'

'You are asset–rich. One of your properties must be sold to pay off the debt.' The advocaat purses his lips. 'Maybe two. You understand you may not take possession or commence renovations until these legalities have been completed. I have a possible buyer for the keep on this headland.' He points to a remote island on a map on the wall. 'A ruin. No use to you. The buyer would satisfy the whole debt.'

The skin at the back of my neck prickles. But the sight of all those zeros is too much. I sign a piece of paper accepting liability for the death duties as itemised. On another piece of paper I sign over any rights I have to a mediaeval keep on another island.

The paperwork finished with, I straighten in my chair and glance again at the map on the wall. It extends beyond Zeeland to the area around Rotterdam. The island, home of the keep I have just given away, is highlighted in orange and adjoins one of the royal estates.

★

THE COMPANY OF MEN

'Lady Juliana?'

Judging by his brimming wheelbarrow, the man addressing me must come from one of the farms.

'I haven't seen carrots as red as those for years,' I say.

The farmer breaks off an end, wipes it on his corduroys and offers it to me. My stomach rumbles.

'We saw the flag,' he says.

'Silly of me to hoist the thing.'

'Yes. It was.' He grins. 'You will want to know about the rents. We've been expecting an adjustment for years.'

'How much are you paying?'

'Three farms. All paying ten euros per week for two and a half hectares each.'

'And the houses?'

'Come with the land.'

Soft sunshine bounces off the wet walls of the farmhouse behind him, an early nineteenth-century building with a tall triangular roof and black-pointed masonry walls. Through a diamond-paned window I glimpse a blazing fire.

'Please come inside. You look cold. This is the lady, Ma.'

His mother inches up close, examining my face. 'I remember you when you were a toddler. You followed Count Siegfried everywhere.'

'You remember my grandfather?'

'Of course.'

'Do you remember my parents, Jack and Janna?'

'Jack was in the Resistance. Janna in Dachau. The eldest boy Justien was murdered near the end of the war.'

An awkward silence fills the room.

'Take no notice of her,' the farmer says, pointing to his forehead. 'Memory all over the place.'

The old lady retreats to a corner by the fireplace while her son brews coffee and makes pancakes. I drink three cups and gulp down everything he puts in front of me.

'You shouldn't fly that standard,' the farmer says. 'It's very old and valuable, ceremonial, to be used for the Queen's birthday and such. There's another flag somewhere, not valuable, the wildlife people used it from time to time.'

'You can't walk in after fifty years and expect everything to be as it was,' the old lady says. 'When Jack Stolburg left, he didn't care what happened to us. Went to Australia, didn't he? Made a fortune. Never showed his face in the Netherlands again.'

Papa didn't make a fortune in Australia.

We lost everything.

5

Blurred

Joanie and I are washing dishes as *Götterdämmerung* fades into a Romantic, German twilight.

'The boys are getting on well,' Pearl says as she brings in the last of the plates from dinner. She is limping, due to a fall she sustained soon after I left, and every now and then she wobbles to one side as if drunk. But not everything has changed while I was away. There is no humidity, no suggestion of rain, and the air is dusty and scratchy at the back of my throat.

'I would like to sit outside for a while.'

The boys are already on the veranda.

'Juliana,' Frederick says. 'Oscar tells me you are not fond of Wagner.'

'My mother had an extended vacation in Dachau.

She heard quite a lot of Wagner there and developed an aversion to the music.'

'For God's sake,' Oscar says. 'Take no notice, Frederick.'

Frederick's backside is on the veranda railing, taking centre-stage to a half-circle of chairs around him. A full moon picks out silvery flecks in his hair. I wonder what his surname is. Oscar didn't mention it when we were introduced. Lifting an eyebrow, he flashes a mouth of perfect white teeth. His gaze has been fixed on me most of the evening. He has ignored Joanie, which tends to be her fate. Now he turns to her with a ravishing smile. 'The meat was done to perfection. The parsnip puree was to die for.'

'Right,' says Joanie, 'I'm off to bed. With Pearl throwing herself around like a drunk there's only me to muck out the horses in the morning.'

The screen door bangs shut behind her.

'I don't seem to have charmed your Joanie,' says Frederick, brushing Oscar lightly on the arm.

'I have to go to Canberra tomorrow,' I say, 'if you'll excuse me. Still a bit weary from the flight.'

'I have an appointment in Canberra,' Frederick says. 'I could drive you. We could do lunch. What time is your appointment, Juliana?'

'Eleven o'clock.'

'I'll pick you up before ten.'

I cannot think of a graceful way to refuse.

The still, dry crackle of the night air magnifies all sounds. I am at our bedroom window, hoping for a breeze, when I hear feet on the gravel. Oscar is walking Frederick to his car. They stop for a moment, looking up at the full moon. My husband touches the other man on the shoulders. He pulls him gently towards him. Their bodies do not touch. Their kiss is chaste.

Frederick has anticipated I will be in Canberra public servant mode and is wearing a suit when he comes to collect me. He negotiates the drive carefully. The land around Goulburn seems blasted. Signs at the edge of town warn of level-five water restrictions.

'What comes after level five?' I say.

'That's when you drink your own piss,' says Frederick. 'Do you mind if I listen to this? Work.' He inserts a CD into the player and beats time on the steering wheel. 'Damn the bloody girl. Too slow. Now, the next phrase is important.' He thumps hard on the steering wheel. His hands are powerful, with spatulate fingers. 'Ah, yes.' He exhales slowly. 'Orgasmic.'

Like fucking my husband?

'What is it a répétiteur does?' I ask.

'Rehearses someone, or a group of people, into a role. It is *the voice* I am interested in, although one must also pay attention to the stagecraft.'

Frederick is a good driver, edging into faster lanes when it is safe to do so, never exceeding the speed limit.

'Is this meeting in Canberra important to you, Juliana?'

'Not in the great scheme of things.'

'What I mean is, are they going to reharness you?'

'This old warhorse is out to pasture for good.'

'Oscar says you were some sort of spook.'

'One of my husband's fantasies.'

I'll kill Oscar, after I cut off his dick.

'Am I making you uncomfortable with my questions?'

'Nope.'

Sheep are grazing on the bottom of Lake George. A distant heat haze gives the illusion of water. The lakebed is vast. Alien.

Hoe is't in't vreemde land? Nog steeds vreemd?

What is it like in that strange land? Still strange?

On the rim of hills on the far side of the lake, wind turbines stand motionless, their blades outstretched.

'Like the wings of frozen pterodactyls,' says Frederick.

'Don't you want to know where my appointment is?'

'Russell Offices, I assume. Department of Defence. Know it quite well. Someone I knew worked there.'

We enter Northbourne Avenue and Frederick executes a complex turn at the roundabout. He deposits me at the rear of the building. 'My appointment is at the university. Shall we meet in the National Gallery foyer? At midday, say? You can get a taxi there, can't you, darling?'

How dare you call me darling . . .

The interview that puts the full stop next to my career takes place in a room containing two chairs and one standard–issue table. Whenever I interviewed persons of interest, I provided them with a homely, comfortable room – all the better to throw them off balance. I am disappointed that the end of my working life is to be moderated by a nondescript chap in a shoebox without a view.

'Long career, Miss Stolburg. Recruited when you were eighteen.'

'Yep.'

'Vietnam, Cambodia . . .'

'Everywhere.'

'You will receive a pension equal to that received by a brigadier general. Indexed for life. Discretion . . .'

'Guaranteed.'

By the time I am on the other side of Lake Burley Griffin, my long years of service to the Commonwealth of Australia have been crossed out, rendered as meaningless as the stupid water spout in the middle of the lake. The spout's been turned off, in consideration of the drought.

I arrive at the concrete bunker that is the National Gallery of Australia half an hour early. Time enough to repair make-up and tuck in all the recalcitrant parts of my body. From my handbag I extract a small leather box. How improbable the Stolburg coat of arms seems inside this ladies' room. Or anywhere in Australia.

'Are you all right?' a woman applying globs of lipstick to an already bright mouth asks. 'You look miles away.'

'Just back from Europe.'

'That will do it every time. Cheers, dear.'

From the leather box I pluck pearl drop earrings, a pearl necklace and a ring of voluptuous diamonds. Thus armed, I go to meet Frederick.

The doors sweep aside for him. He checks his watch. Stands still. Looks around. Without Oscar beside him, he is tall. Not quite six foot; broad shouldered, slim hipped; suit carefully tailored, perfect at the crotch, not baggy and not unforgivably tight. He wears quality leather shoes, well polished but not too new. He is the epitome of elegance and male grace. He is so beautiful that for a moment I long to see him naked.

There are two sorts of beautiful males: narcissists who flaunt their beauty and are thus diminished by it, and those who take their beauty for granted and are annoyed when someone admires them. Frederick senses an appraising glance. Sees me. A fleeting cloud crosses his expression; the jaw tightens. Then he is himself again.

'Tickets for Munro,' he says to the woman behind the front desk.

His name is Munro.

It means the peak, the apex, Philly said all those years ago.

'Juliana, are you all right? You're white as a sheet. We'll do the exhibition first, shall we, then lunch? I've booked us a table in the sculpture garden restaurant. Your colour's better now.'

As Frederick and I surge through the rooms our bodies nudge and collide. He thrusts back his head to study the ceiling. 'This lighting is fantastic. Lighting is my thing, you know. Some singers I work with are very ordinary to look at. Lights can transform a singer.'

'What about the voice?'

'Most voices by the time they get to me are good. I make them better. I've made a few voices great. The singers have to allow me to bring out the persona hidden within the voice.'

The visiting exhibition is one that compares Monet with the Japanese tradition. There are the inevitable waterlilies and haystacks. It is the Japanese works, the ones that reveal something of their European influences, that captivate me. I cannot tear myself away from Utagawa Hiroshige's *Evening View of Saruwakacho Street*. Women going about the daily business of providing for their households. Women caught behind upper-storey windows gazing abstractedly at life below. At the heart of the picture are four onlookers: a dog and three cats.

'My grandmother was part Japanese,' I tell Frederick.

Their affair is so new I assume he and Oscar are still at the stage of imparting to one another things about themselves, not matters to do with the people in their lives.

'Oscar told me.'

I am surprised to find my cheeks wet.

'Jet-lag,' I say.

'There is also the matter of misplacing your career.' Frederick's voice is soft, sympathetic. 'You could not have expected that to desert you just yet.'

'I had burnt out. My masters and I recognised that.'

He nods knowingly. Knowing nothing.

Our table, close to the pond, is in full sun. 'Do you think it will be too hot?' he says. 'I think it might.

Let's start with a glass of bubbly. I'll only have two as I'm driving. You may have more, Juliana.'

He takes charge of the drink, the menu, the relocation of the table and the conversation. We speak of many things: his job, music, art galleries we love and hate, the drought. Neither of us mentions Oscar. A gap opens in the conversation and we watch a waterbird rise from the waterlilies. It trips over a sculpted human head before settling back, after some hysterical to-ing and fro-ing, in its original spot.

'May I look at your ring?'

Frederick takes my hand and removes the extravagant cluster of diamonds. This feels intimate.

'Family piece?'

He holds my hand to put the ring back on. I do not want him to do that and take back my hand. The waiter comes with the bill. Frederick flips a platinum credit card on the tray.

Champagne, the ennui of a hot afternoon, makes my eyes heavy. I force out a few pleasantries. Then I am asleep in the passenger seat. I hear the crunching of gravel and assume we are back at the farm.

'Thought you might like to see my house,' says Frederick. 'I'll ring Oscar and ask him to join us. After dinner he can take you home.'

The last thing I want to see is your house.

I don't want to have dinner with you and Oscar.

I want to be supplied with a script so that I can negotiate this scene with dignity.

'Yes, that would be lovely.'

His house is not what I expect. Goulburn is a city

of late Victorian architecture. Frederick's house looks like a 1920s bungalow. Art nouveau lilies are carved into the woodwork. High ceilings are encrusted with floral plaster. I pause in front of a blue-grey Hans Heysen watercolour, then an ochreous Albert Namatjira scene of zigzagging mountains. There's a delightful nook in the entrance hall for the telephone. A room he calls the library houses a television and walls of records. In the sitting room is an enormous Persian rug, and in the dining room a toffee-black grand piano. A honey trap for men?

On top of the piano are photographs. One is of a man strikingly like Frederick. This man is vain about his looks and his ability to charm both sexes. He is wearing the uniform of a brigadier and standing in front of Victoria Barracks in Melbourne.

'My brother,' Frederick says, taking the picture from me and putting it back on the piano. 'Did you ever meet Michael? Oscar says you began your career in Defence in Melbourne.'

'I knew Brigadier Michael Munro.'

I take a second look. The red insignia on the man's cap, shoulders and lapels has faded to a pale pink. The photograph must have been taken shortly after he returned from Vietnam for the second time.

'Is there a photo of you, Frederick, in the costume of a chorister at St Paul's Cathedral?'

'How do you know about that?'

'Michael mentioned he had a brother who was a boy soprano. He hoped you might become a gifted tenor.'

'I didn't.'

Delicately wielding a huge knife, Frederick pops wafers of green lime in three glasses and adds gin.

Oscar arrives in the usual way: legs, arms, angles. He stops at the doorway, debating which of us must be kissed, and opts to do us both. He kisses me on my left cheek (my worst side) and Frederick on his right. There is a heavy, civilised silence. Frederick's face looks flushed. My husband does not seem to be paying the younger man the attention he craves.

'Did you enjoy your day, darling?' Oscar asks.

'Yes,' Frederick and I answer simultaneously.

Frederick wants to know what music we'd like to hear, and when neither of us answers he walks out and chooses *Tosca*, with Maria Callas in the title role.

Tosca was his brother Michael's favourite opera.

I have fallen asleep again. I trained as a psychologist, a social scientist, an observer of people. Any half-trained psychology student could point out that falling asleep while having dinner at someone else's house is avoidance behaviour. I am alone in the sunroom. They are in his bedroom, off the veranda. I see their shadows against a holland blind. Frederick's arms are stretched out along the windowsill. Oscar is moving rhythmically behind him. A few minutes later they return to the sunroom.

'Pudding?' asks Frederick. 'I have the doings of a trifle.'

'Do you know where the term "holland blind" comes from?' I reply. 'After William of Orange ascended the throne in the Glorious Revolution of 1688, there was a relaxation of window taxes. Big glass windows became fashionable. Unfortunately, the sun fades upholstery. So blinds were invented whereby those inside could look at the world outside yet remain unseen. At the same time their precious furniture was protected. There was a downside, though. At night those inside were revealed to the world if the light of a lamp was behind them. This double treachery appealed to the English sense of humour and the term "holland blind" entered the language.

'I want to go now.'

'I'm that sorry, Juliana.' Pearl is listing badly, body bent to one side. The labrador follows her from kitchen table to refrigerator, hoping to be fed.

'How do you stand it, Jules?' Joanie asks.

'I knew what I was getting when I married Oscar.'

I knew what I was getting. In 1976, when I told my superiors that I was marrying a lecturer in the English department of the Australian National University, Oscar was subjected to ASIO scrutiny. His sexual orientation, I was warned, was 'blurred'. Over the next few years, whenever he had a homosexual encounter I was informed of the fact in an eyes-only memo. I never told him he was being watched, or that I knew of his affairs. When my job moved me overseas his hopes of an academic career evaporated. Wherever I was posted he found work at one of the international schools, teaching the children of high-level diplomats and senior military officers. Eventually the security services stopped paying attention to Oscar's sexuality. He never slept with the enemy, whoever the enemy happened to be at the time.

'Frederick thinks he might be able to get me a job as an assistant répétiteur,' Oscar says later that night. 'I thought something part-time might be useful.' He looks around at the mess in our bedroom, books and papers scattered all over the floor, a packed suitcase in one corner. 'This is most unlike you, Jules.'

'Not much point unpacking, is there?'

Following me around the world, there are parts of Australia as new to Oscar as they are to me. I don't remember the underground train service from Central Station to Circular Quay feeling so relentless, or the carriages so filthy. I don't remember Australians being so fat, so badly dressed, so broadly accented yet so eager to please. Oscar's face at this first-hand experience of Sydney is a mixture of disdain and pride. The train hurtles from the tunnel into Circular Quay alongside the hazardous blue of the harbour and the art deco exuberance of the bridge.

'The Opera House is quite mad.' His hand trembles in mine.

'Juliana and Oscar entering yet another opera house,' I say, hoping to ease his tension.

'I am not sure I can do this, Jules. Frederick thinks I can. I'm not so sure.'

I drag his face down until it meets mine. He has to bend his body almost in half. 'You will be marvellous.

Your musical knowledge is encyclopaedic. Your skill at the piano is more than adequate. Frederick says you don't have to be a great pianist to be a répétiteur.'

'I'd love the chance to do something else,' he admits. 'I'm sick of teaching. But I don't want to look an idiot in front of Frederick.'

He is waiting for us, deep in thought, in the lobby of the artists' entrance. Head bowed. One foot touching the wall behind.

Within beauty both shores meet and all contradictions exist side by side. I can hear Philly quoting that passage as though he stands beside me.

I wonder if they'll kiss. I have become used to their kisses of greeting. But this is Frederick's workplace. He kisses me on both cheeks, strokes my European jacket – 'Nice' – and shakes hands with Oscar. 'Follow me.' The bowels of the Opera House are crammed with people and objects. 'These corridors meander. Rather like the Danes.'

Oscar and I exchange glances. We have attended many Australian diplomatic functions overseas, with the Opera House a constant backdrop, and are surprised to hear the building so easily disparaged.

'Looks like a dog, sings like an angel,' is Frederick's verdict on one well-known soprano.

'Making her up is a nightmare,' he says of another.

He bestows a withering glance on a man passing by. 'We had a thing once. Can't stand him now.'

Frederick's office is a rehearsal room. A group of singers are humming to themselves by a grand piano. They are instructed to perform the quartet from *Così fan tutte*. 'You're all over the bloody place!' he shouts after a few bars. 'Longing! Longing! You are not going to the supermarket.' One girl fluffs a note and he bangs the lid of the piano. 'You silly tart. Oscar, see what you can do with this lot.'

Oscar moves towards the piano with long, hesitant strides. He scrapes back the stool to accommodate his legs. Plays a few chords to familiarise himself with the instrument. Then he nods. Suddenly the ensemble sing in unison and with great emotion. Twice he stops them to correct slippages of time. Satisfied, he turns to Frederick.

'You'll do,' Frederick says. He flashes me an impish grin that I do not acknowledge. His manipulation of this scene is not subtle enough to warrant my praise.

I trail behind the men as Oscar is introduced around the building. Faces and names appear and disappear. Responsibilities are allocated. By the time lunch is proposed I am tired and bored. The harbour does all the right twinkly things while we study the menu at a waterside restaurant.

'A bottle of Bollinger,' Oscar orders. 'Jules will pay out of her massive inheritance.'

We watch a crocodile of young children climb the Opera House steps, voices skittering with excitement. 'They are about to be introduced to their first experience of opera,' says Frederick. 'Get them in kindergarten and you keep them for life.'

6

The Nachgeborenen

Mama drew envious glances from the other mothers in the Middelburg kindergarten enrolment line. She was the most beautiful and stylishly dressed woman and I was the best-dressed child in a new frock she'd made from old poplin, even if my post–rheumatic fever looks, my skinny body and lank colourless hair irritated her.

She had taught me the ABC and how to count to a hundred. She read to me in the afternoons when I was supposed to rest. Reading, like sewing, was a way of communicating without having to look at me. As she turned the pages I'd study her avidly, drinking in her porcelain skin, the lustre of her hair, the subtle aroma of lavender water that clung to her clothes. 'Don't stare,' she'd say after a while, and I would switch my gaze to the paintings hanging on the sitting room wall, and try to make out details obscured by centuries of smoke from fires and tobacco. I was not allowed to leaf through other books while Mama read. 'You must concentrate.'

The old kindergarten had been bombed and the new kindergarten was visible behind cold metal railings in the basement of someone's house. The queue snaked down the street. Ahead of us the lord mayor's wife waited with her two children, Fritz and his sister Hansje, fellow survivors of the rheumatic fever epidemic of 1949. I was permitted on occasion to play with the lord mayor's children. The family was Calvinist and of the right social background.

Mama filled in forms and gave them to a round-spectacled man with a stethoscope twisted down his neck.

'*Zo*,' the man barked, 'this is Juliana Stolburg. Into that room, please.'

I joined Fritz, Hansje and two boys in a room away from the other children. We were told to strip down to underpants and singlets. A nurse measured our height and took note of our weight. As she wrote down mine, she clicked her tongue. The man with the stethoscope came in and ran the icy instrument across my chest. I was instructed to cough. He tugged what flesh there was on my arms. Then he held up two fingers on one hand, three on the other and asked if I knew how many fingers.

'Two and three is five,' I said.

He pointed to an ABC chart and asked if I could

108

identify any of the letters. I gabbled the alphabet at him. The others were put through the same tests.

'Call in the mothers,' the doctor ordered. Then he jabbed a finger at the five of us. 'These children are not strong enough to attend kindergarten. They must stay home another year.'

Mama approached the doctor, high heels tapping a dangerous rhythm on the linoleum. 'What are we to do with these children? How are we to keep them out of mischief? They need to begin their education.'

The doctor got to his feet. 'I have spoken. My mind is made up.'

Mama hissed. 'Do you know whose grandchild my daughter is?'

'Yes, *Mevrouw*, Count Siegfried's – and the only one he's ever likely to have, given your age.'

Two red spots rose in Mama's pale cheeks. I closed my eyes to block out the storm. The doctor ran out of the room.

'You are punishing these children because they had rheumatic fever!' Mama yelled after him. She grabbed me by the arm and pushed me out of the wonderful world of kindergarten.

'The children will be ten by the time they start school,' one mother complained.

'Could you teach my children,' the lord mayor's wife asked Mama, 'for half a day every day?'

'I am no teacher. I have not had an education. What I know comes from the books in Count Siegfried's library.'

'Your daughter can count and she knows the ABC. I would be grateful if my two knew that much.'

Papa approved. He believed I was not robust enough to begin school. Another year at home, he promised, and I could bypass kindergarten and enter the first grade. 'And teaching the children will be good for you, Janna,' he said.

'Something to occupy my mind,' she snapped.

'*Ach zo.*'

Four children came to our house on school mornings. Fritz and Hansje, lanky Jankees, son of a department store owner, and round-faced Otto, son of an advocaat. The others were given daily doses of penicillin and aspirin, a regime they'd been told they would have to maintain until they were ten, at least. Because of my allergy to penicillin I took aspirin twice a day. Of all of us, I had been closest to death. I was so skinny Mama refused to bathe me. She said the sight of my bones reminded her of the concentration camp. At bath time Papa would make a point of tugging at my bony knees and counting my ribs. 'How many bones does my monkey have?' And yet it was the others who tired quickest, regularly catching colds and complaining of stiff and aching joints. I had none of those.

Mama called us five children the *Nachgeborenen*: those who come after. Bertolt Brecht's poem, *An die Nachgeborenen*, was one we were all familiar with. It was written in 1939 as Germany invaded Poland, and we'd heard it read out in German and in Dutch on Radio Hilversum. Mama had memorised it in both languages. She recited it to us on the morning of our first lesson.

Wirklich, ich lebe in finsteren Zeiten.

Truly, I live in dark times.

Her eyes blazed and her delicate skin turned

110

even whiter. I looked around at the others. Mama's use of German had confused them as much as it confused me. She was supposed to be Jewish. She had been in a concentration camp, a place spoken of in whispers. Even we, four and five year olds, had imbibed the anti-German hatred that gripped the Netherlands after the war. We'd listened to adults accuse each other of being Nazi sympathisers, and we'd heard them mutter about acts of revenge they should have committed during the war. Yet here was Mama wanting us to learn a poem written in German. 'German is a beautiful language,' she said that morning. 'The Nazis were awful people who made German sound ugly.'

We sat on the floor in the breakfast room, where the Singer sewing machine lived. The breakfast and sitting rooms, both upstairs, had been spared the worst of the bomb damage. Sometimes she sewed or embroidered while we recited the ABC or counted with her. Other times she read to us. She didn't introduce us to ABC primers. She read to us from her favourite novelist, Émile Zola.

We didn't understand Zola's bleak realism any more than we understood Brecht. But Mama's voice mesmerised us. Unlike the other adults we knew, who spoke a clipped high Dutch, Mama's voice had a romantic lilt. It was the lilt of her first language, the Yiddish–Flemish of her childhood. She'd lower her voice to raise suspense. When required, she'd shout. Mama was a natural dramatist and we listened to her voice more than the words. The only children's books she ever showed us were Enid Blyton's *Famous Five* stories. The children in those books were like us, we thought. They adored an island.

Each morning at eleven Françoise arrived with the family bible. Mama went off to prepare cocoa and biscuits, and Françoise would sit on a hard-backed chair at the head of the table with the sun at her back. She'd spread her black skirts around her and fiddle with her white coif. Then, with a key she wore on a belt around her waist, she unlocked the good book. In a high monotone, she'd begin reading. I tried to look as though I was listening. Really I was taking in every facet of her gemstones, absorbing the subtle variations in gold on her neck, wrists and fingers.

Fritz claimed my grandmother's unblinking dark eyes frightened him. We followed Fritz, being slightly older, in most things. We all pretended we were afraid of Françoise. When Mama returned we'd run shouting to her like unprincipled savages and Françoise would snap shut her bible. One day Mama overheard us ridiculing Françoise and her bible-snapping. Worse than that, she heard us refer to Françoise by her first name. In our circle only the men used first names, and then only sometimes.

'The Lady Stolburg is not for the likes of you to speak of by first name,' Mama said.

'Why does the countess still wear the Calvinist dress when everyone else is giving it up?' Fritz asked.

'That is none of your business.' Mama looked at him sternly. We all knew she was capable of throwing a book at our heads if we misbehaved; Otto had earned a bloody nose that way just a week before. '*Ach*, you should have known Françoise when I first came into the household in 1920,' she said. 'She was still a great beauty. Her hair was black as a raven's wing.'

Our world was almost devoid of birdlife. Most birds, even swans, had been eaten during the war. We could not imagine Françoise being young, beautiful or birdlike.

'You just called Lady Stolburg by her first name,' said Fritz. He ducked as Mama threw a book at him.

'The serial is about to start,' said Jankees. He got up awkwardly to stand next to the radiogram. Jankees had a stiffness in his right leg that never went away, and he walked with a permanent limp. The radiogram was a new addition to our lives. It occupied one wall of the sitting room. It consisted of a record player for 78 rpm records and a state-of-the-art radio that received not only Radio Hilversum but also the BBC World Service and the famous Radio Luxemburg. In the late mornings there were serials for children. We loved one serial in particular. It featured aliens who hid underground. You always knew when the aliens were coming because their antennae popped out of the ground before they did.

The part of the alien serial we liked best was the introductory music, the *Ride of the Valkyries*, from Wagner's Ring cycle. We were not allowed to touch the radiogram ourselves in case we disturbed some internal balance. Mama had to switch it on, and she would make us wait until the last possible moment. The lighting up of the dials, the flicker of the needle, was as mystical to us as any church rite. Then at half past eleven the *Valkyries* thundered out of the radio and aliens invaded our imagination.

Sometimes Papa came home for lunch. We could hear his motorbike growling up the street and him pounding the stairs in his American army boots. Then he'd enter the room, tall, handsome and exotic in his long leather coat. The boys idolised him and hung on to that coat, savouring the smell of tobacco, gin and the sea, and Papa's status as a hero of the Resistance.

Papa had acquired a Meccano set from the black market. After removing his coat and settling down at the table with the thick treacly coffee he loved, he brought out boxes of metal rods and tiny screws. He showed us how to make simple constructions and shared with us the deep spiritual relationship Zeelanders have with the sea. At the footings of one of the dijkes, he told us, his men had found a Roman-era statue of the sea goddess, Nehalennia. 'The people of the sea worshipped this goddess before Christ,' Papa said. We learnt that, like icebergs, three-quarters of a dijke is hidden below the surface. Arranging and rearranging the Meccano pieces, Papa demonstrated how the dijkes destroyed at the end of the war were supposed to be rebuilt. We didn't know how hard he fought the government in The Hague for money for the rebuilding, or how little was made available.

It was Papa's idea that Siegfried should tell us something of the history of the Netherlands. The first time Count Siegfried Stolburg strode into our breakfast room-cum-schoolroom in his nineteenth-century court costume, I was as impressed as my friends were. Siegfried's knickerbockers shone at the knee, his white stockings had yellowed with age and his patent leather shoes were cracked. But the coronet, fitted over a velvet cloche, looked like newly minted gold.

At first Siegfried was stiff and formal. He filled us in on the *Batavieren*, a Germanic people who were the earliest inhabitants, then the Roman invaders, then a mixed bunch who called themselves *Nederlanders*, descended from Franks, Romans and Germanic tribes. Suddenly he grew animated, sketching a bewildering collection of kings and dukes as though he had known them all personally. He'd met Queen Victoria in his youth, he'd known the Kaiser, he'd gone on shooting parties in the Scottish Highlands with Edward VII. He had even seen Japan and bowed to the Meiji emperor. We held our breath as he talked of marrying Françoise in 1899 in a far-off place called Nagoya.

'Yes, I married a half-Japanese lady and risked the anger of my parents, the royal family and my fellow aristocrats. What you children have to remember is that my wife's father was a famous Dutchman, a *waterbouwkundige*, a manipulator of water . . .'

'Spanish Jack, I mean Lord Stolburg, he's a waterbouwkundige, isn't he?' said Fritz.

'My son Jack has a special relationship with the sea and the dijkes that have protected Zeeland for thousands of years.'

'Can we hear more about Japan?' I butted in tentatively, not wanting this precious opportunity to disappear in yet another discussion about dijkes.

Siegfried made himself comfortable. He took off his coronet and rested it on his knee. When Fritz touched it, he smiled. 'Go on, boy. Put it on your head. See if it fits.'

Fritz balanced the gold band over his curls.

'The Dutch,' said Siegfried, 'had trading agreements with the Japanese for three hundred years. We weren't masters there in the way we ruled Indonesia. Far from it. The Japanese trusted the Dutch, even put us in their paintings, but they kept us in enclaves. The Meiji emperor wanted to modernise Japan, to adopt western ideas, and Françoise's father, the man the Japanese called the hero of Kiso, became his friend, his adviser, his secretary of state. No other westerner ever achieved that honour. I was on a year-long tour. Nagoya was my last stop. Françoise and her father made me welcome. I had never seen such a beautiful young woman. We were married six weeks later in the Calvinist church there. The emperor came to the wedding – not inside the church, no. He stayed outside in his carriage. We bowed to him as we came out.'

Siegfried reached for his cane. This was one of his bad days, I could tell, when his hip and leg felt as if they were on fire. We watched from the upstairs window as he walked across the road, the coronet dangling around his left arm. He stopped to speak to some church elders, pointing at his knickerbockers and gesturing up to the room where Mama's lessons took place. He saw us looking through the window and smiled, and for a moment he was transformed into the beautiful fair-haired man he must have been in his youth. Then, bent at the shoulders, he hobbled up the steps to his front door.

The next time Françoise and her bible descended on us, I looked for signs of her Japanese heritage. But that woman was hidden far beneath all those layers of black skirts, and I was too young to see past them.

As the year wound towards summer, Mama encouraged us to seek fresh air. We were supposed to rest in the afternoons. That was the mantra hurled at us daily: rest, rest and more rest, the cure for rheumatic fever. Mama knew that too much rest drove us insane. She feared we might become invalids from too much resting. On fine days she asked the other mothers to send along packets of sandwiches and, if possible, a piece of fruit. In 1951 fruit was a luxury and almost unobtainable. We were lucky to have three oranges a year. Whenever I saw fruit in our house I knew Mama had been to the black market.

Before the war there were fruit trees all over Walcheren. Papa told us that when he and his brother and sister went out on horseback, they never took food. They'd pick fruit off the trees, or fish, or shoot a rabbit. They'd cook a meal over a fire. Papa spoke of streams teeming with fish and waterbirds. He filled the sky for us with tales of autumn migrations, when the sky would turn as dark as the day the Luftwaffe blackened it with their birds. He described the birdsong of spring, the first birds trickling in singly, one by one, then slowly, within days, filling the air with an opera of mating songs. Papa brought alive for us the famous Zeeuws horses, so sturdy they could carry a knight in full armour for a whole day. He made us see paddocks where horses roamed and created young.

On sunny days we headed out with our packets of sandwiches, our heads bursting with before-the-war tales, into a shattered landscape. The sound we knew was not the birdsong of spring but the clatter of heavy equipment clearing away war rubble.

'Let's go to Buitenrust,' Fritz said one day. 'You can show us around, Juliana. The Nazis used the place during the war. There's lots of stuff like flags and helmets and things just lying around.'

We coveted Nazi memorabilia. On our forays into the countryside we always hoped to find something with a swastika on it. We never did. The rubble around Walcheren had been thoroughly picked over by British, American and Dutch servicemen.

'Your uncle's buried at Buitenrust,' Fritz persisted. 'Don't you want to see his grave?'

'My uncle?'

'Justien – the Nazi collaborator, the one your father executed after the war.'

'My father didn't execute anyone.'

''Course he did!' my companions shouted. 'He was head of the Resistance. Betrayal got you a bullet to the back of the head. Yeah! Everyone says so.'

'Papa wouldn't have executed his brother.'

I could feel tears coming.

'Come on, Juliana,' said round-faced Otto, poking me in the ribs, 'take us to Buitenrust.'

I had never been there on my own. I hesitated. Buitenrust was surrounded by barbed wire and impossible to enter from the road. But there was another entrance, one Siegfried had shown me, from the fields. Forgetting doctors' orders not to run, we raced each other until the broken spires of Middelburg were out of sight. We ran and ran until we were left breathless, under a sky written over by white clouds, not noticing the black clouds gathering in one corner.

The German bunkers on the property gleamed wet and angry. There were weeds everywhere and fences with writing on them. Mama had introduced us to Zola, Brecht and Enid Blyton, but we had not learnt to read little words attached to fences. We crawled through one set of fences, then another, until we came to the first of the bunkers. The manor house was visible in the distance. But it did not interest us nearly as much as the round concrete shapes left over by the Army of the Third Reich.

In front of one of the bunkers was a slight slope. Fritz told Hansje – tiny, white-haired Hansje – to go up and peer into the terrible black mouth. We did not ask ourselves why he didn't volunteer to go himself.

'What can you see, Hansje? Swastikas?'

'Well . . .'

'A photo of Hitler?'

'Maybe.'

'Skeletons?'

Hansje screamed. 'I can see skeletons!'

Summer storms in Zeeland can arise out of any unnoticed corner. Suddenly the sky darkened and lightning danced around us. Hail the size of cherries pelted us. We ran off yelling hysterically. We knew we had to avoid the poplars, which drew lightning to the ground. Arms and legs flailing, we crawled under the first fence we came to. We were in a pockmarked field. Wires poked out of holes. Fritz and I looked at each other.

'*Aliens!*'

After the hail came giant raindrops, and we wandered from hole to hole, touching the wires, oblivious to voices shouting at us. There came a gap in the storm, and that's when we heard them.

'Children. Listen carefully. Walk to us on tiptoe.'

They were army men with loud hailers. We stepped slowly towards them. The nearer we got, the angrier their faces looked. They pulled Hansje roughly through a fence, her fine white hair catching in a barb, making her cry. Next they jerked Otto through, then Fritz, then Jankees. I held back, wanting to go last. When it was my turn I took a step back and gave one wire a last, delicious tug.

Mouths opened in horror but no sound came out. Hands beckoned me urgently. Some of the soldiers started to run. But I was on Buitenrust land. My family had owned this land for nearly eight hundred years. I wasn't going to be told what to do by strange men. I sauntered nonchalantly to the fence.

As I crawled through, the ground rumbled. 'Hurry! Hurry!' A mine had exploded, setting off a chain reaction of more explosions, sending dirt into

the air and shockwaves ringing through my head.
When I came to, I was covered head to foot in dirt,
and lying next to me were soldiers who were also
covered in dirt. A few metres away lay Otto, weeping.
I laughed. A man – the boss – slapped me.

'Hey,' one of the soldiers said, 'that's Count
Siegfried's granddaughter. Her father was Spanish
Jack.'

The man who'd slapped me grunted. We were
roughly dusted down and loaded onto an army truck.
They asked where each of us lived and began dropping
us off, explaining to the parents what had happened.
At the mayoral residence the lord mayor answered
the door. He dragged Fritz inside by the ear.

I was the last child on that truck by the time
we approached our house. Papa was fitting a new
front door, replacing a temporary door made from
packing-case wood. Some of the soldiers saluted him.
Others touched their caps with an index finger. '*Zo*,
Jack, we found your daughter at Buitenrust. Some
mines exploded, no one hurt.'

Papa shook me by the arm. 'Didn't you see the
signs?'

It was the first time he had ever shouted at me.

'We saw signs,' I said, 'but we can't read little
words.'

Tears squelched from my eyes as Mama flew out
the front door, throwing the packing-case door to
the ground. Stuck in the bosom of her dress were
pins, a needle and some thread. Before Papa could
supply her with a sanitised account, the soldier who'd
slapped me said, 'We found the girl and her friends

playing in the minefields. Pulled a wire, didn't she? Made a mine go off.'

Mama's blows rained about my head. Her lips withdrew from her teeth. The tip of her tongue stuck out. Papa grabbed her and pulled her away, but not before she had delivered a hard kick to my upper thigh.

I did not cry.

I never cried when she hit me.

I watched Mama as she burst into tears. Then I turned to the soldiers. 'Thank you for bringing me home. You may go now.'

'Miss high and mighty,' I heard one of them say.

Papa ran a bath and scrubbed me carefully, avoiding the purpling bruise on my thigh.

'Why did you go there?'

'We wanted to find Nazi stuff. Hansje said she saw skeletons in the bunkers. Is it true Uncle Justien is buried there? Fritz says he is.'

'Justien died at Buitenrust, that's true,' Papa said. 'Look here, took us twelve years to have you. Appreciate it if you don't die just yet. I'll go up to the school tomorrow. After the holidays you and your friends had better start first grade before you blow up the rest of Walcheren. I don't know what all the fuss was about, those mines were half defused. You might have lost an arm or a leg at most.'

Papa used black humour to paper over the cracks caused by his war. He drank too much gin, sometimes half a bottle a day, and smoked as many cigars as the black market could provide. Yet he held our family together.

That night, round-faced Otto was the first of the

Nachgeborenen to die. His heart, battered by rheumatic fever, stopped while he slept. The rest of us were not told until after the funeral.

Mama did not recover from the Buitenrust incident. She stayed in bed, refusing all sustenance other than sweet biscuits and tea, and sank into silence. After a few days of this she packed a suitcase while Papa was at work and took me across the road to my grandparents' house. She did not say a word. She didn't need to. We knew she was going home to Oma and Opa.

Françoise stood behind me, holding on to me, as Mama dragged the cardboard suitcase she'd brought back from Dachau away with her. I waved and waved. She did not turn around. When Papa came home, Siegfried and Françoise said they did not think they could cope with me.

'Has she been naughty?'

No, they assured him, they were simply too old. There was also the matter of the other children Mama was teaching. Honour demanded that the responsibility she'd accepted be fulfilled. 'Six years since the war finished,' Françoise said. 'Janna must learn to put it behind her. As we have done.'

Françoise's new gold-rimmed reading glasses accentuated the dark of her eyes. She poked the glasses under her coif, coiled them round her ears and opened the bible.

To everything there is a season, and a time to every purpose under heaven . . .

A time to kill, and a time to heal;
A time to break down, and a time to build up

Without warning I began to cry great, galloping sobs. The adults asked me over and over why I was crying. 'She never cries.' I wasn't yet old enough and didn't possess the words to tell them that Mama, I thought, would never recover from the war.

No one else in Middelburg could look after me, so Siegfried summoned his daughter Katrien home. She immediately informed us that she had been on her way to Scotland with Wilhelmina for the ex-Queen's annual sketching holiday. 'Her Majesty understood I had to attend to *het kind*,' Katrien sniffed, shooting me one of her ice-blue glances. I was always *het kind*, the child. She never referred to me by name.

Katrien took up residence in the chair next to Mama's sewing machine. Mama's chair was left empty. Although it was high summer and schoolchildren were on holidays, the education of the *Nachgeborenen* continued. Brecht and Zola were banished with a double sniff. '*Truly, I live in dark times* – bah. Brecht spent the war years in America. He should have been in London during the Blitz. Then he would have known about hard times. They sent Mary of England, Queen Wilhelmina and us ladies away in the middle of the night once, bombs falling around us, to an awful place in Norfolk. It was cold and damp. You should have heard their Majesties swearing at the *Duitsers*. Those were hard times.'

We hardly dared breathe, hoping for a crumb or two more from the royal world Katrien lived in. Instead she flung open an ABC primer and a new phase in our lessons began. Fritz reminded her that elsewhere in the Netherlands it was officially school holidays.

'You children are behind. You will not be when I have finished with you.'

Katrien demanded our full attention. We were not allowed to jiggle, giggle, whisper, pull at our hair or — the Calvinist God forbid — poke a finger into noses or ears. Our group was strangely lopsided without Otto's sweet smile. We were not allowed to speak of him in front of Katrien. Whenever she was out of the room we whispered fast-fading reminiscences.

'Do you remember his giggle?' we'd say.

'I teased him for being like a girl,' admitted Fritz.

'He helped me with my reading,' said timid Hansje. 'I get mixed up between *ij* and the Greek *γ*. Do you think Lady Katrien will notice?'

Françoise continued to come at eleven o'clock to read to us from the bible. Siegfried came only once. Katrien corrected him on a point of history and he stomped out. 'I will take the children for educational walks around Middelburg,' he said.

Hansje was terrified of Katrien and cringed whenever my aunt's cold and oval-shaped eyes fell on her. Hansje was also a fidgeter. We all were to a degree. Aching joints made it difficult for any of us to sit still. One morning, while Fritz was reading aloud, Hansje was squirming in her chair and crossing and uncrossing her legs. Finally she put up her hand. 'Please, Lady Katrien ...'

'Not now.'

Hansje scrunched up her face. From beneath her skirt, a stream of urine oozed along the chair and down onto the carpet.

'Take her home,' Katrien growled at me from behind clenched teeth.

'She's my sister,' said Fritz, 'I should be the one to take her home.'

'You, boy, will clean the carpet.'

I walked ahead of Hansje to the lord mayor's residence. The back of her pretty skirt was wet. When she tried holding my hand I shook her off, furious. As I rang the lord mayor's doorbell an imp who lived not too far below the surface of my brain took control.

Ze 'ebt int broek gepiest.

She's pissed her pants.

I said this in Zeeuws dialect to the lord mayor's wife. Then I ran off home.

That evening, the lord mayor and his lady called on Siegfried and Papa. 'The government in The Hague wants all of us to speak high Dutch,' said the lord mayor. 'Not these ignorant dialects.'

'I find the dialects charming,' Siegfried replied.

'Speaking dialects the Germans couldn't understand saved lives during the war,' said Papa.

'The war is over,' the lord mayor said. 'It's as if you Stolburgs think you have your own kingdom down here in Zeeland.'

'Have a gin why don't you, Lord Mayor,' said Siegfried.

Katrien railed and stormed and glared at me. 'How did *het kind* learn dialect?' Siegfried shuffled uncomfortably, hoping I would not give him away.

★

My grandfather's favourite destination on our 'educational rambles' around Middelburg was the weekly cattle market, held in a small square between the backs of tall houses. In the middle of the square a pavilion was divided into stalls, and inside each stall were brass rings. Tethered to these rings, by the nose, were bulls.

Siegfried seemed to know every farmer and to speak all the dialects of Zeeland, even those from the most remote islands. The women wore the *klederdracht*, the traditional costume of the region, while the men donned black pantaloons, short jackets and colourful scarves. Siegfried was unmistakable in his three-piece tweed suit and oxblood red riding boots, a riding crop tucked under one arm. He'd point to me and tell the farmers, in dialect, that he'd brought his little girl and her friends with him. '*Ebt meske en't vrientjes mee.*'

Siegfried came alive at the cattle market, and although we were young, we knew that what we were seeing was a disappearing world. We adored the dialects, especially the words for urinating and defecating: *piesen en poepen*. And the steaming, snorting bulls entranced us. Whenever a cow was paraded through the market, farmers would tickle their bulls' genitals and make gigantic sheaths appear.

After a few weeks of looking after me, Katrien decided it was time to visit Mama. We marched along the streets of Middelburg to the railway station, with Katrien gripping my hand tightly, not acknowledging the locals who doffed caps or nodded to her, wearing her overcoat buttoned to the neck so that potential ruffians could not spy her necklaces. Our ferry ride across the Schelde was calm, but still Katrien leaned over the railing to vomit as we approached Breskens. She remained a bluish-green colour when we boarded the bus on its meandering journey through the villages of Flanders.

'Oma will give you something for your stomach,' I said. 'She always fixes me.'

They were not expecting us. Oma and Opa were flustered. They rushed around, getting in each other's way, desperately trying to find something to offer Katrien. Oma gave her a piece of almond cake and Opa a bunch of flowers wrapped in one of his handkerchiefs.

And Mama was not pleased to see us. She was dressed to go out, in a suit and smart hat.

'I'm going to Bruges,' she said. 'On the next bus.'

'Can I come?' I asked. I knew all about Bruges, the home of the black market. I wanted so badly to visit that magical place.

'I wouldn't mind going either,' said Katrien.

'Don't be silly.' Mama waved one dismissive hand at us. 'Katrien, you're wearing a fortune in jewellery. You, Juliana, you're too thin.'

I wanted to point out that Katrien could leave her jewellery with Oma and Opa. But *you're too thin* echoed around my brain. Opa intervened, suggesting I go with him to inspect the pig. At least that's what I thought his gestures meant.

Every year Oma and Opa fattened a pig to sell to their Lutheran neighbours. It lived in a shed and was fed kitchen slops, and once a day it was released into the orchard so that the sty could be cleaned. It wasn't given too much freedom, though, lest it run off some of that lovely fat so prized by the Lutherans. The slaughter of one of Opa's big round pigs was an eagerly awaited annual event in the village. Local legend claimed he had a secret recipe that made his pork more delicious than any other. Some villagers enjoyed killing their pigs slowly, laughing as the animals scurried about squealing, blood spraying out of their mangled throats. Opa prided himself on killing his pigs quickly and humanely. And he never, I knew, ate any part of the animal.

When we got to the sty Opa gave me his gold watch to set. The watch was a half-hunter which he wore strung across his waistcoat. He had never learnt to tell the time. Oma and Opa rose with the sun and went to bed at sunset. Their parents had lived the same way. My reading ability was haphazard, but I could tell the time. Ever since I could toddle I'd accompanied Siegfried around the longcase clocks in our houses, watching him move the hands and make minute adjustments to the weights.

I wound Opa's watch then set the hands to match mine. Papa had given me my little gold watch, on a thin leather strap, for my fourth birthday. I was allowed to wear it on special days. As visiting Mama could be considered a special day, I had put it on that morning. When I finished winding and adjusting the hands of Opa's watch I announced the time. 'It is now . . .'

Opa repeated what I'd said. He shook his head at my brilliance. '*Ist niet wunderlich. Wunderlich.*' He held the watch to his ear to make sure it was ticking, then he put it back in the pocket of his waistcoat.

We returned to the little house and stood outside, eyes fixed on the Breskens road, waiting for the bus carrying Mama to reappear. I don't know how often I stood in that spot over the years, each time expecting to see not a bus but a black coach with four horses. Katrien waited in Oma and Opa's parlour, for hour after hour, and after a while I went in to entertain her. I showed her the cunning bed inside a cupboard where Oma and Opa slept.

'Where do you sleep when you're here?' Katrien asked.

'In the kitchen in front of the stove. Opa made me a bed from fruit cases.'

Katrien stared straight ahead. Her spine did not touch the chair-back. Mama's bus did not return.

Finally, at the end of that summer of 1951, the *Nachgeborenen* were allowed to go to school. 'The Germans are coming back to our island,' the headmaster said on our first morning. We sat on a freezing gymnasium floor as he wandered around us. 'Not as conquerors this time, but as tourists. Some of them might ask you for directions. This is what I want you to say if any German asks you the direction to anywhere: "*Meneer* or *Mevrouw*, I am a polite Dutch boy or girl and, with respect, I must point out that as you found your way during the war, so you must find your way now.'"

After school I rushed home to practise my speech. *I am a polite Dutch boy or girl and . . .*

For months afterwards my friends and I would stand next to unsuspecting tourists, hoping they might ask us for directions. No one, of any nationality, ever did.

7

The Singing Turned to Yowling

I have never known Oscar to be interested in the sport of kings. Yet he, Frederick and Joanie have gone to Randwick for the races.

'I love the races,' Frederick declared this morning. 'All the themes of the opera are there.'

Joanie likes them, too. 'The races are the only chance I ever get to dress up.' She looked odd out of jodhpurs, in her crimson dress and green blazer.

Pearl, Dog and I have stayed in Goulburn waiting for the family doctor. Pearl woke this morning unable to move. 'Me legs have turned to jelly but they feel heavy as lead,' she said. Oscar took her to the toilet and Joanie helped her wash. Then they put her in bed. Dog is pacing back and forth, unable to decide whether to keep his mistress company or follow me.

'Juliana. Sorry. Can you help me please?'

By the time I get to her she is half in, half out of bed. 'Sorry, love, I need the toilet again. Me bloody legs won't work. The physio says I did something to my back. But I don't have backache, it's just me legs.'

She leans on me with such force that I am afraid of collapsing under her. Between us we manage to position her on the toilet seat. She is able to lift her nightgown by herself. I catch an accidental glimpse of a smooth pubic mound and a sprinkling of white hair. The journey back to her bed leaves both of us exhausted.

'I couldn't half do with a drink right now, Juliana. As my old dad used to say, the sun has got to be over the yardarm somewhere.'

Ever since Frederick became part of our lives, there is always champagne in the house. I prepare some triangular smoked salmon sandwiches and bring out Pearl's Waterford flutes.

'I don't usually like champagne,' she says, 'but I could get used to this Bollinger. I suppose you and Oscar had stuff like this all the time.'

'We became accustomed to a high standard of living.'

'Are you going to be all right, Juliana, when . . .?'

'When the three of us decide how to conduct the next part of our lives?'

'That's it. I've always admired that crisp way you speak. I often think, that's right, couldn't put it better myself. I suppose that comes from being a diplomat. You couldn't muck around with words in those situations. I wish you would fight for Oscar.

I know he loves you in his way. Maybe if you'd had kids?'

If only you knew, Pearl, how hard we tried.

'I didn't learn to speak this way from being a diplomat,' I say. 'Shortly after my family arrived in Australia we met a man who became a great influence on all our lives. He taught me to speak English the way he and his family spoke.'

I am determined you will not speak with a Dutch accent, Juliana. That was what Philly said.

'Oh,' says Pearl, 'you were a little tyke when you came out here, weren't you?'

'A month off my thirteenth birthday.'

'I never knew that. You've been married to Oscar near on thirty years and I don't know any more about you now than I did the day you two were married. Remember how pretty the garden was? You looked that lovely with your dark hair. He was that proud of you, Oscar was. And we had a laugh, didn't we, about how you two met.'

One of my colleagues thought I needed to meet a man and arranged a BBQ where I was to be introduced to a friend of his called Oscar. I chatted to a tall blond man and we discovered we both loved opera. It turned out this was another Oscar.

'What were the chances, eh? Two blokes called Oscar at the same BBQ. That was my old Dad's name, did I ever tell you that?' Pearl has finished her champagne and eagerly accepts another. Who knows how we will stagger to the toilet when she needs to go again. Ever since I met her she has seemed an eternal sixty-ish. In the last few days her wrinkles have deepened and her voice has developed an old-lady wobble. I leave her as she drifts off into a teary doze.

'Juliana? Juliana? I can't feel me legs.'

I find her poking the sharp end of a pair of nail scissors into her left thigh. 'Look!' There are scratches all over her legs where she has repeated the experiment. Her nightgown is wet and there is the unmistakable smell of shit. 'I'm that sorry, Juliana. Don't know how that happened.'

'I'm going to ring the doctor again. And an ambulance.'

'Not before we've cleaned up this mess. Please, love.'

Pearl's soiled nightgown is the first item removed. I roll her over and wipe between her buttocks with the sheets. I roll her back the other way and put a fresh sheet under her.

'You better get some air freshener after you call that ambulance,' she says.

The others return from the races laughing, exuberant. The laughter stops when I tell them an ambulance has taken Pearl away. Oscar and Joanie leave immediately for Goulburn Base Hospital. Frederick stays behind. I can't think why and retreat to the upstairs bedroom. He follows me and without so much as an introductory cough enters the room. 'I thought I might do something about dinner. Oscar and Joanie will want something when they come back.'

'*I thought I might do something about dinner,*' I say in a camp, lispy way, not that there is anything lispy or camp about Frederick.

The beautiful façade cracks. His glorious eyes fill

with moisture. 'I'm sorry, Juliana. I didn't mean for all this. So sorry. It was just . . .'

'A fuck with a married man?'

'No. Yes. Maybe.'

An odd moment comes over us and we hug. Then quickly part.

Frederick is a thoughtful and inventive cook. He plonks down three bottles of bubbly and lays four places at the table. 'God I hate these Royal Doulton dinner plates.'

'Oscar and Joanie gave this set to their parents,' I say.

We exchange a conspiratorial look.

'Pearl is in the neurology department,' Oscar says gloomily. 'They're talking about sending her to Sydney.' He downs a glass of champagne in one gulp. 'Frederick might as well stay here tonight. You don't mind do you, Juliana?'

★

When the *Nachgeborenen* went to school I fell so deeply in love with numbers that for a while adding and subtracting was more important than reading. I was bewitched by the certainty that one and one made two, and I raced ahead of my classmates in search of other examples of this beautiful exactness. Mama had returned from Oma and Opa's home in Flanders and in the evenings she resumed her sideways stories from behind the Singer sewing machine. I listened to her melodic voice while I filled sheet after sheet of white paper with black numbers.

'Mama, 1930 from 1935 leaves five. What did you and Papa do in the numbers from one to five?'

'We wanted to get married in 1930. But we were only twenty. Too young. Your father was sent to Indonesia and I was sent back to Oma and Opa. Then I went to Bruges to learn dressmaking and tailoring. We were finally allowed to marry in 1935.'

I did not ask why Papa was sent to Indonesia or she to her family. I knew by now that Mama's stories came together like the pieces of a Meccano set, with metal rods and tiny screws holding all the parts together in a turbulent balance.

She continued, 'Justien saw us kissing in the orchard at Buitenrust – that's what caused all the problems.' She cackled. 'The Stolburgs got rich before the war, when everyone else was poor. Their rubber trees in Indonesia had never made much money. Suddenly they were a precious commodity. Rubber for American cars. The Germans and Japanese must have bought Stolburg rubber, too. Well, all that wealth was lost in the war. Not before Jack and I had a two-year honeymoon, though. *Ach*, those were the best times.'

Mama brought out her wedding album, a slim volume, and I pored over a group picture of the wedding party on the steps of the Oostkerk. Mama's wedding dress is black. The lace around her waist is black. They are all in black. Prince Bernhard, Papa's best man, is the only one smiling. Justien is leaning over Mama as if he would like to eat her.

'Typical Calvinist wedding,' Mama said, shoving the album back in the bookcase. 'Everybody miserable.'

★

In the summer of my first year at school, Papa took my friends and me sailing on the estuaries and waterways around Walcheren. Our boat was a flat-bottomed mahogany yacht called the *Scottish Princess*, named after a distant ancestor, Mary, the daughter of James I of Scotland, who'd married a Stolburg and brought the wool trade with her to Zeeland. Before the war Papa moored his yacht in front of the Rue du Commerce. He and Prince Bernhard sailed all over the Zeeuws waterways while the penniless prince pursued the Queen's daughter. Knowledge of secret inlets, of islands that existed only at low tide, of which way the water ebbed and flowed, would serve both men well during the war.

On our sailing trips, Papa fired our imaginations with stories of spies and heroes, sparing us the tales of villages where all the men and boys were executed because Allied servicemen had hidden there. Fish were rare in the post-war years, the catches reduced by the trauma of the sea battles in the English Channel, but Papa always found something. He would land our yacht on an uninhabited island then cook whatever he'd caught over an open fire while we pretended to be Resistance fighters. We'd skulk in the bushes, sneaking up on innocent fishermen and yelling, 'Hands up! Hands up!'

During the war Papa anchored the *Scottish Princess* below a tower in the fishing village of Veere, where the princess herself had lived in the fifteenth century. Night and day the Germans manned that tower overlooking the estuary. They were hoping to spot members of the Resistance or, the biggest prize of all, Prince Bernhard, commander-in-chief of the Free Dutch Forces who were exiled in England.

Soon the legend spread beyond the islands of Zeeland: how Jack Stolburg, second son of Count Siegfried Stolburg, moored his boat beneath the Scottish princess's tower and pretended to be a simpleton fisherman. 'The Germans didn't know I too could speak German,' Papa said. 'I brought them a brace of fish every few days and they talked in front of me as though I didn't exist. *Poor Jaapie. Can't even speak Dutch properly. Can only speak some silly dialect.* They never connected me to my other identity as Spanish Jack. I pretended to admire their uniforms. And that's how I learnt all their plans.'

How Papa laughed as he told us that.

He never mentioned his brother, or what had happened to him.

While pretending to fish, Papa would pick up Allied spies and take them to a meeting spot in the English Channel. Three times his English counterpart couldn't make the rendezvous. Three times Papa had to sail his boat across the Channel and up the Thames, flying the orange flag of resistance and the tricolour of the United Provinces, so that the British wouldn't shoot at him. He could have stayed in England, safe in the court of Queen Wilhelmina. But each time he returned to his beloved Walcheren. He was in his early forties, streaks of white colouring the hair above his ears, when he told us this. His olive skin tanned easily. His mouth curled into a smile.

I was consumed for most of that year by the excitement of turning six the following January. Five seemed so spiky, gangly. Six, with its lovely round bottom, was mature, grown-up. I could not wait to be six.

The year had begun with the death of George VI. Katrien accompanied Wilhelmina to England for the funeral. Soon, a new Queen, the young Elizabeth, entranced us. The weekly magazines were full of pictures of her and her husband, the handsome Viking prince, and their children. Our own Dutch royal family, with the exception of Bernhard, seemed pedestrian by comparison.

Christmas was abnormally white; usually we didn't get snow till January. The temperatures were so low that most of the congregation didn't go to church for the Christmas morning service. The doll co-opted to play the part of the Christ child had a smattering of frost across its eyes, making the baby look dead before we'd had a chance of rejoicing his birth.

The cold continued into January 1953. My sixth birthday, the day I had longed for, passed unmarked beneath a deluge of snow drifts. The schools couldn't get enough coke to keep us warm. We had to wear extra layers of clothes. Sometimes we were sent home. Even when the stoves were burning all out, only the children sitting closest could feel any warmth.

And then, on 31 January 1953, school was cancelled altogether. The weather that day was considered extreme. Mama stayed in bed. 'You can come with me, monkey,' said Papa. He rugged me up and put me in the sidecar of his motorbike. I loved going with Papa to wherever his crews were working. I'd watch cranes and machinery operated by men who looked puny beside the might of the sea. Papa had spoken often that January of unusually high seas pounding the tops of the dijkes. But never before had I accompanied him on a day such as this.

Our motorbike was buffeted across the road. Papa braked hard to avoid a hurtling roll of barbed wire. From the sidecar, through slits of glass, I could see Papa hunched over the bike, his leather coat flapping, goggles covering his eyes, a scarf over his mouth, a pilot's helmet on his head. The wind worried at one of the sidecar windows, trying to work it loose. I couldn't fix the window without removing my mittens, and I had been told never to take my mittens off in winter. A terrific gust of wind ripped the window clean away. Sleet came sailing in.

Papa slowed down as we reached the outskirts of Vlissingen. We stopped in a street of iron-clad buildings. At the end of the street the sea poured over the top of a parapet. But Papa wasn't looking at the sea. He was staring at the dreary buildings.

'Papa, what are you looking at?' I yelled through the wailing wind.

'These shipyards are where the Germans took Dutch men and boys as slaves to fix their ships. I hate this place. We should have bombed it to the ground when we had the chance.'

He popped me back in the sidecar before I could tell him one of the windows was missing.

Crowds had gathered on the boulevard at Vlissingen, facing the snarling Schelde. Whenever a wave hit the seawall and made it over the top a cheer went up. 'Fools,' Papa muttered. The crowd parted for Papa as he walked along, me hanging onto his coat. 'That's Spanish Jack,' I heard men say to each other, followed by another whisper I had heard all my short life. 'The brother, *ja*, Justien, the collaborator, they say Jack executed his brother himself. Wouldn't let anyone else touch Count Siegfried's heir.'

Papa stared at the Schelde for the longest time, at the point where the river meets the English Channel. Then he said, 'There's a wall of water there. We have to get back to Middelburg.'

A few miles outside Vlissingen a mini-tornado hit us. With a lurch that threw me upside down, the sidecar was wrenched from the motorbike and flew off into a ditch. I was unhurt. The capsule I had travelled in since I was a baby was wrecked. After feeling me all over to make sure no bones were broken, Papa buttoned me inside his coat and we rode off again.

Mama had prepared a lunch of bread and cheese. She was listening to a music program on Radio Luxemburg. 'Juliana looks like a drowned rat,' she said, yanking off my wet clothes. Papa turned the dial to the BBC.

This is the BBC World Service . . .

I can still mimic those crisp, sharp consonants. We heard how flooding had killed three hundred people along the English coast. A storm surge in the Atlantic and the highest tides in living memory had combined to batter the Channel. Papa's face paled as he crouched over the radio to absorb every comma, every full stop, of the weather report.

'It's all right, Papa,' I heard my child's voice say. 'That's England.'

He turned around slowly.

'Child, the water has to come back.'

He ran from the house to fetch his parents. Françoise arrived with a saucepan of pea soup. 'Siegfried hasn't had his lunch yet. He and Jack are raising the Stolburg standard.'

'All this nonsense for wind and flooding in England,' Mama grumbled.

I looked out the window at my grandparents' house. Flying high from the roof was the Stolburg lion and the orange flag. 'To the attic, everyone,' Papa ordered. Then he got back on his motorbike and headed for the dijkes. In the remaining hours of daylight we tramped up and down stairs, conveying valuable items to the attic. I grabbed my dolls and the Meccano set. We fixed up coke heaters and tried plugging holes in the roof. Siegfried looked old and frail. Yet he managed to get a crystal radio working. It was on this radio that he had listened to Queen Wilhelmina's broadcasts from England while he was held under house arrest.

Françoise and Mama mocked our precautions. Middelburg, they scoffed, was the highest point of Walcheren, and we lived in the city's epicentre. In the flooding of 1944 the water had not risen beyond basement level of the houses on the Heerengracht. We dined on soup that had been warmed on the coke heater. Mama arranged a selection of paintings, one of them a Rembrandt, in a corner of the attic and draped a fur coat on top. She and Françoise sat themselves down on piles of warm rugs.

At eight o'clock the storm out at sea abated. In its place was a starry night sky.

'This is ridiculous,' Mama said. 'I'm going downstairs to sleep in my own bed.'

I begged her not to. 'Papa told us to stay in the attic, remember?'

'Always playing the hero. Where was he when I was betrayed to the Nazis? In England, that's where, on that stupid boat of his.'

Siegfried and Françoise fell silent. Françoise took off her white coif, letting her long hair tumble down her back, and lay beside Mama. I had never seen my grandmother without her coif. The hair at the front was white; the rest of it was a rippling black wave. I stayed with Siegfried, next to the radio. At nine o'clock the electricity died. Through the attic window we could see not a single light in or around Middelburg. Siegfried switched on his crystal radio.

This is Radio Hilversum. All residents of Zeeland are warned to move to high ground. This warning applies particularly to the islands of Tholen, St Philips and Walcheren . . .

Siegfried's hand reached for mine. We lived in the flattest province of a flat country. There was no high ground to go to. In the past, church bells rang to summon the populace in times of danger. But the Germans took all the church bells during the war. Few had been replaced. Unless you had a crystal radio there was no way of heeding the warnings. The radios produced at the Philips factory in Eindhoven required electricity. All that night, Radio Hilversum and the

BBC sounded their warnings into an ether where few people could hear.

At eleven o'clock a soft singing rose in the distance. Siegfried hugged me close. Mama and Françoise slept on. The singing turned to yowling. The last word we heard on the crystal radio before it too died was *typhoon*. Mama woke when the house started to shake. Other homes in the Heerengracht collapsed. In the hour before twelve the wind screamed and screamed.

At midnight the wind dropped. There was a profound silence. We looked at each other, hoping that maybe the people of the sea had been spared.

Then we heard a crack so deep heaven must have been ripped asunder. And another. And another. The dijkes of Zeeland broke one by one.

Zeeland disappeared that night under waves more relentless than all the armies that had ever invaded us. Papa found some air-raid sirens that had been put away in storage after the war. The sirens wailed and wailed. Across the road the Stolburg lion was ripped from its flagpole. The pole snapped and fell to the street. The coke heaters in our attic gave off a dim light, enough for me to watch Siegfried weeping, his head on his knees. It was the first time in my life I had seen a man cry.

At dawn we looked out the window. Middelburg had more or less survived. Beyond the city was nothing but water and an occasional protruding chimney.

'Now I know there is no God,' Mama said.

Françoise and Siegfried stood for a long time in front of the attic window. Her head rested on his shoulder. I could not see the white of her hair. All I could see was the black. For a moment, in the ghostly light of that morning after the flood, I glimpsed the glamorous part-Japanese girl she must have been half a century before.

'I can't give any more,' Françoise said.

She never spoke again.

We heard a sound we would hear many more times over the weeks and months, the sound of a motorboat, and a crier, shouting, 'Water! Water!' In the new land of the sea created that night in 1953, drinking water became a scarce commodity, one that could not be bought in the black market or any other magical place.

At first we thought our two houses in the Heerengracht had escaped the worst. But within days the basements flooded as water seeped to the surface. Then the ground-floor rooms turned soggy. Papa eventually made it out to Buitenrust. The horses Siegfried had acquired to revive his stud had drowned in their stables.

Opening my bedroom wardrobe one morning, I could not find one article of dry clothing. Everything reeked of mould and sewage. Damp crawled up the walls. We moved to the top storey, knowing how lucky we were. Every day we heard tales of people who'd clung to chimneys that terrible night; people who'd watched helpless as loved ones drowned; people who'd listened as their cattle, locked in byres, squealed to their deaths.

The rescue operation, led by the Americans, happened quickly. Thousands were evacuated. Some never returned. Queen Wilhelmina, clad in layers of mink, hauled herself out of retirement to share the grief of her former subjects. Prince Bernhard, in the same sexy uniform he'd worn during the war, was everywhere: hopping in and out of helicopters, directing the cameras onto the tragedy, as if he was the one coordinating the rescue effort. Papa, too, was everywhere. And nowhere.

Overnight he became a celebrity. But we heard of what he'd done only in fragments. In 1944, after setting the dynamite charges that weakened the dijkes in preparation for the British bombers, Papa and his comrades had ridden the last of the Zeeuws horses to warn villages and towns of the coming flood. Nine years later, on the night of 31 January, Papa repeated this epic quest, riding his motorbike into the ground to alert all those living closest to the dijkes. Much of this was in vain. As he said, 'In 1944 the weather was with us and the flood came on gradually. This time our enemy was the sea.'

Papa was decorated for his efforts. On top of a hastily repaired dijke, Mama and I were presented to Wilhelmina. Through a wind that did not let up for weeks, I heard the ex-Queen say, 'The child looks like you, Jack.'

But Papa's face was grim. He had begun his campaign of blaming the government in The Hague for the tragedy. Fewer lives would have been lost, he said, had adequate money been provided to fix the dijkes properly after the war. He laid his allegations in the press, on radio and in the *Tweede Kamer*, the lower house of parliament. The bulk of the money had been spent in the north, on the reclamation of the Zuider Zee, and the citizens of the land of the sea, Papa said, had paid the price in blood.

At the end of February a death toll was released: eighteen hundred souls, a quarter of a million head of cattle, and all the arable land reclaimed since the liberation flood. Deaths from influenza, pneumonia and heartbreak over the ensuing months were not counted in the statistics.

Some Zeelanders, needing someone other than a dispassionate God to blame, turned on anyone with a German name. Stolburg was the most German name in the province and one night a swastika was scrawled on Siegfried's front door. The damp and mould kept climbing through the centuries-old fabric of the buildings, and Papa suggested we move to Buitenrust. The manor house there was not practicable. So we moved into the gatehouses: my parents and me in one, Siegfried and Françoise in the other, all of us still living opposite each other but in homes a fraction of the size.

Françoise never put her coif back on, or reopened her bible. Sometimes she murmured to herself in Japanese. Siegfried knew a few words, and he said them to her over and over, but it was not enough to ease whatever was troubling her. The Calvinist god who had sustained her most of her life had deserted her.

In the gatehouses there were open fireplaces where we tried to burn wet timber. Françoise spent her days huddled in damp blankets, staring into the feeble flames. She refused all food except for broth and water. Her long hair was becoming matted, and I offered to brush it.

'Spring will be here soon, Grandma. Papa says the water will go down then and we can walk in the park.'

My prattle stopped her murmuring. A few days later she could not get out of bed. She died one afternoon while I was brushing her hair. I knew she was dead. I kept on brushing until her hair, white and black, lay fanned out across the bed, either side of her face. Then I went to find the adults.

Françoise was to be interred under the floor of the Oostkerk. But when the stone slabs were lifted the crypts were found to be full of water. It was a time of so much death that the government in The Hague, alternating between neglect and interference, looked away when Françoise was buried in an unmarked grave at Buitenrust, with the intention that she be reburied at the Oostkerk later. I peered into the deep hole and saw a mound of old hessian bags, similar to the ones Siegfried used in the stables. Papa lowered the coffin. He attached a rising sun, one he'd fashioned from lead, to the lid. Siegfried leant on Papa as we walked back to the gatehouses. The ring the Meiji emperor gave Françoise on the occasion of her marriage was on the little finger of Siegfried's right hand.

Apart from a few minor pieces given to Mama and me, Françoise's collection of jewellery went to her daughter, Katrien. Papa and Katrien argued about the black-pearl choker with the blood ruby. Papa thought it should be kept for me. 'But I live and work with royalty,' said Katrien. 'I need to keep up appearances.'

A six year old, she said, had no use for such a thing.

I adored life in the gatehouses. Every night I was allowed to choose whether to sleep in Siegfried's little house or with my parents. Most nights I chose Siegfried. In his gatehouse, the room that was my bedroom had an alcove with a ceiling so low no adult could stand up. I stored my books and toys in there, creating a nest. Together, Siegfried and I explored Buitenrust. I'd help him set a chair upright, or paper over a window against the weather. There was no question of us attempting to fix anything properly. We had a roof over our heads. Many did not.

Papa spent more and more time at home. His outspokeness had lost him his job. Siegfried could not understand how the government in The Hague could dismiss his son, and he wrote to Queen Juliana, ex-Queen Wilhelmina and Prince Bernhard, pleading with them to intercede. Katrien invited Papa to visit her at Het Loo and arranged for him to meet with Bernhard. But the men argued and never spoke to one another again. Papa busied himself dismantling the water-ruined stables that for two hundred years had stood either side of the driveway. Siegfried, for as long as he could, helped.

In 1953 there was no spring. There was no renewal, no resurrection. Wherefore art thou God, we asked ourselves. Cold gales were followed by weeks of rain, swelling creeks and rivers that were already overflowing. I squelched around Buitenrust in boots filled with mud. Living outside the city, I saw less and less of my friends. When school reopened I walked the two kilometres between school and the gatehouse four times a day. We were sent home every lunchtime in the hope we would get a hot meal. I'd gulp down a few mouthfuls, turn around and trot back to school. I became so thin it got on Mama's nerves.

'You look like you've just been released from a concentration camp,' she snapped.

I tried eating more. I could not gain weight.

Mama and Papa argued about the sewing machine, which he said took up too much room in our little gatehouse. She complained he was always underfoot now that he didn't have a job. He tinkered with his beloved motorbike but couldn't get it back in working order. She screamed, 'You're too old for motorbikes!'

I played outside until evening came, when I could not stand the cold any longer, and then I went to Siegfried's and we played games or read. We pretended not to see the shadows behind the curtains of the other gatehouse arguing.

Mama hated living in the gatehouses. She refused to enter the manor or venture anywhere near the German bunkers. I could not understand why she loathed them so. Surely the Germans were long gone?

'Come on,' I begged her one afternoon, when it was just the two of us. 'The bunkers are fascinating. You can climb up the slope and look right in. One of them is set up like a kitchen. We can have a picnic and cook in the bunker.'

Her silence should have told me I was approaching a dangerous perimeter. But I kept on.

'Mama, come on, the water in the creek is flowing really fast. We can make paper boats and then I'll cook for you in the German kitchen.'

'Leave me alone!'

She lashed out, forgetting that she held a cast-iron pan. I heard the sound of my skull cracking above my right ear. I felt blood in my mouth and blood coming out my nose. Then nothing. When I woke I was in Flanders with Oma and Opa. I stayed with them for the rest of that miserable summer. Every week Papa collected me on his stuttering motorbike and took me to a doctor in Antwerp, who examined my skull and asked about headaches and nightmares. I had become a sleepwalker and sleep-talker.

★

Korngold's *Die tote Stadt* is on Oscar's record player. My favourite aria is playing: *Mein Sehnen, mein Wähnen.*

My sighs, my tears.

My tears have smudged the pages of a book I should never have reopened.

Frederick knocks. 'All right to come in?'

I feel disconnected, unplugged. Turning to him, I trip over my feet. He holds me up in a soft embrace. Oscar finds us like this.

'The stallion is dead,' Oscar says. 'And Pearl has a tumour on the spine.'

★

Siegfried died while I was away with Oma and Opa during that false summer of 1953. Papa fetched us from Flanders in a borrowed Ford station wagon. Oma and Opa understood the significance of the occasion; I was surprised to see them curtsy to Papa. He had brought me a black armband to wear.

Papa used his fast-dwindling stocks of influence to create a grand occasion. Grand Duchess Charlotte came from Luxemburg. The House of Orange sent Wilhelmina. Siegfried was carried out of Buitenrust in a coffin made from the timber of his beloved stables, and placed on a gun carriage. Four ill-matched horses had been found to pull the carriage. On either side of roads scarred by the misery of the flood, the people of the sea lined up to pay their respects. Once the carriage arrived at the station, on the other side of the great canal, Papa and the men who had followed him in the Resistance loaded the coffin onto a train. The body was taken to Luxemburg, where the Stolburgs first rose in the ninth century. There, in a church below a castle in the clouds, a crypt was opened to receive a man who had risked the wrath of his fellow aristocrats by marrying a half-Japanese girl. The Meiji emperor's ring was given to Mama.

On the morning after Siegfried's funeral I wake convinced that men with torches are outside my window. The alarm clock next to my bed says it is two o'clock. From the window I see a small procession head towards the farmhouses on the edge of the estate, Papa and Siegfried leading the way. Two men follow, and they are holding another man between them. Then I am near the German bunkers.

The captured man cries.

I didn't mean it.

He turns his head in my direction, and I see that he has fine blond hair and shining blue eyes. He is kneeling at the hole where surely we buried Françoise weeks before. Papa is holding a gun to the man's head.

And then I hear two shots.

'Juliana! Juliana! Wake up.'

The wind and the cold hit me.

'You are sleepwalking,' said Papa. 'In your nightdress and bare feet.'

'I saw Uncle Justien,' my teeth chattered.

'Shush. Shush. Justien died long ago.'

From my bedroom, I heard Papa tell Mama that he found me near Françoise's grave.

'Jack,' Mama said, 'we must leave here.'

8

To the Bottom of the Earth

'It's not benign or anything,' Joanie assures us. She is talking about Pearl's tumour. We do not have the heart to tell her she has 'malignant' and 'benign' mixed up. In Pearl's case the terminology hardly matters. A neurologist has declared that the tumour must be removed and Pearl will most likely be left a paraplegic. As for the dead stallion, it's as if he is asleep in his stall, the body still warm to the touch. 'I'll ring the knackers,' Joanie says.

Frederick takes one look at the horse and says he's going home. 'Urgent things to attend to.' His car roars down the drive, raising a cloud of dust.

'He'll be back,' I say.

Oscar throws up his hands.

In her four-bed ward at Goulburn Base Hospital,

Pearl is full of indignation. The room is barely big enough for two beds. 'Men in the same ward as women. Whatever next?' Her voice lowers to a whisper. 'See that bloke, Juliana? They sat him up on the pot this morning and I saw his whatchimacallits. How do you like that?' As she speaks, the old man giggles. A tiny woman in a pink dressing gown comes up to her.

'Haven't seen you for ages, Mum.'

'I'm not your mum, love. So how's the stallion?'

I tell her the stallion is doing as well as can be expected. Joanie snorts at this and walks out of the ward. We can hear her banging on a vending machine. Before Pearl completely loses the power in her legs she will be taught to use a wheelchair. A physiotherapist is helping her to strengthen her arms. Her arms ache from the half-hourly dumbbell exercises. The operation to remove the benign tumour will happen at St Vincent's Hospital in Sydney. 'Then they want to stick me in some rehabilitation place. Well, they can stuff that for a start. I'm coming home.'

'Maybe there are some skills they could teach you in rehab, Pearl?'

She sets her mouth into a hard line. 'There's things to be worked out with the farm. Oscar will have to do his bit. And there's that land I gave him.'

'Oscar has just got this job as an assistant répétiteur. As for the land, that may not come to anything. Frederick has a house, after all.'

Joanie drives us home along the street where Frederick lives. His house is set well back. Its sheer height and sprawling width, the four columns at the front entrance, make for an imposing sight. She slows the car. 'Garden looks good. Must have recycled water. One of the few gardens in Goulburn that hasn't gone to God.'

In the pre-dawn Oscar crawls into my bed. I no longer think of it as our bed. He does not speak. Just lies there. He reeks of sex. 'You stink. Go and have a shower.' He leaps out of bed and storms into the bathroom. Yet again, I see the outline of his long body through the pink shower curtain.

'Do you want me to fuck you?' he says. 'I could, you know. Or would you prefer Frederick to fuck you?'

'Frederick is one of the most beautiful men I have ever met. I cannot, however, imagine the possibility of him fucking me.'

Oscar collapses on the bed, laughing. 'Frederick is gorgeous, isn't he?'

One last time – I am determined it should be the last time – Oscar makes love to me. He has learnt some new moves. The sex is better than it's been in a long time. He grabs my buttocks and squeezes me in a way that is new to our relationship.

'What a pity you've gone gay,' I say at the end.

'Not bad for a guy who's nearly sixty. Two people in one night.'

And with those words from him and a kick from me that leaves him yelping, our marriage is over.

★

Frederick looks around with distaste at the
St Vincent's Hospital waiting area. Joanie and Oscar
make themselves comfortable. The surgery could take
hours. 'I'll take Juliana off with me.' He summons
me with a wave. Placidly, stupidly, like a dairy cow
needing to be milked, I follow.

He walks into the understorey of the Opera
House as though he owns the place. On the piano in
the rehearsal room is a pile of mail. Most of it he drops
unopened in the rubbish bin. He tucks an embossed
envelope with a European stamp on it in the inside
pocket of his jacket. I watch him rehearse some young
singers. Frowning, uninterested, he barely bothers
correcting their timing or breathing. When the young
people leave he turns to me. 'Would you like to come
to my apartment? We can have lunch there.'

I wonder how much a répétiteur is paid. Driving up
to Frederick's apartment building, an art deco complex
with harbour views on the Kirribilli side of the bridge,
he reads my mind. 'I inherited some money from my
parents. The car was part of a messy "divorce" when
I split up with my last man. Have you got anything
decent to wear, Juliana? There's a ballet tonight. Oscar
and Joanie will be at the hospital forever.'

'I have the jeans I'm wearing.'

'Then we must shop. You could do with some
stylish clothes.'

For the second time that day I feel like an in-
convenient parcel. Again I say nothing. Instead I ask the
way to the bathroom, where I hoist my bra up an extra
notch and smear onto weary lips at least three coats of
a fuchsia-pink lipstick I was given in a cosmetics shop

in Luxemburg. A pin prick of fuchsia lands in the silky white sink. My hand reaches for the tap, but I leave the pink wax for Frederick to deal with.

Lunch is a sandwich and a glass of white wine on the small balcony. Below us people gather to watch a flotilla of tall ships weave their way up the harbour. One of them is a replica of the *Duyfken*, the Little Dove, the Dutch East India ship that bumped into the Australian coastline in 1606. The water is as unmoving as a mirror, yet the boat bobs like a dove.

'Tell me about the man you had the messy divorce from.'

'Oh, him. Singer of course. Not as good as he thought he was. He believed being openly gay would be bad for his career. A looker, you see, women adored him. And men. He started getting roles above his range. He was too young to sing the big stuff they were demanding of him. I tried to warn him but the flatterers were everywhere. In the end there was nothing for it. I had to help him and hope his voice wouldn't be destroyed. All for nothing. He developed nodules on the vocal cords and I got bored with the boy. He does croaky musical comedies now, Christmas specials for the old ladies. He has a new man, a sycophant.'

'And you have an older man.'

I do not want to go shopping with Frederick. Trailing behind him, saying nothing, I am shown materials and colours I would never think of wearing. 'Avoid white. You are too old for white, Juliana. Cream, pale tan, light blues – those are good colours for you.'

At a hairdresser's near David Jones he supervises my hair and make-up. 'Don't pull the hair back from her face. Let it fall, let it soften her brow. Your eyes are your best feature, outline them.'

Frederick's fingers tug at my shirt's second-top button. 'Not too much cleavage, thank you.'

He lifts my chin and turns my head sideways. 'Never go out the door without pink blusher. Pale is ageing.'

Finished with me, he submits to a haircut and shave. 'Plenty of moisturiser to keep my skin supple. Not too much hair off the front.' Twisting and arching his neck in the mirror, he judges what he sees. But he does not preen. Frederick is not vain about his looks.

For the rest of the afternoon he is an attentive companion. At regular intervals he rings Oscar for updates. Pearl is doing well. She has no feeling in her legs but she is talking. Frederick tells Oscar he is taking me to the ballet: *Spartacus*.

Oscar took me to see *Spartacus* on our first date thirty years ago. Later, we made love with the adagio from Act III playing in the background. I wonder what music Oscar and Frederick made love to the first time.

'Too much posturing and thumping,' Frederick says at the end of the performance. 'Saved by that sumptuous adagio in Act III.'

Oscar and Joanie have decided to stay with Pearl. 'Juliana shall sleep here,' Frederick tells Oscar. 'I'll take the couch. She can have my bed.'

The bedroom, like the whole apartment, like the house in Goulburn, reveals nothing about the man except that he is fastidious. There is nothing kitsch, no lapses in taste. Valuable ornaments are studiously placed. Dozens of white shirts hang ready for the man to slip into.

Near dawn I wake and see the Little Dove, festooned with lights, still bobbing. The fuchsia blob in the sink has been magically removed.

★

With the death of Françoise and Siegfried, we were three. We saw little of Katrien, and on those occasions when she did visit dreadful arguments broke out between her and Papa about how to rescue his career and our sinking fortune. At a time when the Netherlands was in a frenzy of rebuilding and reclamation, Papa was unemployed and seemingly unemployable. He had crossed a line and could not find the way back. He did not even seek formal recognition as the heir to Siegfried's titles. 'I cannot afford the death duties. So what's the point?'

We stopped going to church except on high feast days. Church elders and acquaintances had called on Siegfried daily. After his death, no one visited. In the local press people called for the German bunkers at Buitenrust to be destroyed.

Most of my friends left Zeeland after the night of the flood. Books became my companions. Evenings in the gatehouse – a concert playing on the wireless, the three of us reading – were bliss for me. For Mama and Papa, who now had little to say to each other, the hours before bed must have been torture.

The Middelburg library provided Mama with the new realist works of the period, novels that mocked the pre-war aristocracy and class system. The library was supposed to represent a sort of freedom. But it became another form of torture. The library was narrow and mean and borrowers were not allowed to wander the stacks. Books had to be requested through a window, by title and author, and failure to provide either of these meant there would be no books that week. Mama, who had grown up in a community where illiteracy was the norm, lived in fear of losing the ability to read and to write. And she dreaded not having anything to read.

'Mama,' I cried, 'look out! A puddle!'

Lifting her eyes from the book resting on her bicycle handlebars, she swerved suddenly. '*Ach*, Juliana,' she moaned, 'I have to know how this book ends.' She bent her head back over her handlebars and resumed reading. We parked our bikes outside the forbidding library and waited for Mama to finish the last chapter. Then she rapped on the window. 'Now,' she announced, 'I must borrow the next book in the series.'

The whole of the Netherlands was obsessed with a series of books about the life of a country vet named Doctor Vlimmen. Mama had just completed the second volume. The librarian, a woman, checked the back of Mama's book to make sure she'd returned it by the due date. If a book was late, the borrower was banned for a month. Through the window I could see shelf after shelf of books I was not allowed to touch.

164

Papa refused to come to the library, saying books were for reading, not for hiding away.

'The next one, please,' Mama repeated.

'Name of author and title?'

'The author's the same as the one I just returned. The next book is called *Vlimmen contra Vlimmen*, I think.'

'I can't work with what you think. Author and title?'

'Author is *Meneer* Roothaert,' Mama stumbled. 'Title . . . the one I just told you.'

'No.'

The window was slammed down. Mama knocked once more. 'I'll remember in a moment.' The window stayed shut. Mama's library was denied her that week. 'The books have been imprisoned,' she sobbed that night. 'The librarians are warders.'

'Then why go there, Janna?'

Mama gave Papa a steely look. 'I will become a Resistance of one.'

And resist she did. She bought a Remington typewriter and taught herself to type. She began firing off letters to the Middelburg Council, then to the newspapers, complaining about the library's draconian ways, until gradually others began to express their outrage and the library had no choice. It opened its doors. Librarians stood at the end of the aisles, watching anxiously for damage, while Mama and all the other patrons let their fingers glide along the books.

In the children's section we were not allowed to ask for books. We were given books considered good for us: religious, sickening, moralising tracts, or books years too young for me. 'Mama,' I pleaded, 'can't you do something about the children's section?'

But Mama had exhausted all her nervous energy. She could not rouse herself to fight on my behalf. I did not ask Papa, who walked aimlessly around the estate completing small and insignificant tasks. He threatened to blow up the German bunkers with dynamite. 'They're on my property,' he said. But the provincial government, on orders from The Hague, had them heritage-listed. The local Zeeland newspapers who'd wanted the monstrosities destroyed were now demanding that they be preserved. 'Aristocrats,' it was claimed, 'are curators on behalf of history.' Papa gave up. He fenced the bunkers off so we couldn't see them from the gatehouse.

One day Katrien proposed a two-year exile from the Netherlands. Two years, she suggested, would be time enough to repair our fortune and for Papa's ignominy to be forgotten. Mama and Papa proceeded to while away the next two years, from 1955 to 1957, arguing about where we were to spend this exile. Papa suggested Israel, as he was sympathetic to the Jewish desire for a homeland. But Mama was not about to swap one religion-riddled society for another.

'Too many Jews,' she said.

Papa mentioned South Africa. Speaking Zuid-Afrikaans, he reckoned, was sort of like speaking Dutch.

'Too many *zwartjes*,' Mama said.

'America?'

'Bah. Too much of everything.'

★

Then came a phone call offering Papa a prestigious-sounding job in a place at the bottom of the earth. A Dutch company, a firm of wool exporters, wanted him to take up a directorship in Melbourne. I told my teachers: *We will be away two years*. Then, our fortune restored, Papa would resume his rightful place in Dutch society among the depleted ranks of the aristocracy.

Our properties were rented out and the farms tenanted. Belongings were sold to raise money to help establish ourselves in the new country. The Rijksmuseum accepted a Rembrandt. Ancient porcelain and delftware that had survived the bombing of Middelburg and the two great floods since went for a pittance. The Netherlands, Europe, was crying out for the new; we Stolburgs were dinosaurs nibbling on the last green shoots around Buitenrust, about to become extinct.

Mama was convinced Australia could not possibly supply her with the buttons, zippers, cotton threads or bolts of material she needed. She bought boxes and boxes of these, insisting that the Singer sewing machine and Remington typewriter come too. Papa placed ads in the local and national papers for the sale of the *Scottish Princess*. I went with him to Veere, the fishing village, where we slept on the yacht for four days: cleaning, painting, polishing the brass, restoring the ropes. 'Wait and see, Juliana, the buyers will come flocking. This boat is of historical interest. She belongs to a famous family. She has a wartime connection.'

When the day of the sale came, one person turned up.

'I am Jack Stolburg,' Papa said, holding out his hand.

The man did not remove the cigarette from his mouth as he shook Papa's hand. 'I'll take some measurements.' The man walked up and down the jetty, casting his tape measure about.

'Of course,' said Papa, 'you know the history?'

'Can't sell history.'

I noticed the man's shirt was dirty around the neck, and his jacket had food stains. He was a scrap merchant. He named a scrap price.

'But I am . . .' Papa's face went taut.

'I know who you are all right. All over for you aristocrats. Good thing, too.'

The man handed Papa a roll of money. Papa bit his lip and handed the greasy roll to me. We stood beneath the tower erected by our ancestor, Mary, as the scrap merchant borrowed one of the dockside cranes and dumped the *Scottish Princess* in the back of his truck. He broke the mast to fit it alongside the rest of the yacht. He bundled the sails roughly together. The anchor he couldn't be bothered with. He tossed it in the water. On our way back to Middelburg, Papa smoked two cigars in quick succession, something I had never seen him do before.

Mama was waiting for us outside the gatehouse. 'How much did you get, Jack?'

Papa shook his head, leaving me to explain. 'I would have liked the anchor,' he whispered to me later.

The government body that was to rent our house at Buitenrust agreed not to enter one room – the ballroom – and it was here that we did our final packing. We covered everything in sheets and locked the doors. We walked away secure in the knowledge that the possessions to furnish our future life in the Netherlands were waiting for us under dust sheets. Mama still refused to enter the manor house. Yet somehow, Papa and I felt sure, two years in Australia would be long enough for her to overcome her fears. On the day we left Middelburg I wandered one last time from room to room, listening to the castle's creaks and groans, trying to decide which room would be mine upon our return.

We spent our final weeks in the Netherlands with Oma and Opa in Flanders. They had no real clue as to where we were going. They thought we'd be able to visit on weekends and worried about which buses and ferries they'd catch when it was their turn to visit. Mama's bachelor brother Piet, a farmer, was someone I had seldom met before. Suddenly he seemed to drop in on Oma and Opa nearly every day, asking Papa endless and horribly real questions.

'How long will the trip take, Jack?'

'Five weeks.'

'Will it be hot all the time in the new country?'

'The summers are hot. Winters in Melbourne are mild, I believe, like spring in Zeeland.'

'Does the same sun shine down there or is it a different sun?'

Slowly, listening in, Oma and Opa began to understand that where we were going was far, far away.

'We will write,' Papa promised. The old people looked at him helplessly. Mama searched the village for someone able to read our letters to her parents and perhaps write the odd letter to us. She sewed a smart dress for Oma we knew the old lady would never wear. I strolled around empty lanes, searching for a landmark, any landmark in the featureless landscape, to imprint on my brain. I came back in the evenings, my absence not noticed, to hugs and cuddles from grandparents whose language I didn't understand. I studied their faces, memorising the colours of their eyes, the creases in their smiles, the feel of their skin.

Papa had brought with him to Flanders an old Spanish trunk damaged in the flood of 1953. The base and part of one side had rotted. He tore away the rotting timber to make a new trunk. He created a false bottom and showed me how to lift the panel. Underneath lay two secret compartments. One contained all our papers and a metal strongbox for money and jewellery. In the other Papa hid a large pistol I had never seen before.

'The Americans came looking for this gun when they had control of Middelburg during martial law,' he said. 'I told them to look wherever they wanted. They searched and searched all our properties. Never found my gun.'

'Why didn't you want them to find it, Papa?'

Carefully he wrapped the gun in a chamois cloth. I noticed his initials – J.S. – engraved on the barrel. He put it back in the trunk and closed the false bottom.

'This gun,' he said, 'was with me all during the war.'

On our last morning Oma refused to come out of the shed attached to their cottage. She threw her apron over her head. We had to kiss her through the fabric. Her shoulders shook with weeping as we boarded the bus to Breskens. I waved and waved and kept waving, long after the village and my grandparents had disappeared from sight.

Katrien and two of her friends, courtiers, came to see us off in Amsterdam. Dressed in evening clothes, they were an incongruous sight as they ran up the gangplank. Over the years, Katrien had become an elegant, austere woman. She wore a mink jacket and long velvet skirt, the black pearls draped round her neck and down her flat chest. 'We don't have much time, Jack. Mahler's Fifth tonight. You know how busy it gets around the *Concertgebouw*.'

Her companions shook hands with Papa and wished him well. They nodded at Mama. One of the men gave me a five-guilder coin.

'Two years will go by quickly, Jack. Don't forget to write your memoir of the war. *Tot siens*.'

A chauffeured car whisked them away, even though visitors were not required to leave yet.

The ship was called the *Johan Van Oldenbarnevelt*. I had completed my primary education and had mastered a smattering of Dutch history. 'Oldenbarnevelt,' I explained proudly, 'was known as the pensionary from Rotterdam and was beheaded by Prince Maurits of Oranje-Nassau for being troublesome unto God. The poor man was so crippled he had to be helped up the scaffold to have his head removed.'

'Don't be a show-off,' Papa said. Nevertheless, he spent many hours of our journey from the Netherlands to Australia raging about the insanity of shipping owners who named their ship after a traitor to the Protestant cause.

★

The news from the hospital is unchanged. Pearl probably won't regain the use of her legs. Oscar and Joanie will stay with her for another day. 'You and I,' says Frederick, 'might as well go back to Goulburn.'

'Tell me about the letter from Luxemburg.'

Frederick flinches. 'How did you know?'

'Oscar and I lived in Luxemburg for eight years. You learn to recognise the stamps. I saw you put that letter in your coat pocket.'

'Well,' says Frederick, 'I have been offered a job at the Philharmonie de Luxembourg. I applied before . . . before Oscar. Didn't really think I'd be in the running. Seems I was.'

He hands me the letter. The contract is for three years and the terms are generous.

'Does Oscar know?'

Frederick shakes his head.

'I can't,' I say, 'imagine him wanting to return to Europe.'

★

On the upper deck of the *Johan Van Oldenbarnevelt* we had three cabins to ourselves: a bedroom for Mama and Papa, one for me with an adjoining bathroom, and a sitting room to receive any friends or acquaintances we might make in our travels. The *JVO* was too small for its six hundred passengers. The larger lower-deck cabins had been subdivided to hold several families. Our three cabins were comfortable but hardly luxurious. Papa complained that the chairs were vinyl and the beds too narrow.

We were still in the English Channel when we sat down at the captain's table for our first shipboard dinner. Almost immediately we learnt that the captain and first officer were Catholics and that Mama was going to suffer from seasickness. A prawn cocktail turned her face a translucent white. Then she vomited into her napkin. As Papa and I lifted her into bed, I could feel the twiggy bones of her legs and arms. I tried holding a wet cloth to her forehead but she pushed my hand aside. She allowed Papa to sit by her.

It was still daylight, so I went exploring. I discovered schoolrooms, a small library and a cinema. Lower down in the ship were the first- and second-class kitchens. Huge liquidy vats steamed and gurgled in the latter, while in the first-class kitchen dainty portions were being assembled on plates.

'Hey,' a voice called out, 'what are you doing? Children are not allowed down here.'

'I am twelve, nearly thirteen. I'm not a child.'

'*Zo*, you must be the Stolburg child. I am the purser. After the captain I am the most important person on this ship. See how magnificent my uniform is?'

I nodded politely. The purser's faded blue coat, with its rusty-looking braid epaulettes, was far from magnificent.

173

'My mother is sick,' I said. 'I was just looking for something to do.'

'Come with me,' said the purser, 'I'll put you to work. I suppose your father won't let you mix with the Catholic children on board. Well, we won't tell him I come from a Catholic family. I've forgotten the last time I went to confession.'

And so, while Mama was confined to her cabin, laid low by a retching that did not stop, not even when there was nothing, not even water, left in her stomach, I became the purser's assistant. I put pieces of paper to do with passengers in files. I took care of people's telegraph forms, relaying their messages of homesickness and the second thoughts they were having about migrating to the new country.

In his spare time the purser collected stamps. He had four bulging albums filled with stamps from all over the world, and he'd begun a fifth. He showed me how to soak letters so that the stamps came away, how to apply sticky hangers to the back. He was particularly keen on stamps produced by the Third Reich during its occupation of Europe. From catalogues he taught me to identify the gaps in his collection. Hitler's raging visage was unmistakable; I wondered how so much rage could be contained within just one brain. I learnt to recognise Goebbels and Goering, and Speer the delusional architect, and Rommel the soldier, a decent man caught in an indecent war. Mussolini's big head and post-box mouth made me laugh. Franco looked as if he would be happier being a matador. And the Japanese emperor was pathetic.

The purser had served with the Dutch merchant

navy since before the war and was due to retire.
Like many wanderers, he had no wife or children.
'Make sure, Juliaantje,' he said, 'that you have plenty
of children to keep you warm in old age.' He called
me by the diminutive of my name. For the five weeks
I spent in his company I called him *Meneer*.

Mama's inability to keep food down worried the
ship's doctor. She lost an alarming amount of weight.
Papa and the doctor debated whether or not we should
get off the ship at Gibraltar so she could be hospitalised.
I told my friend, the purser, we might be leaving.
'Huh,' he said. 'Seasickness! Doctors give you pills and
injections and tell you to stop eating. Sailors tell you to
keep eating and keep drinking so you don't dehydrate.
Here, take this to your mother. Make her drink it. And
tell her to eat *bischuit*. She will recover. Anyway, what's
wrong with her has nothing to do with the sea.'

Believing the purser to be correct in all things,
I went away clutching the sachet he'd handed me and
a packet of the wafery, round *bischuit* to which the
Dutch are addicted. Papa was up on deck studying
the Rock of Gibraltar through his binoculars. Mama
was alone in her cabin.

'Mama,' I said, 'here is something the purser says
you should drink.' I emptied the sachet into a glass
of water and held her head still while she drank it
down. Her hair was stringy, her nightdress stained.
The sachet – an old remedy for seasickness, the
purser assured me – contained granules of gelatine
that expanded when they came in contact with
liquid and filled the stomach. Mama managed to
keep the concoction down.

Then she croaked, 'I don't want to leave the ship. I want to go to the new country. A cup of tea, please.'

Our cabin had a jug, along with our own cups, saucers and teapot. I fixed her a weak tea and two rounds of *bischuit*. While she ate I opened the book of stamps I had started to assemble: leftovers and rejects from the purser's collection.

'What are those?'

I was so unused to Mama expressing interest in anything I did that it took me a while to answer. 'Stamps,' I said. 'From all over the world. I've been helping the purser with his collection. He's got books and books of them, Mama.'

'Show me.'

By the time Papa returned from his scrutiny of the Rock of Gibraltar, Mama was bewitched by the art of stamp collecting. To our surprise, her interests coincided with my friend the purser's: she was fascinated by what we came to refer to as the 'Hitler stamps'. 'These little squares of paper,' Mama said, 'helped rule an insane empire.'

I repeated what she'd said to the purser.

'*Ja*,' he replied. 'Quite so.'

He found an empty stamp album for Mama to begin her own collection. I badgered crew members for stamps. The purser gave me messages to relay to Mama about how to conduct the business of stamp collecting, about the tools that were required: a fine pair of tweezers, hangers, catalogues that gave prices (Hitler stamps, alas, were worthless). As we edged through the Suez Canal, Mama sat up on deck. When we got to Aden she was well enough to leave the ship and Mama, Papa and I scoured the old sea town for stamps and stamp albums. Papa bought hand-rolled cigars in a tobacconist's and asked the man whether he happened to have any stamps.

The tobacconist brought out leather albums filled with Arabian scenes, all of them in pristine condition. He also had a couple of boxes of unsorted stamps. Papa asked him about Hitler stamps. The tobacconist darted behind a curtain and came back with an envelope. Mussolini's face peeked out from under the flap. 'Worthless!' The tobacconist's long, striped robes wobbled as he shook his head. But Mama was adamant. These were the stamps she wanted. The tobacconist threw up his hands and accepted a small sum of money from Papa.

Papa was eager to encourage Mama in anything that absorbed her mind, anything that took her away from depression and anxiety. I extended my badgering to fellow passengers, even the Catholics, asking if they had any stamps they'd like to sell. Each purchase concluded with a gentle enquiry about Hitler stamps. By the time the *JVO* was cruising down the side of Western Australia, Mama had filled almost one whole album with stamps arranged neatly by country, and where possible by year. But it was her second album, the Hitler album, that really consumed her. In another tobacconist's, in Fremantle, she unearthed a prize discovery: a complete set from the 1936 Berlin Olympics, twenty stamps for five shillings, featuring the architecture of one Albert Speer.

We nosed towards Melbourne in the first week of December 1959, expecting hot weather. To celebrate our arrival Mama and I wore pretty summer dresses, and Papa a lightweight suit with a Panama hat. Then we hit Melbourne and the weather was freezing. We stood shivering in our dresses on the dock at Princes Pier, watching the other migrants pile onto buses bound for the migrant camp at Bonegilla. They sang cheerful marching songs as the buses carried them away.

We were waiting for someone from Papa's firm to pick us up when the purser approached. I had already said my goodbyes to him and had promised to write letters to his address in Rotterdam. 'Here,' he said to Mama, 'I am sick of collecting stamps. I am going to start on something else.' He presented her with four albums, including the one they both treasured: the Hitler stamps. Before Papa could extend a hand to thank him, the purser had disappeared into the ship.

Still we waited for this person to collect us and take us to the place where we were going to live. And waited. We had a suitcase each. The rest of our belongings were to be offloaded from the ship and placed in storage, probably until the new year. The waterside unions were in favour of an Indonesian push to add Dutch New Guinea to their empire and new Dutch migrants were the lowest of their priorities.

After an hour we realised no one was coming to collect us. We had the address. We would have to find our own way. Papa had some money he'd changed into Australian currency, and he went to speak to a man in one of the dockside offices.

'My good man,' said Papa, 'would you arrange a taxi for us? We are going to a place called Elsternwick.'

Papa had learnt English before the war and spoke the language flawlessly – but with a British, upper-class inflection.

Whatever the good man said in return did not please Papa. We slouched away from the docks, our suitcases trailing along with us, until we stumbled across a tram that promised to deliver us to the city. We climbed on board, suitcases bumping up the steep tram-step. All we had were ten-pound notes. The conductor circled back and forth, hoping we might find change. He stared at us, disgusted, when we got off the tram without having paid our fare.

We were standing in front of some concrete construction, squat and grey. It was the Melbourne Town Hall. Papa looked up at it, frowning a little, as he cleaned his glasses with a monogrammed handkerchief.

'So new,' he murmured. 'Not even eighty years old.'

9

Rattle, Whoosh, Crash

'Elst-ern-wick,' Mama said loud and slow. 'Come on, Jack. We have to find Elst-ern-wick.'

We stood still for a few minutes while crowds lugging Christmas parcels jostled past. Finally another tram rattled by: *Elsternwick*, it said. Elsternwick sounded like a village, with a grand town square, a place where there would be plenty of people you could ask for directions. We hopped on the tram and it resumed its rattling journey.

'Do Australians worship heathen gods?' asked Mama, pointing out the window. We followed her gaze and saw the most astonishing building, a building not unlike the pyramids we'd caught a glimpse of in Egypt.

'What is that building, please?' Papa asked a red-faced woman sitting nearby.

The red-faced woman said, 'That's the Shrine of Remembrance, darl'.'

Papa lifted his hat and thanked her. 'I have no idea,' he whispered to us, 'what that place is for.'

We passed Prince Henry's Hospital and Papa wondered which Prince Henry. Elsternwick, it turned out, did not possess a grand town square – or even a sign to indicate we had arrived. The tram rolled on and on, until eventually a fellow passenger took pity on us and told us that we had long passed Elsternwick, and that we'd better catch another tram back. This time, Papa, fuming, succeeded in hailing a taxi.

Our destination looked, from the outside, like a pleasant enough bungalow. Inside, the place had been divided into flats and rooms; Papa's employers, it dawned on us, had found us accommodation in a rooming house. The proprietor was a rambling old woman who told us that our immediate neighbours were 'a lovely German couple'. Waiting for us in the sitting room was a round little man, his hat crushed in his hands. He rose eagerly to greet Papa.

'Count Jacobus,' the round little man said.

'I have not taken my father's titles,' Papa replied. 'I am Jack Stolburg.'

'Oh, well, that depends on. The firm prefers you to be known as Lord Stolburg at the very least.'

'May one ask,' said Papa, 'why you were not at the docks to meet us?'

A long explanation followed about a sick wife and an unreliable car. When it was over Papa instructed him, 'You may pick me up in the morning.'

'Oh, I don't do that. In Australia everyone finds their own way to work.'

'Even the director of a company? *Zo*, please write down directions so I will know how to get there. You may leave now.'

Before he left, the round little man handed over a parcel. 'Compliments from Hart,' he said. Hart was the name of the wool exporting company of which Papa was now a director. Inside the parcel was a black and white Kriesler radio.

We immediately invented a name for the fat envoy from Hart: 'Mr Dikkertje'. In Dutch, *dikkertje* means *little fatso*. Mama pranced about copying his cringing way of speaking.

I don't do that . . .

Oh, that depends on . . .

I bowed down before Papa and addressed him as 'Lord Stolburg'. That made him smile. Then we switched on the Kriesler radio and found a music station playing the latest pop tunes. 'This will have to do,' Papa said, 'until the things come from the ship.' Among the possessions still to be unloaded was our beloved radiogram.

The next day, while Papa went to work, Mama and I explored the streets and shops of Elsternwick. We were shocked. Everything looked old-fashioned, rundown, dirty. By mid-morning the day was boiling hot. Mama swore her high heels were sinking into the bitumen of the footpaths. We entered a butcher's shop where men and women stared at us. '*Got*,' Mama gasped, once we were back out on the street, 'those people were Jews. Who could have known there would be Jews in the new country? I thought they were all dead.'

Our new home had a sitting room and one bedroom between three of us, with a curtained-off kitchen and a bathroom we shared with the other tenants. We had endured many privations in our lives, but Mama and Papa did not intend to live in a rooming house. The search for an appropriate home began immediately.

For the few remaining weeks of the school year I was enrolled at Elsternwick Primary. The Grade 6 teacher's name was Miss Nedewell. On the last day of term, knowing we were moving house and I would not be returning, I went up to Miss Nedewell and offered her my hand. In my thick Dutch accent I said, 'Thank you vurry much, Miss Nerr-do-well.'

'Nedewell! Nedewell!' the woman screamed.

In our sitting room, in the days before Christmas, the Kriesler radio played over and over the big hit of 1959:

Honey in the morning
Honey in the evening
Honey at suppertime
Be my little honey
And love me all the time

Mama could not stop the stupid song fizzing round her head. She sang it, hummed it and danced around the table every time it erupted out of the black and white box. Papa and I were delighted to see her happy. Maybe the new country would be good for her, after all.

★

Oscar and Joanie have returned from the hospital feeling despondent. Plans must be made. The year is turning to autumn. Soon I will have to go back to the Netherlands to sort out the beginning of the end of my family. Oscar still does not know about Frederick's job.

Joanie – blessed, squared-off Joanie – is the only one able to articulate what needs to be said. 'First off, Pearl can't live here. It's no good you looking like that, Oscar. Facts is facts. She won't be able to get her wheelchair around this house. There are steps and turns everywhere. Furniture sticking out. And she'll never get in the shower. I'm not going to break my back lifting her.'

'What about Juliana? Can't she help?'

'In case you have forgotten, big brother, your marriage is broken up and you've gone gay. You can't expect your ex-wife to look after her ex-mother-in-law. Jesus, Oscar, sometimes I wonder where you keep your brains.'

'I only meant for a little while. We were married nearly thirty years. You don't just get rid of that overnight.' Oscar looks at me for confirmation.

'Our thirtieth anniversary is tomorrow,' I remind him. Oscar groans. Frederick looks embarrassed. 'Anyway,' I say, 'I have to go back to the Netherlands and Frederick has some business to attend to in Luxemburg.'

Frederick's eyes flare. The skin around his nose turns white.

'You have to go to Luxemburg?' Oscar huffs. 'And you told Juliana but not me?'

'Telling Juliana just happened. Anyway, you could take over my duties at the Opera House while I'm away. You could,' he adds, 'sort out the Pearl problem as well.'

'Thanks,' says Joanie, 'but I can sort out the "Pearl problem" all by myself. I've been running this stud for years. I'll be running it when you and your boyfriend have moved on to wherever. Why don't the three of you bugger off to Europe? You can mess up your lives over there.'

Dog lets out a sudden howl, startling us. Before Joanie can catch him he runs outside.

'I do not want to go to Luxemburg,' Oscar says quietly. 'Juliana's posting was supposed to be for two years. We stayed for eight. I really, really do not want to go to bloody Luxemburg.'

★

In the new year, the new decade of the 1960s, we moved into a two-storey Edwardian house in the well-to-do suburb of Malvern. Our dead-end street was called The Avenue. Mama questioned Papa about how this fine house could possibly be afforded. We had brought money with us but the whole purpose of our exile was to rebuild our fortune. Papa explained that Hart had helped him buy it with a piece of paper called a *mortgage*. This meant that when we returned to the Netherlands we would sell the house for a handsome profit.

Our furniture had still not arrived. We wandered around empty rooms, imagining where we'd place our possessions. The large dining room would be perfect for entertaining and our oak table was big enough to seat all the new friends we'd surely make. We would line the study with Dutch books, and Papa would write his war memoir there. Next to the spacious modern kitchen was a tiny sewing room for Mama. 'And,' she exclaimed, 'a closet where I can hang clothes in progress.'

Upstairs, the bedrooms had French doors opening onto a wide veranda. The veranda wound all the way round the house. My new friends could sleep over, and we'd sit out on the veranda in cane chairs, reading books and exchanging confidences and looking down at the garden, which was a sodden, emerald green. Night and day, all along The Avenue, sprinklers whoosh-whooshed water onto saturated lawns.

On the day our goods were released from the docks and dumped on our gravel driveway, I collided in the street with a tall, blond god. Both of us were reading while walking, and then *crash*.

'Whoa,' said the god. 'What's that you're reading?'

I showed him my Enid Blyton book and the Dutch–English dictionary I carried with me everywhere.

'I'm Philip de Vere. Everyone calls me Philly. Who are you?'

'My name is Juliana Stolburg and I am a Dutch girl.'

'I can see you're a girl. Rumour in the street has it your father's some sort of aristocrat. Must say your English is not too ghastly. I might make you my project for the summer hols. Think I'll call you Jules. What do you say to that? Now, why don't you take me to meet your parents.'

I nodded. I had no idea what the god with the sort of Dutch-sounding name was talking about. But he seemed to want to see our new home. Mama fluttered about offering cups of tea, clearly affected by this golden creature. Philly wandered around our oversized oak furniture, touching the carved gargoyles and opening and shutting drawers. He admired our paintings. He lamented their refusal to hang straight. I nodded at his every sentence.

'Everything in this country is either too big or too small,' Papa said. He pointed to the floor. 'I've had to pile the Persian rugs one on top of another.'

'Lord Stolburg, this is a Ruysdael! Wouldn't mind showing it to my pa.' Philly pounced on a silver salver. Engraved in the middle were the Stolburg lion and Siegfried's titles. 'What does all this say?'

'Something like *Lord of the Islands*,' said Papa.

'I see,' said Philly. 'Yes, I think I see.'

When it was empty the house had seemed elegant. Our too-big Dutch furniture reduced the space and revealed awkward corners. Only the radiogram and Papa's boxes of 78 rpm records looked at home. As soon as Philly saw these he declared himself in classical heaven. Papa frowned at such blasphemy but happily rearranged the necessary transformers and machinery to play the operas Philly selected. 'Not too much Wagner,' Papa said softly. 'My wife is not sympathetic to Wagner.'

Philly told us he was studying to become a psychiatrist. He had passed his bachelor exams in medicine and surgery and was now embarking on his specialist course. 'My family can't understand my interest in the mind. They're in newspapers, you see. They report what people do. I am more interested in why people do what they do.'

We nodded knowledgeably. Papa understood what he said; I understood some of it. Mama never became proficient at English. Yet she claimed she understood Philly.

For the rest of that January, during the school and university holidays, Philly undertook to teach me English. 'We will concentrate on conversation. Grammar will follow. Not before eleven o'clock, mind, I'm not human before then. We will walk around Malvern unless it's too hot. If it's hot, we will sit in your garden. I am determined you will not speak with a Dutch accent, Jules.'

He praised Papa's English. 'Your father,' he said, 'could be an English gentleman.'

Philly was the oldest child of a family who lived in a ramshackle Gothic-style house at the top of The Avenue. His ma, pa and two siblings had big, generous voices that curled around corners, up and down staircases and out onto the street, often to the neighbours' horror and annoyance. Philly introduced them all to me: his parents Uther and Morgana, brother Arty and sister Griselda. When I told Papa he chortled. '*Ach*, I have that book somewhere – *Morte d'Arthur*. You will understand when you read Malory.' I hadn't realised they were nicknames.

Philly was tall like Papa but made of slender stuff. In every way – physique, colouring, character – he was a sort of cuckoo in his own family. They didn't question why a 26-year-old man should take an interest in a twelve-year-old girl. That was the sort of thing Philly did. And Philly, everyone in his family agreed, could do no wrong.

On our strolls around Malvern – 'Mol-vurn not Mahl-vurn' – he succeeded in eradicating the Dutch from my voice. 'Rain falls out of the sky. Not rai-in fahls uit ov de skoi.' He passed onto me, without meaning to, an upper-class accent and his family's peculiar speech mannerisms.

'Philly, is that Jules child here again? Did she bring her clogs?'

'No, Arty, she's brought her jim-jams, though.'

My brain started to swirl. 'Please,' I said, 'only Catholics and peasants wear clogs. And what are jim-jams?'

'Pyjamas,' said Arty.

'Catholics and peasants,' said Griselda, 'that's a bi-i-it intense.'

Philly tried explaining to me some of the de Vere family dynamics. 'Morgana comes from a frightfully good family,' he said. 'Uther's people are self-made.'

Apparently 'frightfully' and 'good' were words that belonged together at certain times but not others.

'Do you like baked beans on toast, Jules? 'Cause I'm just throwing some together.'

'Oh, yes,' I replied, 'frightfully good.' I could see

by the frown on Philly's face that I'd got something wrong.

Philly loved to lie in till midday. He'd bemoan the fact that tempus was fugiting, whatever that meant, then stay in bed anyway. Sometimes I'd get to his house at half past eleven to witness his arrival downstairs.

'Ah, the boy is among us,' Arty would announce. 'All bow to the golden child of genius.'

The housekeeper would place tea and toast before him, then, after a while, a pot of coffee. Morgana had never been known to cook and wafted through the morning room in a variety of drooping clothes my mother would have thought deplorable. Philly ignored me and the rest of the world until he had drunk two cups of tea and the entire pot of coffee.

'Ah, there you are, Jules. What shall we do today? I know, we'll go to the pictures. Anyone else coming?'

Arty then drove however many of us there were to picture theatres, tennis courts or the beach. Philly did not drive and was not about to learn. 'I know I won't be any good at it.' Arty and Griselda drove him everywhere. He was their eccentric older brother and they adored him, that's all there was to it.

Early on, Mama expressed reservations about Philly spending so much time with me. Papa explained to us that Philly wasn't the sort of man who was interested in girls 'in that way' and I was quite safe. Mama nodded as though she understood.

Our next-door neighbours in The Avenue were an elderly couple who grew blue hydrangeas the size of dinner plates in their front garden. Their name, according to the sign on the gate, was Fuchs. 'Hello Mr and Mrs Fucks,' Mama and I yelled out in friendly greeting, only to see the elderly couple scuttle away. 'Those Fucks next door are very rude,' Mama said to Papa that evening. Papa nearly choked on his ice-cream.

One afternoon as we roamed Malvern's streets Philly said quietly, 'Your folks are rather precious, Jules. Papa all old world and terribly 1850s. Mama had a ghastly time during the war, I suspect. No other family?'

'Mama has parents back in the Netherlands. And a brother.'

'They didn't end up you know where?'

'Where?'

'In a concentration camp. Jewish and all that.'

'Oh.' Groping for the right words, I tried to tell Philly the family history as I understood it. 'Papa was a boss, leader of the Resistance. Mama was in Dachau with . . . with political prisoners. The Nazis didn't realise she was a Jew. The Germans hoped Papa would give himself up. Siegfried and Françoise, my grandparents, were in house arrest. But they didn't tell the Germans where Papa was.'

'How did the Germans find your mother?'

'My uncle, Papa's brother, was . . . was traitor.'

'A collaborator, do you mean?'

I consulted the dictionary and agreed that was what I meant.

'I see,' said Philly. 'Siegfried – fascinating name.'

Papa lamented the lack of a Calvinist congregation in Melbourne. He discussed this with Philly and they decided the St George's Church of England on Glenferrie Road was the place for us to worship our Protestant God. One Sabbath morning we marched up The Avenue and perched near the back of the church. Philly, for once rising before mid-afternoon on a Sunday, followed after us, swiping lazily at bushes protruding onto the pavement, and then sitting not in the pew with us but in the row behind. I looked around, wondering at the twinkle in his eye. Mama twisted around several times to stare at his white suit and pale blue shirt.

Soon Papa was scowling. On the stained glass windows a cowering dragon was about to be pierced with a sword by a youth who didn't look strong enough to administer the death blow. The vicar entered to a series of curling trills from the organ. Boys in long white gowns followed, one of them carrying an ornate cross. Behind them came a man swinging a brass object gushing incense. Papa exhaled mightily and pushed us out of the pew and out of the church. He stalked up Glenferrie Road and down The Avenue as stiff-legged as a Prussian. 'Philip de Vere, what do you think you were doing suggesting that place could be suitable for us? *Gotverdomme.*'

'I thought Jules might enjoy the colour and spectacle, Lord Stolburg. Protestantism can be a bit earnest.' He whispered in my ear. 'Jules, what was that Dutch oath?'

'Papa was asking God to damn his soul.'

'Dear me.'

For a few days there was tension. But Philly's natural charm was irresistible. He was made of the stuff of mischief, a mischief tempered with wit and intelligence. As soon as his holidays were over, the indolent youth disappeared, and was replaced by a man who worked night and day among the saddest cases of insanity: the psychotics, the severely deluded, the ones whom society had deemed incurable and then discarded.

For my thirteenth birthday, in that blissful January in the first year of the 1960s, Philly arranged a party at his parents' house. There we were introduced to the mysteries of the Australian barbecue and that indescribable delicacy: burnt sausages. Our fathers got tipsy together. Mama somehow communicated with Philly's mother. Griselda presented me with a shell necklace I knew I'd never wear. Yet I treasured it. Arty gave me his collection of Mary Grant Bruce's Billabong books and said, 'I enjoyed these when I was your age. Might borrow *Captain Jim* off you every now and then.'

Mama thought Morgana odd. 'Why does she wear her hair down her back like that? And do you notice the white streaks, Juliana? That Morgana should go to my hairdresser.'

Mama visited a hairdresser on High Street every Saturday morning. Every second week Papa went to the same place for a trim. Mama wanted my hair cut in the same neat bob I'd had since I was five but Philly intervened, saying dark hair like mine should be left to grow long. Mama sniffed, saying it would only straggle down my back. Papa agreed with Philly and thus my hair was allowed to emerge from its childhood bob. The longer it grew, the more I saw Françoise sneaking out from behind my features. In time I became used to people saying, 'You don't look Dutch! You don't sound Dutch!'

I knew our exile was temporary. By the end of January I was afraid it might be too temporary. Even the cicadas – from the first early-morning soloist to the thrumming afternoon orchestra – seemed to sense our urgency. Those cicadas plagued our lives. We were assured they were unusually loud that summer. Uther reckoned it was the loudest they'd been since the war. We longed for the hours when The Avenue was in shadow, for that was when the cicadas drowsed. The moment the sun came out the orchestra cranked up again.

Papa slept badly. Often he sat smoking on the veranda outside my bedroom. I liked waking up during the night, smelling the sweet aroma of his cigars, listening to the soft rustling of pages of whatever book he was reading by torchlight. He had never been a great bible reader but now he began reading the Book of Psalms over and over.

A few days after my birthday party Philly and his parents visited. Mama handed around little savouries and cups of tea and coffee. Morgana said she'd prefer a beer.

'Do women drink beer in Australia?' Mama asked me, shocked, while we were in the kitchen making club sandwiches. When we rejoined the others she decided to try a glass. She wrinkled her nose. She sipped deeply. Within minutes of drinking her first and last glass of Australian beer she was pale and swaying. I grabbed her arm and helped her back to the kitchen.

'No! The toilet! Quick!'

With a violent lurch from her innards, Mama threw up all over the kitchen floor.

'Lady Stolburg, dear lady, you've been ill.' Philly put a damp dishcloth to her head and guided her upstairs. 'I'll be back down in a minute, Jules, to help you mop up.'

I cleaned and scrubbed quickly, determined that Philly should not mop up Mama's vomit. Then I ventured upstairs.

'Has your mother always been so thin?'

She was lying on the bed, moaning, clutching her stomach. Philly lifted Mama's hands and showed me how her wedding ring and the Japanese ring slipped up and down her fingers. I told him about her seasickness on the boat.

'What about menopause?'

I didn't know what he meant.

'Periods. Does she still have periods?'

I looked at him blankly.

Mama couldn't get up the next day. She was able to swallow and keep down weak tea and thin slices of bread but nothing substantial. The cicadas began singing mid–morning, signalling another hot day. I sat on the veranda with a book and my dictionary, within earshot of Mama. I had begun the Billabong books. They were set on a country property around the First

World War and I relished the word pictures: of the children Norah and Jim and their good mate Wally, and the innocent adventures they had on horseback. It was everything I believed Australian country life to be.

Philly found me engrossed in *Captain Jim*. The illustration on the cover – tall, blond Jim – looked a little like Philly, who by now felt sufficiently at home in our house to walk in unannounced. He pulled out a book of his own about the reproductive systems of males and females. Patiently he explained that soon I could expect to bleed once a month. 'Griselda calls it the curse. Bit of a nuisance when she wants to go swimming. She gave me this packet of Modess and pins for you. You pin the pads to the inside of your undies. On heavy days you may need to double up.'

He then outlined the process of sexual intercourse between men and women, and how life is created. He also said something Papa had said once before: that he himself was a man who was not interested in women 'in that way'.

'There are laws,' he said, 'that would prefer it if men like me didn't exist. My family, bless them, don't believe in those laws. That's all you have to know for now.' Then he said he wanted Mama to see a colleague of his who specialised in women's problems.

That afternoon Papa came home with a car. One of his fellow Hart directors was returning to the Netherlands and had sold Papa his 1955 Daimler Conquest. Mama was well enough to get up and inspect this important addition to our lives.

'A Nazi car,' she hissed.

'No,' said Papa. 'This car is English. Like Jaguar. There are almost no miles on the clock. She is as good as new. Does ninety miles per hour top speed. And look, Janna, at the leather interior and fruitwood dashboard.'

Mama went back to bed while Papa took me for a spin in the Daimler. Turning out of The Avenue, forgetting that in Australia cars drive on the left side, he almost collided with a tram. We stopped for Philly who was walking home along Glenferrie Road, reading a textbook.

'Divine car. That two-tone effect – burgundy and tan – very smart. Arty will be impressed. Afraid I don't drive. Hopeless at it. Can't drive and no good at cricket. When you're a bit older, Jules, you should read Freud on the interpretation of dreams.'

As we drove off again, Papa said to me, 'Do you understand everything Philly says?'

'No, Papa.'

'But he likes the Daimler, don't you think?'

'Yes, Papa.'

We were in a heatwave so hot the leaves fell from the trees. The cicadas that jangled all our nerves bothered Papa more than anyone. Sometimes I found him in the study, smoking a cigar, his fingers in his ears. Mama blamed the war. The guns and explosions he'd had to endure, she said, made his hearing sensitive.

Late one Sunday afternoon, while the rest of the street dozed and tried to get cool, and when Papa could not stand the screaming frenzy of the cicadas any longer, he opened the false bottom of the Spanish trunk, took out the pistol with the initials J.S. engraved on the barrel, went to the top of the house and fired three volleys up The Avenue. The cicadas fell silent.

Our neighbours didn't go to the trouble of calling the police. They already had us catalogued: Papa was a crazy Dutch aristocrat, Mama was a crazy war-damaged Jew and I hung around with the de Vere family, who prided themselves on being crazier than anyone else on The Avenue.

Papa taught me how to drive and maintain the Daimler. I'd clean spark plugs, drain the radiator, check the oil level. On the hottest of the heatwave days, he woke me early and we drove along the empty roads of Malvern, Toorak and Armadale. Some of Toorak's leafier streets enchanted him. Maybe, he fretted, he should have looked in Toorak before buying our house in Malvern. I knew all about the piece of paper called *mortgage*. I was afraid his company might give him another one of those papers and we'd have to leave The Avenue. But Papa assured me there was no point moving. We were only going to be in Australia a short while.

When the time came for Mama to visit Philly's colleague, the gynaecological specialist, she did not feel ready to negotiate the trams on her own. I sat in the waiting room at Prince Henry's while she and Philly went in. Philly was rarely without a smile. But when they came back out his face was grim. He and Papa talked in the study that night for a long time.

'Your mother will have to have an operation,' Papa said. 'The Germans treated her badly. Philly's colleague says it was a miracle you were born at all, Juliana.'

10

The Fork in the Road

Papa was a *waterbouwkundige*. Mama and I had no idea what his function was at Hart, other than that he was a director. A party celebrating the company's tenth year in Australia was planned for the Dutch Club in South Melbourne. Mama was excited. She decided she would design a dress for the occasion. In the Myer Emporium on Bourke Street there existed one whole floor of buttons, cotton threads and needles, along with swathes of material.

'I don't even need to make up the patterns,' she said. 'They come in packets. All you have to do is unfold them and pin them on.' She told Philly's mother she was making a nightdress.

'Think she means evening dress,' said Philly.

'Yes,' said Mama, 'a nightdress is what I am making.'

Surely, I thought, a dress worn to a night-time function was a nightdress. But I could see from Philly and Arty's eye-rolling that we had used the wrong word again.

'The nightdress I am making is from gold mat-er-ial,' Mama said.

Philly and Arty rolled around the floor like puppies. Morgana gave them friendly kicks.

'Ow, Ma, not in the national treasure.'

As we trudged home, Mama and I sighed in unison. 'I don't understand what was so funny, Juliana. And what is this treasure?' The English language was a minefield as treacherous as anything left behind by the Germans.

A few days later Mama modelled her creation in the sewing room, where she had installed full-length mirrors. She twirled on tiptoe to highlight the way the dress flowed down her slim body. 'Let us dance, Lady Stolburg,' said Philly. They waltzed around the room and the gold tulle of the material made Mama seem light and ethereal. 'Doesn't she look the thing, Morgana?' Philly said as he hoisted Mama high above his shoulders.

Mama giggled. 'I love dancing. Jack hates it.'

Morgana bent down for a closer look, studying the seams and the cut. Mama showed her the original pattern. She asked me to explain to Morgana how she had altered the design so that the tulle overskirt sat below rather than above the waist. 'Does your Mama change patterns like this all the time?' Morgana murmured, 'Bloody genius.'

We had been told 'bloody' was a bad word and

warned not to use it. But Morgana de Vere was not like other women in The Avenue. Mrs Fuchs next door whispered that Mrs de Vere was a 'bohemian'.

'I like *La Bohème*, the opera, very much,' Mama replied.

On the night of the ten-year party Papa drove us to the Dutch Club. 'Look at that!' He clicked his tongue. 'The German Club is right next door.'

He parked the Daimler carefully beside a car he was positive belonged to a Hart employee, and we sat down at a table with the other directors and their wives. The men cast admiring glances at Mama. A tinny band provided background music. We ate ham and pea soup in the sweltering heat and when the first course was finished our table emptied and couples got up to dance.

'Lord Stolburg?'

It was the grovelling voice of the round little man we had met at the rooming house in Elsternwick. By his side was a fat woman. She wore a fur stole. Her face, surrounded by fox, looked waxy.

'We thought you might like help with being Australian,' she said, beaming.

With a sumptuous wave, Mr Dikkertje introduced his wife. 'We know all about Australia,' he said. 'We came from Holland in 1955.'

'We are not from Holland,' Papa said. 'We are Zeelanders. The provinces of Noord and Zuid Holland are to the north of us, in every sense.'

'Oh, that depends on.'

Mrs Dikkertje shoved Mr Dikkertje aside. 'For instance,' she said, 'my husband's name is Johan. But in

Australia he is John. My name is Marijke. In Australia I am Mary. What is your name, Lady Stolburg?'

'Janna,' Mama answered.

'Then you must be Jan. And you?' Mrs Dikkertje pointed at me.

'I am Juliana Stolburg.'

'Ha! You will be Julie.'

She looked at Papa. She decided against re-arranging his name. 'What a lovely thing,' she said instead, her eyes lighting up at the sight of the Meiji emperor's ring.

'You must come and visit us at the house we are building in Black-burrrn,' said Mr Dikkertje.

'Yes,' agreed Mrs Dikkertje, 'and then we will visit you.'

Mama and Mrs Dikkertje exchanged phone numbers.

'Janna, you must never, never speak to those people,' Papa said as we drove home in the Daimler. 'He is not a director. The only reason he's never been sacked is because he's Protestant. And she . . . *Gotverdomme*.'

Mama was close to tears. 'I didn't get to dance,' she said. 'And no one even noticed my nightdress.'

★

'God damn it!' Oscar has jammed a finger during the excruciating process of moving Pearl from the car to her wheelchair. The wheelchair has to be positioned beside the passenger door and a plastic board inserted under her bottom. She must then manoeuvre her body into the wheelchair by means of this plastic board.

'Transferring takes my breath away,' she tells me, tears in her eyes. Dog sniffs at Pearl's feet, reacquainting himself with his mistress.

'Hurry! To the toilet!'

It takes all of Joanie's and my strength to haul Pearl out of the wheelchair and onto the toilet seat. Then we haul her up again to lift her skirt and lower her underpants. By the time we have accomplished the task she's wet her pants.

'I have to poop now.'

'You go back to the boys, Jules,' says Joanie, not wanting me to see her mother weeping.

The boys, though, are not hanging around. 'Oscar's coming home with me,' says Frederick. 'Bringing Pearl home from hospital was traumatic. He needs some quiet time.'

'Fuck off then,' I say.

Frederick raises one elegantly defined eyebrow. 'I daresay some sort of fucking might take place, Juliana.'

'Stop it you two,' says Oscar.

Pearl is exhausted. She has gone to bed. She wants to know how the stallion is. 'Where is he, Joanie? He's usually in the home paddock about now smooching for oats.' When we do not answer she asks again.

'You tell her, Jules. I've had enough.'

Thus it is me who tells Pearl that her dreamy-eyed stallion survived the snakebite yet died soon after of an unknown cause. He never, I guess, really recovered from that encounter with the snake. Some essence was leached out of him. He languished. Then he died.

Pearl turns her head to the window, searching the skeleton of her farm for meaning. 'He was my last stallion. I can't start again. Anyway, I don't have me legs. What's the point? What's the point of anything?'

Joanie might be able to continue the stud, I say.

'Horses are a mug's game – tell her that from me. And where's Oscar in all of this? Tell me that, will you, Juliana?'

Oscar and Frederick return in the morning with a picnic basket. They have brought lunch: there is a thirtieth wedding anniversary to celebrate. Both men kiss me. There is nothing to differentiate their kisses, nothing to suggest that one of these men is my husband. The spat with Frederick is forgotten. The two of them have chosen an anniversary present for me, a gold bracelet in a Roman design.

'Morgana de Vere would have liked this,' I hear myself say.

★

Morgana thought I should study Latin at my new school in Malvern. Philly was surprised Papa would not allow me to attend a private school. But Papa, as a committed Calvinist, believed in the separation of church and state. He'd supported the post-war efforts in the Netherlands to ban all forms of private schooling, and the private schools in Malvern had a religious affiliation he disliked.

As it turned out, Morgana did not need to suggest Latin. The French class was full and the only other choice was German. 'You'll love Latin,' Philly promised. 'That dear old language creaks like a rusty door hinge. But it provides the building blocks for everything else.' Morgana showed me her collection of bracelets and necklaces made from Roman coins. 'I think the heads are so noble,' she said.

My first weeks of high school were confusing. Philly was working long hours at the hospital and had little time to spare. For a time I was convinced I knew as much Latin as English. I was plunged into a world of togas and spears and characters with musical names. Scipio Africanus. Julia Pompeia. Then there were the beguiling phrases.

Carthago delenda est
Carthage must be destroyed

Where in the world was Carthage? But Philly was right. I did love Latin. I delighted in discovering the origins of words.

I did not make friends, though, preferring to sit at a table in the school library reading any book I liked. No one told me what to read; we were encouraged to read whatever we fancied. I brought home simple children's books for Mama to get the hang of English. She learnt enough to shop and to conduct undemanding conversations. But she never fell in love with the language, and never mastered it.

She seemed happier than I had ever known her, despite the serious operation that was only a few weeks away. She wrote home every week to Oma and Opa but grew frustrated that they could not reply other than through a village letter writer. They sent one letter for every four of hers. 'Never mind,' she said. 'They will want to know what we are doing, that we like the new country.' In one letter Mama wrote proudly: 'Juliana is a Latin scholar. Her best friend, a young man, is studying to be a doctor of the mind.'

Mrs Dikkertje began calling on Mama when I was at school and Papa at work. She was always gone before I got home. Sometimes I'd glimpse her behind the wheel of her Volkswagen. The VW made her seem even fatter and more venal. Then one afternoon I came home and Mrs Dikkertje was still there. Philly came over to help me with my mathematics. I liked arithmetic and geometry but hated algebra. Mrs Dikkertje was drinking lemonade and nibbling at a hunk of cake. She was as blonde as Philly. In every other way they could not have been less alike.

'*Zo*, de Vere, that is a Dutch name.'

'Actually,' said Philly, 'it's Norman-French.'

'No, this name is Dutch. Definitely.'

'Madam, I assure you the name is Norman-French.'

'Jan is telling me you are some sort of brain doctor.'

'Jan? Ah, you must mean Janna, Lady Stolburg.'

Mrs Dikkertje managed to look embarrassed and furious at the same time. '*Ach*, those silly titles. They are disappearing from Holland.'

'Really! And what about the rest of the Netherlands?'

'We talk about *Nederland* as Holland in Australia.'

'Lord Stolburg doesn't,' Philly said.

Mama had never been in the habit of tucking me in or wishing me goodnight. But that evening, she crept in while I was reading.

'Mrs Dikkertje thinks Philly might be *homo*,' she

said. 'She thinks you shouldn't be friendly with him. I told her this was none of her business as long as your father approves. Philly's family has been kind to us. I think this friendship with Philly is acceptable. Being homo has nothing to do with women, I know that much.'

'No, Mama.'

She was operated on in March. 'All her women's parts had to be removed,' Papa said. Philly stayed with a friend for the two weeks Mama was in hospital and I took his bedroom in the de Vere household. His window looked out on a huge plane tree and it was by this window that I read *Morte d'Arthur*. The Arthurian world of gallantry, chivalry and the seeking of an impossible holy grail was not so far removed from the myths told about my ancestors. I longed to possess enough English to tell Philly about Charlemagne's nephew, Siegfried, the same Siegfried who founded the Stolburg dynasty and haunted Philly's favourite Wagnerian opera, *Götterdämmerung*; and to tell him about my grandfather with the same name.

Philly was Mama's most frequent visitor and sat with her for long periods as she lay pale and small beneath the bedclothes. She hardly spoke, claiming the anaesthetic had removed all her knowledge of English. Philly asked me teach him some Dutch phrases.

Goeden morgen, Janna. Hoe gaat het met U vandaag? Hebt U pein?

His efforts made Mama laugh. I was sitting with her behind the curtains one day when I overheard the gynaecologist say to Philly, 'There was dreadful scar tissue. Nazi bastards.'

Mama came home still thin. 'I want to learn ballroom dancing,' she announced brightly. 'There's a place called Leggett's Ballroom where the Dikkertjes go dancing.'

'Over my dead body,' said Papa. He had begun reading the bible, and now he snapped it shut. It was as if Françoise were back in the room with us.

Mr and Mrs Dikkertje were keen dancers and had photos of themselves swirling and twirling their fat bodies across ballrooms all over Melbourne. Papa never saw these photos as they didn't dare visit when he was likely to be home. But I delighted in flicking through them, pretending to be impressed, so that I could later regale Philly and the de Veres with the most accurately revolting descriptions. Arty reckoned I had the makings of a 'prize bitch'. Apparently that was a great compliment.

Mr and Mrs Dikkertje lived in a garage while they were building their Blackburn house. Our Malvern home and our crates of European possessions convinced them we were rich. We became a source of plunder to the Dikkertjes. Silver boxes, oriental vases and Meissen shepherdesses began disappearing. Papa didn't seem to notice. I did. Whenever I questioned Mama about a missing piece, she'd say, 'Oh, Mrs Dikkertje liked that little thing. Poor dears, they have to live in a garage.'

Mrs Dikkertje had convinced Mama that she was her special friend. Mama had never had girlfriends before. I loathed Mrs Dikkertje. Yet I rejoiced to see Mama happy. Her silences, her chronic depression, were replaced with laughter and purpose.

Papa brought home every stamp that came into the Hart mailroom and Mama attended to her stamp albums with the avidity of a born scholar. She delighted in finding minute differences in design, or watermarks, and she filled notebooks with neat copperplate handwriting on matters to do with philately. When the availability of Hitler stamps dwindled, she collected Australian wildlife. And then Antarctica. 'No one,' she said, 'likes the Antarctica stamps except me. You wait, they will be valuable one day.'

As soon as the de Vere family learnt of Mama's hobby they began dropping piles of envelopes into our letterbox. Arty gave her some stamps to do with the 1956 Olympic Games in Melbourne. 'Philly and I went to a few events,' he said. 'I cheered like anything. Philly sat in the stands reading a book.' Mama declared these stamps to be among her favourites. 'No other country has anything like them. *Ach*, what a pity so many were produced. Rarity is everything in stamp collecting.'

Philly had begun another phase of his psychiatric career and now worked long hours in a locked ward. Some mornings, when I walked up The Avenue's rippled footpath to catch a tram to school, I'd meet him coming down. At times he was so physically and mentally exhausted that he could not locate a smile.

'Philly takes everything to heart,' Uther said to me one afternoon. I put down my schoolbag and removed the straw hat scratching at my forehead. 'Look here, Juliana, I'll get right to the point. Philly is depressed. Which is not like him. Don't suppose you could find time to cheer him up? He gets on well with you.

Perhaps you could call around during the day, when he's off duty? Morgana and I are never home. And Arty and Griselda are no use, no use at all.'

'Are you depressed, Philly?' I asked my friend the next day.

It was nearly four in the afternoon. He was still in bed. Circles had created blue sketches under his eyes and his chin was covered in a fine golden down.

'Tired. Bloody, bloody tired.'

'Everyone is afraid you're depressed.'

'Are you the emissary, Jules, from an uncaring world? Never mind that. Get under the sheet with me. Take off those horrible shoes. And the socks. Positively indecent to wear socks in bed. I'll read you some Shakespeare.'

My English was still too shaky to grasp much of the sonnets. Philly recited something about a dark lady and love.

'Are you in love, Philly?'

'Yes. What a bore.'

'Another man?'

He sighed. 'I am in love with a man who does not love me. He refuses to acknowledge his homosexuality. Do you understand, Jules?'

'I think so.'

Our two years were up. It was time to return to the Netherlands. At the end of spring Papa asked Mama and me into the study. Behind his desk two long windows looked out on The Avenue.

'I need to stay another year,' he said. 'I haven't made quite as much money as I'd hoped. Hart want me to stay. There are uncertain economic conditions ahead.'

He looked worn out. Mama was overjoyed. She danced around the house and launched into an orgy of dressmaking.

I wanted to go home.

Yet I did not want to leave Philly.

Our two-year exile was extended to three. Papa had decided on a fork in the road, thinking he was doing the right thing.

And that made all the difference.

I had just started third form at high school when Papa found me outside my bedroom one night, bent over the veranda railing, searching for something below. Mama said sleepwalkers could not come to any harm. An acquaintance in Middelburg sent her Dutch women's magazines every month, and in one of these was a homily on sleepwalking. In the 1960s the Dutch busied themselves studying the generation born just after the war. Sleepwalking and sleep-talking were common afflictions. Sleepwalkers, it was believed, were protected by God and could not harm themselves, no matter where or how far they roamed.

Papa consulted Philly. Philly told him sleepwalkers frequently injured themselves and he suggested I come see him at Prince Henry's on Saturday mornings; maybe he could help.

His office where he saw outpatients was at the end of a dark corridor. I expected to lie on a couch and be asked questions. Instead he put me to work filing stacks of papers by their hospital codes. When I finished doing that he told me to read. At the age of fourteen, with the help of my Dutch–English dictionary and Philly's medical and psychological dictionaries, I read about sleepwalking, sleep-talking and personalities subjected to early childhood stress. He encouraged me to write down my reflections. 'In any language you like.'

The man Philly loved who did not return that love was a fellow psychiatric resident called Ivan. He too saw outpatients on Saturday mornings, and he was in the habit of dropping in on Philly between appointments. Whenever Ivan came into the room Philly blushed and fidgeted.

'Your girlfriend here again, Philly? What did you make of my patient X? Do you concur with my diagnosis?'

'Sorry, Ivan. Afraid I can't see X as a psychopath. Severe delusional schizophrenia. No malice involved, other than to himself.'

I flicked through Philly's dictionary of psychiatric terminology, trying to keep up.

'Should the child should be listening to this conversation, Philip?'

'Jules is a psychologist in training. She has the sort of brain ideal for the epidemiological aspects of our sport.' Philly paused. 'Not, perhaps, the type of personality to deal with the clinical aspects. I would hate to see her become a psychiatrist. I rather fancy she will end up a social scientist.'

That night, I said to my parents, 'I am going to be a social scientist.'

After consulting our dictionaries once more, we decided I was going to be the sort of scientist who studied people and their interactions with others. When I woke hours later out of a deep sleep, peering down from the veranda and listening to the pattering of rain on the windows, I wondered if I was walking in my sleep again. Below me on the grass, shivering in shirt sleeves, was Philly.

'Jules, can you let me in?' He staggered into the kitchen. The back of his pants was covered in blood.

I was not dreaming after all.

'I've got a slight problem. Couldn't think of anyone else. Not the sort of thing to share with the family.'

We had two upstairs bathrooms and another one downstairs that no one used, which is where I took Philly. He removed his clothes and stood under the shower. He was covered in bruises. It was as if he'd been kicked. The water was hot but he was white with cold.

'I've got a piece of glass up my bum, Jules. Tried to remove it. Couldn't make the bastard budge. Stuck sideways, you see.'

Blood was running down his legs.

'Do you want me to call a doctor,' I said, 'or an ambulance?'

'For God's sake. No. I want you to remove the glass. There's a medical bag at home. Get that, will you? Here's my key. Don't wake them, whatever you do.'

I ran up The Avenue to Philly's house, letting myself in through the back door. I wanted to wake Uther and Morgana. I wanted to say that Philly needed a doctor. I stood before their door. I almost knocked.

Instead I went up a flight of stairs, switched on a light and found the medical bag in the bottom of Philly's wardrobe. I stood before Uther and Morgana's door again on the way back down. Then I crept out.

Philly was where I'd left him – in the downstairs bathroom, clinging to the sink.

'Good girl. Give me the bag. These are fine needle-nose forceps. I'm going to wash them in the hottest water. Now, listen, Jules. The glass is stuck in the right side of the rectal canal. I want you to feed the forceps up my arse, close the tines around the glass, pull to the left, turn the glass slightly and feed it out of my bum. Can you do that? I'm going to bend over and part my buttocks.' He bent over and his head touched his knees. Blood poured out of him. 'That'll stop in a minute. Get some gauze, throw some disinfectant over it and clean my arsehole as best you can. Good girl. Oh, Christ. That hurt. I'll just take a deep breath.'

As gently as I could, I fed the forceps into his rectum, found the glass, pulled it, turned it, tugged it. It was out. I managed to catch Philly just as he fainted. I couldn't hold him up. All I could do was ease him to the floor. Then I went to make a pot of tea. When I returned he was sitting on the bathroom floor, still naked and so pale I was afraid he might faint again.

'I'd better go back to your house,' I joked, 'and steal some clothes this time.'

Philly's clothes lay scattered and bloodied. I held him while he sobbed. 'Sorry, darling. Sorry. You shouldn't have seen this.'

'What happened to you? Did you fall over and sit on a piece of glass by accident?'

'Yes, that's it. I had to use a public toilet. Slipped on the step and landed on some glass. Embarrassing. Got rather dirty, I'm afraid. Don't say anything to anybody. Good girl. I'll have this tea then I'll be off home. You go back to bed now.'

In the morning I checked the downstairs bathroom. There was no sign that Philly or anyone had ever been there. The next day was a Saturday, the day I visited Philly at Prince Henry's. He was in his office as usual, sorting through paperwork.

Ivan did not call in on Philly that Saturday. But I did see him later, as I was leaving. Ivan had a black eye, gauze in one nostril and he did not speak to me.

★

Being a public servant has its advantages. Within a day of Pearl's return I have arranged all sorts of home help. Three times a week someone will help bathe her. A housekeeper will drop by weekly to clean the house. A district nurse will check regularly that she doesn't develop pressure sores and ask about her bowel motions and the frequency of urination. A physiotherapist will give her exercises to counteract muscle wastage. These are stopgap measures until more permanent arrangements can be made.

'I really have to leave soon,' I say.

Affairs in the Netherlands demand my attention.

'Go,' says Joanie. 'We'll manage. This mess is no longer your concern. Take the other two with you.'

'Joanie!' her mother barks. 'Juliana is a part of this family.'

'Yeah? And what does Juliana know about hard work, about making ends meet. I've never known her to be without beautiful clothes and expensive jewellery. All those places she and Oscar lived in . . . I didn't even get married. Never been out of Australia.'

According to the calendar, autumn and a break in the weather should be upon us. But more than ninety per cent of New South Wales is drought declared. The dams around Goulburn are empty — crazy paving mudflats. The city has become the media face of the drought. Visitors are asked to donate water to cafés. The pubs are no longer able to wash glasses. The shire council is considering a sewage recycling scheme.

The upstairs bedroom is unbearable, even without the heat of Oscar in my bed. He sleeps downstairs. At other times he is with Frederick. To hear him arrive home in the early hours is unusual. I find him sitting in a cane chair on the veranda, long legs folded under his body.

'Are you crying?'

He doesn't answer, just looks at me, face wet with tears.

'Frederick hasn't made his mind up yet,' I say. 'He intends to visit Luxemburg first.'

Oscar is so much bigger than me. Yet he is lean, and when I gather his body in my arms it has a precious fragility.

'I love Frederick,' he says, simply. 'I love him. Do you understand, Juliana?'

'You adore him and I am sure he adores you.'

Please let that be true.

Please let history not repeat itself.

'There's another problem,' he says. 'I don't seem to have any money.'

Oscar is a decent man. He recognises that Joanie is the one who has worked the stud for thirty years and has said she should get everything. He earned a reasonable salary at the international schools wherever I was posted. He has accumulated modest savings. There is no denying he sacrificed his career to follow me around.

'I will buy Pearl into some sort of place out of my settlement from the government,' I say.

'Thank you, darling.'

After a while he falls asleep upon my chest. I always expected our relationship to end after a few years and now thirty years have passed. I thread my fingers through his hair. He is thinning on top.

Don't hurt him, Frederick.

Towards dawn, with Oscar still asleep, I dream of Luxemburg. A boy possessed of a voice of such searing beauty that hearts shatter when his careless eyes fall on them is singing a Kyrie.

Lord have mercy on us.

★

Philly never once referred to that night. For weeks afterwards he was clearly in pain, barely able to walk at times. Morgana complained that he hardly ate and when he did eat it was only soft, mushy food. The next time I visited him at Prince Henry's he seemed distant. Ivan, he said, had transferred to another hospital. 'There is no need, Jules, for you to come here again,' he said. 'The sleepwalking seems to have stopped.'

Papa was moody and easily irritated. Tired, he said. Tired of the Melbourne winter. Tired. He had never slept well since coming to Australia and in the winter of 1962 he hardly slept at all. The Daimler was his sole pleasure. He drove round and round Toorak, Malvern and Kew, returning home grey-faced in the early morning. He had been a drinker since the war. Now he was an alcoholic. He drank a glass of whisky or gin as soon as he finished work for the day. 'I'll be myself again,' he promised, 'when we return home.' But the empty gin bottles accumulated in the garage. His skin turned florid. My handsome, dashing father had disappeared.

He was angry with Mama about Mrs Dikkertje. 'Her husband is nothing at Hart. I don't want them to presume on a supposed friendship.'

'I don't have anyone else,' Mama cried.

A letter came from school saying I had a tendency

to daydream. Yet if a teacher asked me a question, I knew the answer. Papa was worried. 'Are you bored?' I told him I couldn't wait to resume my real education. I wanted to go home to the Netherlands and study at least four languages at gymnasium level. I did not mention the part of me that wanted to stay − the part that couldn't bear the thought of leaving Philly.

But Philly had moved out of The Avenue and into a weatherboard cottage in East Prahran.

'He says he needs to be closer to the hospital,' Arty said. 'I used to tease him about not being able to drive. Do you think that's why he left, Jules? I didn't mean it. I think he's really clever. Could you come with me and talk to him? Please?'

We went to East Prahran in Arty's battered Austin. The cottage was small, the furniture modern. The prints on the walls carried the signature of someone called Kandinsky. A large informal area at the back was flooded with light. 'I've bought this place,' Philly said.

'Did you have to have a piece of paper called *mortgage*?'

The brothers looked at me oddly.

'You're not coming home, then?' said Arty.

'I need quiet. I'm working nights. There's too much distraction at home. Walking from Prince Henry's to Malvern is just too far.'

'I could pick you up.'

'Thanks. Better this way.'

Arty and I drove off in silence. Finally, he spoke. 'He could catch the tram, you know. Something's happened. Don't know what.'

Papa missed Philly wandering in and out of our house as much as I did. 'Wouldn't mind talking to him. There's a pain in my left arm I just can't shake.' Then we heard Philly was leaving for England, to Cambridge, to study for six months. I wrote to him at Prince Henry's, urging him to visit Zeeland, telling him he could come see us in Middelburg in a few months' time. He never replied. 'Left for England without saying goodbye,' Papa said softly. 'Poor boy. He is troubled by something.'

August in the southern hemisphere can be the cruellest month. Spring softens the air and buds appear on the trees, then with a thrust of betrayal winter returns for another bitter round. On 10 August 1962, less than a week after Philly left, Papa did not come home from work.

11

Where Are You, Philly?

Papa had taken the tram that day, saying he'd slept too restlessly to risk driving. Mama and I waited until nearly seven in the evening before ringing Hart. There was no answer on the switchboard. No answer on Papa's extension. Mama rang Mr and Mrs Dikkertje. No answer there, either. We checked the afternoon newspaper, turned on the radio and television. Maybe there was a tram strike? 'I could go and get him in the car,' I said. 'If I only knew where to go.'

We waited one more hour. Then I walked to the police station on Glenferrie Road. They didn't know of any accidents. Plodded back past the de Vere house. I considered asking Morgana and Uther for help. All the lights were on. I couldn't make myself go inside.

When I got home the Dikkertjes' Volkswagen was parked in the drive. Their grating voices – a rolling *r*, a gurgling *g* – were coming from the dining room. Mama sat at the table, shrunken, as small as one of the hedgerow birds that flickered between the shadows on our island of Walcheren. Mrs Dikkertje was holding her arm. Mama flinched at her touch. Mr Dikkertje marched around the table, a farcical ball of Aryan rectitude.

Zo, het kind.

So, the child.

I said nothing. My voice held fast in my chest.

'Well, Lord Stolburg has died. He had a heart attack at work. An ambulance was called and he was taken to the Royal Melbourne Hospital, but he had another heart attack there and died immediately.'

'Yes,' Mrs Dikkertje said, 'it was a coronary conclusion.'

You fool. You mean a coronary occlusion. You don't know how many of Philly's medical books I've read by now.

'She's smiling, John,' Mrs Dikkertje said. 'What does she mean by smiling?'

I found my voice. 'At what time did my father die?'

'Your father died at approximately ten o'clock this morning,' Mr Dikkertje replied. 'I was with him. I went to the hospital in the ambulance.'

It was now nearly nine o'clock at night. Papa had been dead eleven hours.

'Why,' Mama asked quietly, 'did it take you so long to let us know?'

224

Mr Dikkertje blustered. 'The phone was engaged. And . . . You know. Things to organise when a director of an important company like Hart dies.' We listened to his voice run down.

'Anyway, Jan, the funeral must be arranged,' Mrs Dikkertje said. 'We will need money – and the Daimler. It is unthinkable, Julie, that your mother should be driven to the funeral in our Volkswagen. Your mother says she does not know where the keys are.'

'I am fifteen. I can arrange the funeral.'

They burst out laughing. 'Ha. She thinks she can arrange a funeral. Don't be ridiculous. What do you think, Jan, isn't that ridiculous? But, you know, to be serious, just for a small time, we must have money for the funeral, a director of Hart, an aristocrat, cannot be sent off like, well, like . . .'

Mama stared into the distance. I wondered if she might collapse. I thought of the strongbox hidden beneath the false bottom of the Spanish trunk. And I thought, suddenly, of something Papa had said recently – 'In case anything should happen to me' – as he took the strongbox out of the trunk, put it in his dressing room and gave me the combination to the lock.

I raced upstairs. Inside the strongbox was nearly five hundred pounds, Papa's will, his life insurance policy and his medals, those he'd won during the war and the ones he'd been awarded after the night the dijkes broke. There was also a leather box I had never seen before bearing the insignia of a golden lion. Sometime in 1953 Papa had been made a knight of the Order of the Golden Lion, the highest honour a Dutch monarch can bestow.

I took three hundred pounds and locked the strongbox. Papa's pistol, I reminded myself on the landing, was still in the Spanish trunk.

'We must have the keys to the Daimler.' Mr Dikkertje was panting heavily from climbing the stairs. He was standing so close I could smell pickled herring.

'You may borrow the car on the day of the funeral,' I said. 'Not before.' I pushed past and ran downstairs with the money. 'I will ring the Dutch embassy,' I said. 'Papa's will says his body must be returned to the Netherlands, his medals placed on the coffin.'

'Oh, that depends on,' Mr Dikkertje said. 'Your father loved this country. Yes, he told me this definitely, one day at work, how much he loved this country. He could be buried here easily.'

I gave Mama the three hundred pounds. She counted it, put it on the table and the Dikkertjes grabbed it. They forgot about the Daimler. Mrs Dikkertje offered to stay overnight. Mama shook her head. After they left we stayed sitting at the dining table till Mama, without speaking, left the room.

I rang the Dutch consul's office and was told to call back in the morning. The embassy in Canberra said the same thing. Walking up to the top of The Avenue, there was only one place in the whole world I wanted to be. I didn't ring the doorbell, or wander in the back door without knocking, but just stood beside the dark and untidy garden gazing up at the house. Philly was gone, and he hadn't said goodbye. I wasn't old enough to understand that his leaving was a retreat into himself.

I walked back. And began to pack. For home. Mama lay in her room, staring at the wall, not acknowledging me when I checked on her at midnight. I made her a cup of tea, sweet and weak, in case her stomach was bothering her, and brought it in on a tray. She turned her back.

Throughout that long first night I sat in Papa's chair in the study, dozing intermittently, before showering and putting on his favourite dress: a high-necked, low-waisted, red viyella that I liked to wear with black tights. I pinned the bluebird brooch to my collar. The watch he gave me for my fourth birthday sat on my wrist, marking the time since he left.

Mama refused breakfast with a shake of her head. I waited until nine then began making phone calls from the study. The smoke from Papa's cigars was trapped in the fabric of the curtains, in the books and carpet. The Dutch consul promised to contact Aunt Katrien. Papa's will, I said, stipulated that his body be returned to the Netherlands and buried with his ancestors. Papa's will said no such thing. He hadn't left any instructions as to the disposal of his remains.

'Your guardian has already been here,' the voice on the other end said. 'He tells me you are only fifteen. You had better leave this to older and wiser heads.'

'But I do not have a guardian.'

'*Ach*, he has shown me a piece of paper signed by your mother. If there is anything further we can do for you in the future please let us know.'

'I don't need your help in the future. I need your help now,' I said into a dead telephone.

I confronted Mama. 'Did you sign a piece of paper giving Mr Dikkertje guardianship over me?' Her eyes were fixed, pupils dilated. She had withdrawn into catatonia, that place she'd retreated to at Dachau, allowing her tormentors to do to her whatever they wanted.

The Dikkertjes' Volkswagen was likely to pull up in the driveway any minute. Opening the strongbox, I saw that Papa's life insurance policy was worth three thousand pounds, enough for Mama and me to re-establish ourselves in the Netherlands. Then I read the will once more:

> In the event of my death and in the event that my daughter, Juliana Stolburg, has not reached the age of eighteen years, I appoint Dr Philip Arthur de Vere MBBS to be my said daughter's sole guardian.

Mama was not my guardian. Mr Dikkertje certainly wasn't. Philly was. From beneath the Spanish trunk's false bottom I retrieved Papa's pistol.

The Dikkertjes had no intention of knocking. I heard their feet on the gravel and knew they'd come in by the back, where the door was usually left unlocked. I sat in Papa's chair behind his desk and waited.

'She doesn't seem to be here,' I heard Mr Dikkertje say from the dining room. 'Perhaps she's gone to school.'

'Perhaps,' said Mrs Dikkertje, 'she's with that homo doctor. Jan is upstairs. Can't speak. It must be true what they say – she's mad.'

Mr Dikkertje giggled. '*Gotverdomme*, I can't find the keys to the Daimler anywhere.'

'I'll look in Lord Stolburg's study, that mister high and mighty . . .' Mrs Dikkertje squealed. 'John! John! She's got a gun!'

Mr Dikkertje made as if to leap around the desk and grab the pistol out of my hand. Then he stopped.

'My father,' I said, 'taught me how to shoot this gun, just as he taught me to how to drive his Daimler. Come any closer and I will kill you. There is not a court in this land that will blame me. I have lost my father and my mother is upstairs in a catatonic state. Now read this will.'

Stuttering, sweating, although the day was cold, Mr Dikkertje read.

'Dr de Vere,' I said when he'd finished, 'is on his way over here. I expect him at any moment. He does not like you or trust you. The document you made my mother sign last night giving you guardianship over me is worthless. Give it to me.'

'Oh, you need someone,' Mr Dikkertje spluttered, 'someone like us, to look after your inheritance.'

'Anyway – she wouldn't dare use that gun,' Mrs Dikkertje chipped in.

I pointed the gun at her head, released the safety and watched Mrs Dikkertje turn purple.

'You must be insane. Just like your mother. We will call the police.'

'Go ahead,' I said. 'That will save me the bother.'

'You haven't heard the last of us,' Mr Dikkertje said. 'We have already arranged the funeral. It will be a Hart production. Yes. That's what it will be: a Hart production.'

'You won't be allowed at the funeral. Australian children don't go to funerals,' Mrs Dikkertje said, on her way out, tossing the scrap of paper at me Mama had signed. They left the house and drove off in their wretched Volkswagen.

Papa had placed an antique bronze Japanese mirror of Françoise's on one of the shelves in his study. Glittering in the burnished metal, drawing me to my own reflection, were the diamonds in the tail of the bluebird brooch. Gazing back at me was a pale girl with high cheekbones, dark eyes and a long, narrow Stolburg nose. There was nothing of the quiet grace of Mama's Jewish ancestors.

'Mama,' I begged, 'just a sip of sweet tea. A biscuit.'

She lay on her back, rigid. I touched her and she turned to the wall. I knew from listening to Philly that sometimes patients in a catatonic state had to be intravenously fed. Mama was slight and couldn't, I thought, do without food or water. I had won one round against the Dikkertjes but I could not win another without her. I needed her with me. 'Mama, please, Mama.'

That evening, Morgana de Vere rang the doorbell,

came in and hugged me. 'We've just heard the awful news. Rotten luck Philly's left. Can you make do with me? We're so fond of you, Jules.'

I allowed myself to relax in her arms. 'Mama's upstairs in a bad way. That's the worst thing just now. There are some awful people circling, the Dikkertjes, Philly knows them. I need Mama to eat and drink. She was in a sanatorium when I was a child.'

'I'll cable Philly's ship. Might even be able to speak to him somehow. He'll know what to do.'

Morgana hurried out. From Papa's study I could see her running up The Avenue. When the telephone rang I expected to hear Philly's voice. It was Katrien.

'*Ach, lieve Jack.*'

'He's dead.'

Sounds of sobbing; time delayed.

'We need to bring his body back to the Netherlands,' I went on. 'Mama and I are coming back. We can't leave him here. He hated Australia.'

As I said those words, I realised the truth of them.

'*Ach*, child, I've spoken to the consul in Melbourne. It is impractical and expensive to bring Jack's body back. You must have him cremated. That would solve everything.'

'*Tante*, please, can you see Oma and Opa? Can you tell them in person?'

'I can't leave her Majesty. Wilhelmina isn't well. She's eighty-two, you know. I'll arrange for one of the courtiers to call on your mother's parents.'

'Oma and Opa won't understand a courtier. They don't speak Dutch. They'll be terrified.'

Katrien grumbled. In the end she agreed to go and see Mama's parents and tell them herself that the son-in-law of whom they were so proud had died in a country at the bottom of the world.

It was time to put away childish things. I fetched the bluebird brooch and Papa's pistol and placed them in the secret compartment of the Spanish trunk.

There'll be bluebirds over the white cliffs of Dover,
Tomorrow, just you wait and see.

★

Pearl has managed to roll her wheelchair out of the house and onto the veranda. Steady rain trickled all last night. This might be the long-awaited autumn break. Mares are frolicking about the paddocks, bemused by the sensation of wet dirt. Joanie has gone to Cowra to inspect a stallion she's bought off the internet. Pearl is booked into a nursing home with motel-style rooms and fluffy towels.

'Tell me,' she says, 'what's it really going to be like? The bed looks all right. But what's it going to be like? Are there going to be old folks sitting around waiting to die? I expect the truth from you, Juliana. Unvarnished.'

I should present Pearl with the rosiest possible picture of a future where she will find interesting company and lots to do.

'The unvarnished truth,' I say, 'is that the people who run the nursing home will do their best to keep you stimulated. The room is as luxurious as it is possible for money to buy. But it's small. You'll be well looked after and eventually bored out of your brain.'

'Would you book yourself into that place?'

'Not in a million years.'

'Do you think they'll let me have a bottle of whisky in my room?'

'I'll make sure of it.'

'Thanks, Juliana. You're a good girl.' She sighs. 'Oscar told me you're going with him and that Frederick to Luxemburg. How's that going to work?'

'Oscar and I can't quite let go of each other just yet.'

'You must be mad.' She sighs again. 'There's worse things than death,' she says after a while. 'There's living on with a body that's no use to you. Will you look at that. The rain's really pelting down now.'

★

Morgana managed to cable Philly, whose ship was docked at Colombo. He cabled back, saying he had a friend who owed him a favour. 'This friend of Philly's will look in on your mother,' Morgana said. 'She's bound to be in shock. But I'm sure she'll be all right. Be a good girl now, Juliana, and calm down. These people you fear probably only want to help. Philly's friend will be here soon.'

I dreaded having Ivan call on us. I was afraid he'd take Mama away to a sanatorium. On a tray I prepared toast, a boiled egg and yet another cup of sweet tea. I put the tray on the side-table next to Mama's bed.

'You must eat this, Mama. There's a man coming who'll drag you off to a lunatic asylum if you don't eat. I know you can hear me. This asylum won't be like the nice sanatorium back home. This place will be worse than Dachau. Now, eat!'

God forgive me for saying those things to her. Gagging, nearly vomiting, Mama swallowed the food that I held to her mouth. I forced her to drink some water. Then the tea. Her eyes darted about the room. When the doorbell rang she jumped.

'Mama, that's the mind doctor. You must get up. Put on your pretty dressing gown. Sit in that chair with the dinner tray, and we'll tell the man you are perfectly all right now. You had a shock. That's all.'

It was some while since I'd seen Ivan. Opening the door, I realised I hated him almost as much as I hated the Dikkertjes.

'Mama's perfectly fine now,' I said. 'I overreacted. It was kind of Philly to get on to you, Ivan, but Mama really is fine. A terrible shock. That's all.'

Ivan's glance took in our spacious hall, our paintings and ornaments. 'These old houses are gracious. I'm not sure about those boxes the architects are so keen on now. Perhaps I'll look in on your mother all the same. I can't let Philip down. He mentioned she was a holocaust victim.'

'Holocaust?'

'Concentration camp. There's quite a lot of work being done on the effects on those who survived. Dachau, was it?'

'My mother was held among the political prisoners.'

'Political? I'll look in on her all the same.'

I led the way upstairs. 'Mama,' I yelled, 'we're coming. She doesn't speak much English. I will have to translate.'

Mama was out of bed and in the armchair near the window. Not only that, she'd managed to make the bed and put on some lipstick.

'Please don't get up, Mrs . . . Mrs . . . Tell me, how are you?'

Mama said in a low voice, in Dutch, that she was feeling as well as could be expected. She held up the empty plate for him to inspect. She looked him in the eye and appeared calm. Ivan asked her a few more questions. Each time, whether she understood him or not, she looked to me to translate before replying in Dutch.

'This one doesn't look smart enough to work out whether I'm mad or not,' she said.

'No, he isn't. Mama says, Ivan, that she is grateful to you for calling on her.'

'Is he like Philly as well? Doesn't like girls?'

'Mama wonders, Ivan, if you're married or have a girlfriend?'

Ivan smiled. 'Tell her I'm not married and I don't have a girlfriend. That's a good sign, by the way, being curious about other people.'

'Yes,' I said, 'same as Philly.' I turned to Ivan. 'The Dutch word for curiosity is *nieuwsgierigheid*.'

Mama and I mustered weak smiles at his efforts to repeat the word. I escorted him from the house still trying to say '*Nieuwsgierigheid*'. The most literal translation of that phrase is *greedy for news*.

I went back upstairs. Mama was not where I expected her to be. Not in the chair by the window and not in bed. Too late I knew where she was – behind the door.

'I'll never forgive you. Never. For saying those things to me.'

She lifted her arm to strike me.

'You will never hit me again,' I said. I curled my fist ready to return a blow. She crumpled to the floor and wound her body into a tight ball. I did not comfort her. I knew that if I touched her she would lash out.

The next day I returned to school, explaining my absence with a note – 'A minor illness' – that I'd typed on Mama's Remington typewriter and made her sign. I didn't tell anyone Papa had died. I half suspected Mrs Dikkertje was right. Australian children didn't attend a parent's funeral. By 1962, seventeen years after the war, many of my classmates had lost parents prematurely. These events passed with barely a mention.

On the morning of the funeral Mama looked tiny and fragile. She put on a sober two-piece suit. I backed the Daimler out of the garage and left the key in the ignition. I kept all the other car keys. 'Tell Mr Dikkertje,' I said, 'that I will be waiting here for him at four o'clock sharp. If the car is not in the drive at that time I will call the police and report it stolen.'

The Dikkertjes had arranged a lavish Hart production. While I sat through maths, faking an interest in quadratic equations, Papa's coffin was carried into St George's Church of England, where he was given the almost Catholic rites of the Anglican church. He was buried at Springvale Cemetery. Mr Dikkertje drove the Daimler, with Mrs Dikkertje beside him and Mama in the back.

I was waiting in the drive, just before four o'clock, when Mr Dikkertje climbed out. I grabbed the keys, parked the Daimler in the garage and bolted the garage door.

'She shouldn't be driving at her age,' Mrs Dikkertje said.

'Jack taught her,' Mama replied.

The Dikkertjes left in their Volkswagen. I hoped we would never see them again.

We ate silently that night, Mama still dressed in her two-piece suit. There was a knock on the door, then an insistent ringing of the doorbell. Two men on the front porch wanted to see Mama. They were funeral directors. Demanding payment of the funeral bill. When it was clear Mama did not understand, they turned to me. I asked her, in Dutch, what the Dikkertjes had done with the three hundred pounds. '*Nee! Nee!*' She howled like a wounded animal and scurried upstairs.

'We can pay three pounds a week until the debt is settled,' I said. Upstairs, in Papa's dressing room, I opened the strongbox and took a ten-pound note out of the two hundred pounds remaining. The men did not have change. 'We'll take this on account,' they said. I saw them out the door, the three of us pretending we could not hear the howling woman upstairs.

Ivan had left his card with me and I rang the number, explaining that the shock of the funeral had been too much for Mama, that she needed a sedative of some sort. She lay on the bed, fully dressed. I put the bedclothes over her. 'Why has this happened?' was all she said.

Ivan was at the door within minutes. He did not bother looking in on Mama this time. He'd heard the howling from the footpath. 'She'll be righto in the morning,' he said, passing me a month's supply of sedatives.

She wasn't righto in the morning, or any other morning for the next three weeks. She lay staring at the bedroom wall, not speaking. She ate the food I left her. Every few days she bathed. If I met anyone in The Avenue I assured them Mama was all right but needed to be alone. I attended school and in the evenings I packed for our return to the Netherlands.

Hart's headquarters were on Spencer Street, in a seedy area not far from the station, and a week after the funeral I wagged school to fetch Papa's belongings. I hoped there might be a substantial last pay cheque. Papa's office had been tidied away. Some photographs; a diary in which he had made sporadic notes – the beginnings of the war memoir he should have written – sat in a cardboard box. In an envelope on top of the box were two pieces of paper: a statement of his final pay and a record of the last two months' mortgage charges. The amount on the second piece of paper equalled the amount on the first.

I went looking for Mr Dikkertje. I knew he worked on another floor. I found him crouched over a drawing board colouring in a sales graph. When he saw me he jumped.

'What happened to the money my mother gave you for my father's funeral?'

'Oh, that. That all went on the funeral.'

'Then why are the funeral directors demanding we pay them over three hundred pounds?'

'There wasn't enough money, probably.'

'You are lying. You and your wife have stolen our money.'

He looked about nervously. The office was almost empty. 'Look. Look. Here's ten pounds. That will keep you going.'

I took the money. And on the tram back to Malvern I told myself we would be all right. We still had Papa's life insurance to be paid out.

Three weeks later, when the first spring buds were about to flower, Mama emerged from her room. I came home from school to find she'd washed her hair and put on make-up. She was pale and thin but she said, 'Mary Dikkertje rang this afternoon. We're going dancing. I've always wanted to learn ballroom dancing but Jack wouldn't let me. You could drive me, Juliana. And it's Friday so you don't have to go to bed early. You could pick me up at, say, eleven. Can you help me choose a dress?'

'Mama, these people have stolen from us.'

'Mrs Dikkertje explained that. Some mix-up with the funeral directors. The Dikkertjes have already given us ten pounds. They will sort out the rest.'

She was implacable. I could not persuade her to have nothing to do with the Dikkertjes. I drove her to Leggett's Ballroom on Greville Street. Neither of us thought about the implications of me not having a licence or being legally old enough to drive. We never had before, when Papa was alive. She leapt out of the car and skipped through the luridly lit entrance of the ballroom dancing world.

Waiting on the porch when I got home were the two funeral directors. I handed them their weekly three pounds out of our dwindling money supply.

'That's a nice car, Miss. Wouldn't want to exchange that to settle the rest of the debt, would you?'

'The Daimler is worth much more than the two hundred and eighty pounds we owe you.'

'Sure is, young lady. You are young, aren't you? Maybe a bit too young to be driving?'

'I am old enough to be repaying a debt to you.'

· 'Fair enough, Miss.'

At a quarter to eleven I drove back to Greville Street. Standing surrounded by men was a gorgeous woman in a beautiful dress and glittering jewellery. Mama!

'Juliana!' she cried. 'I've had the best time. Whirling and whirling and meeting people. I haven't thought about anything. I'm going again next week. You'll drive me, won't you?'

As we pulled away I noticed the knot of men who had crowded round Mama pointing at the Daimler.

The first inkling we had that the concept of *mortgage* involved the making of regular payments came when we received a letter from Hart saying our bi-monthly instalment was overdue.

Where are you, Philly?

★

Philly wrote to us from Cambridge. He had gone to considerable trouble to cover the front of the envelope with stamps Mama might like. He said how shocked he was at Papa's death and asked me to write to him. I wrote a long letter describing Mama's catatonic state, telling him we didn't have any money and didn't understand what a mortgage was. I ripped up that letter and wrote a short note saying Mama and I were well, thanks; but could he explain how a mortgage worked? At the post office on Glenferrie Road I was told an airmail letter to England could take up to ten days. In twenty, perhaps thirty days, I could expect a reply. I went into the city and paid Hart twenty-six pounds. That left less than a hundred pounds to last us until Papa's life insurance money came through.

Exactly twenty days later I received a letter from Philly. He outlined the ramifications of a mortgage. He asked me what interest rate Hart had been charging. 'Anything above three per cent is usury. Have you consulted a solicitor? Who is the executor of your father's estate?' I looked up 'usury' in the dictionary. Then I checked the mortgage documents in Papa's bottom drawer. Hart was charging five per cent interest. Also in the drawer was a bankbook with a balance of nearly a thousand pounds.

'Dear Philly,' I replied, 'we have not consulted a solicitor. You are the executor of Papa's estate. He also appointed you my legal guardian. Something has to be done to the will but I don't know what "probate" means.'

Next morning I took another day off school. In Papa's favourite red dress, trying to look grown-up, I went into the city once more and visited Papa's bank. I showed the manager the bankbook. 'My mother and I really need some money,' I said. My face burned with embarrassment.

'Only the executor of the estate can access these funds,' the bank manager said. He was an officious man who couldn't be bothered looking at me. 'Besides, we don't do business with minors.'

Mama's dancing became a Friday-night ritual, at first with the Dikkertjes, and then as she began to make friends she ventured out on her own. She was fifty-two with violet eyes, rich auburn hair and perfect skin. She floated around the dance floor on childlike feet in the arms of men who couldn't wait to possess this creature. I had never seen her smile the way she smiled for the bevy of men waiting for her every Friday night in the doorway of Leggett's Ballroom. I had never realised the person I knew as 'Mama' – a person locked away in a private world of anxiety and depression – was a stunning beauty.

Before going out, she would assemble her outfit with consummate ease. 'Think I'll put a scarf around my waist,' she'd say. The scarf, or whatever it was, would be superb.

I didn't want her to wear valuable jewellery. 'But I like to sparkle,' she said, twirling round the room in diamonds and sapphires. And she sparkled and spun like the newest star in the sky.

For the first time in my life I felt lonely. My only confidant was a much older man. And now he was in England. I was hesitant about reaching out to Philly's family: it would only draw attention to Mama's erratic behaviour. I didn't like leaving her alone for too long, so I began driving the Daimler to and from school, although parking too close was perilous in case I was noticed. My teachers said I was distracted, withdrawn. 'Are you all right, Juliana? Your work is slipping. Everything all right at home?'

To all of these enquiries I replied that everything was 'fine, just fine', and I put on a smile so broad it hurt.

Homesickness – a longing for the life that had left us – hit me so hard I thought my heart might burst. I'd hear the voices of Siegfried and Françoise from across the road; the roar of Papa's motorbike; the soft crooning of Oma and Opa; the whirr of a Singer sewing machine. I followed the sound of the sewing machine and there was Mama, in a chiffon creation stuck together with pins, her eyes so bright they looked washed with tears.

'Look, Juliana, an ev-en-ing dress. I'm going to a ball.' She hummed the melody from a Strauss waltz and swayed in front of the mirror. 'How much money do we have?'

'Less than one hundred pounds. There's some more in Papa's bank account. I'm waiting for Philly to tell me how to access it.'

'Poor Juliana. Poor Juliana.' And she gave a delighted cackle. 'I must get back to my sewing. There is another dress I have to make. For Saturday. I shall need five pounds. Another thing your father would not have approved of. A nice man I met at the ballroom dancing has offered to take me to the races.'

12

Rosella Tin Days

'Horses is grand animals,' said the man who appeared at Sunday breakfast. A dot of white lather clung to his ear. He had been using Papa's shaving gear. He wore an old-fashioned suit and a wide tie and his name was George. 'Used to be called Red on account of the red hair I used to have. Red is what they called me when I was boxing.' He feigned a few punches and shimmies that made Mama giggle.

'Caw,' George said, 'look at her face! Don't think your daughter likes boxing, Jan.'

He had danced with Mama at Leggett's Ballroom all Friday evening and introduced her to the races on Saturday. One win – five paltry pounds – and she was addicted. She was also addicted to George and in the months ahead I often heard them have grunting, rutting sex. I had never heard my parents have sex.

'Wouldn't mind going out for a spin today, Jan. Whaddya reckon? We could take that fancy car of yours. Go down to Mornington or somewhere.'

'The Daimler is mine,' I said. 'And my mother's name is Janna.'

'Aw, come on, Jan. You gunna let that toffee nose tell you what to do? Bet I can drive that posh car. No worries.'

Before Mama could ask for the Daimler I'd fled the dining room and backed the car out of the garage. I drove it the short distance to the de Vere house.

'Any word from Philly?'

'Why ask us? You hear from him more than we do, Juliana.' Uther looked at me over his newspaper. I had interrupted the family as they were eating breakfast.

'Haven't seen you for a long time,' Morgana said. 'Everything all right?'

'Mama has a boyfriend. I don't trust him. I don't know what else he wants but he wants the Daimler.'

'So *soon*?' said Morgana.

Arty gave me a huge smile. 'Our garage is empty at the moment. I crashed Daddy's car. You can park your Daimler here until things sort themselves out.'

We went out to the de Vere garage, Arty chortling to himself as we disconnected the battery and locked it in the boot. When I got home there was a note for me in the kitchen:

We have gone out. George opened the strongbox. He

had to borrow some money. He lost at the races yesterday. He'll put it back when he gets paid this week.

Papa's strongbox was on my bed. The top had been prised open; the combination lock was intact. Fifty pounds were missing. The Spanish trunk was on the landing, Papa's pistol safely hidden in the false bottom. I wrapped the pistol inside a towel and walked back up The Avenue.

'More loot?' said Arty, as I swung open the boot of the Daimler. The towel caught on the catch, revealing the loot.

'What a beauty! A pistol – pre-war if I'm not mistaken. Can I have a look?' Before I could stop him Arty had the gun in his hand and was pointing it at a weather vane on the roof.

'Careful!'

Too late. He released the safety and shot the rooster off his perch.

'Bloody hell,' he squeaked, 'if I'd been aiming at that cock I wouldn't have hit him.'

'What are you up to now, young Arty?' Uther stuck his neck out the window.

'Nothing, Daddy. The Daimler backfired.'

'What's that bloody rooster doing on the ground then?'

'Don't know. I think the poor old bird must have had a shock.'

'Why are you and Juliana clinging to each other like that? What's so funny?'

★

'By God,' says Pearl, 'horses is grand animals.'

Joanie has come back from Cowra with the new stallion. He is a sturdy fellow, grey, with a deep chest and pinkish markings all over. Pearl's hands are twitching in her lap. She wants to touch him. 'Why did that lot in Cowra get rid of him anyway? Has he sired any young?'

Joanie hands her mother a piece of paper with the horse's credentials.

Pearl snorts. 'You're bloody mad. What's the point of breeding any more horses, what with the drought and that climate change?'

Oscar and Frederick are perched on the veranda rail discussing Oscar's sixtieth birthday.

'I can't understand your dearth of friends.'

Frederick touches Oscar lightly on the arm. He gives him a look that promises all sorts of consolations later.

'Jules's job required us to be discreet,' Oscar says. 'We didn't make friends outside the circle she moved in. She tended to take that security thing seriously. Calvinist rectitude, I suppose.'

The men leave for Frederick's house. They have a party to organise – a party for the friends Oscar feels I deprived him of. Dog gazes up at me with big begging eyes. I have begun packing for our trip to Europe. I do not know where I will base myself back in Australia, or if there'll be anywhere for me at all. The rose outside the bedroom window is flowering again, the inside of the bloom is a creamy yellow. A last autumn flush. Consulting one of Pearl's gardening books, I see that it is not crepuscule after all but a Gloria Dei, the glory of God.

I'll miss Dog when I'm gone. I'm sorry now that I refused to give him much affection. All he wanted was someone to walk with him.

★

George never put back the fifty pounds from Papa's strongbox. I found new places to store our ever-shrinking funds: at the back of Papa's bible, with the pistol in the boot of the Daimler, under a corner of the carpet in my bedroom. Mama and George searched and I had to change the hiding places often.

'Juliana is like all the Stolburgs,' I overheard Mama whisper. 'She is keeping secrets.'

'You don't say. Wants that knocked out of her,' George said.

All the predators who came into our life after Papa died took something. Even Katrien, his sister, dipped her fingers into the honey pot, assuming the titles that should have come to me. 'Katrien,' Mama pointed out, 'has more use for that mediaeval folderol than you.'

School hours were the worst. I had no idea what Mama might be up to, or who might be visiting. It was while I was at school that the cheque for Papa's life insurance – payable to Mama – arrived.

She was jubilant. 'Look at this letter, Juliana. Three thousand pounds. Mr and Mrs Dikkertje said they can get me five per cent. They went with me to the bank and helped me cash it. Then the five per cent deal was arranged.' Her eyes were shining.

'Mama, why wasn't Mr Dikkertje at work?'

'Oh, he doesn't work for that company, that Hart, anymore. They haven't promoted him. Mary Dikkertje is really furious at them and made him quit.'

'Mama, who or what is the money invested with?'

'The Dikkertjes. They only want the money for a month so they can finish their house. Then they will pay me the interest. Five per cent is good. Look, they have given me an IOU.'

'Mama, the IOU just says they promise to pay you. It doesn't say when.'

'They have given their word.'

'The Dikkertjes have stolen from us. Remember the funeral money?'

Mama's lip quivered. 'But Juliana, they have repaid that money. They told me.'

The men from the funeral parlour had been coming every Friday evening while she was dancing. I hadn't mentioned it. I hadn't mentioned it because I couldn't make her listen.

'You're bloody barking mad,' said George when Mama revealed her brilliant moneymaking scheme to him.

Three thousand pounds would have paid out the mortgage. It would have covered the funeral debt. It would have allowed us to resettle in the Netherlands. It would have put food on the table. Even during the food shortages after the war we had never gone without, there had always been money or gold to buy food from the black market. Now poverty – real, palpable poverty – glared at us.

When the allotted month had passed I rang the Dikkertjes.

'Now look,' they said, 'we don't owe the money to you. We owe the money to your mother. You are just a little girl with a big mouth. We will be a bit longer. Don't worry. We wouldn't let you starve.'

'Look here, Jan,' said George. 'That horse was a certain thing. But you know how trainers are. Told you, haven't I? They're all in cahoots. Don't worry. I won't let you starve. Anyways, there's all this stuff in the house, and that Daimler, that's gotta be worth money. Dunno why it's parked up the road with that de Vere lot. Doesn't make sense to me when you've got a perfectly good garage here.'

George was an amateur boxer of some note in the 1930s. He had a scrapbook of newspaper clippings he called 'me cuttings'. The scrapbook was burnt around the edges. 'Rescued from a house fire, see.' Every time he showed us 'me cuttings' a bit of charred paper fluttered away.

George's other passion was the Returned Services League. He had served in a regiment called the Thirty-Niners, who left Melbourne in 1939 to fight in the war. He served in the Middle East, Cyprus, New Guinea. He was proud of his collection of medals. 'Your bloke didn't get too many, Jan,' he said when I showed him Papa's medals. 'Was he wearing clogs when he collected them bits of brass?'

Mama laughed. George's friends, fellow Thirty-Niners, were made welcome in our house. They were not unlike Papa in that they filled the holes left by their war with alcohol and nicotine. In other ways they were quite different. They liked to mock rather than try to understand.

'You Dutchies didn't put up much of a fight against the Jerries, did ya?'

As for the inscription on the silver salver, on which Mama served the men the last of Papa's gin, one fellow said, 'What's this wog writing?'

To all of this, Mama smiled. All she saw or heard were their cheery faces.

George was a jobbing carpenter at the Rosella factory in Richmond. After work he and his workmates would go to the nearest pub and fill themselves with drink till the pubs closed at six. Within a few weeks of knowing Mama he was weaving a beery path to our house most nights. She complained, once, that he never brought flowers or chocolate. The next evening he brought her a box of Rosella tins. 'The labels is missing,' he said, 'but it's all good Aussie food. See, I told you I wouldn't let you starve. These tins is all beef stew.'

Each unlabelled tin had a code on top. GLPN 362: golden peaches in nectar. SBB 362: sausages and baked beans. We deciphered the codes one by one and I wrote them all down. 'Youse Dutchies are smart, aren't ya?'

Beer was George's preferred drink. Once the last of Papa's gin had been consumed, he told us men who drank spirits were poofters.

'What's poofters, Juliana?' Mama asked me. She didn't understand much of what George said.

'Never mind, Mama.'

He wanted me to call her Mum. Only nonces called their mothers Mama.

'Big girl like you,' he'd tell me, 'should be out working. Eddication's a waste of time for women. They get pregnant – never lift a finger again.'

The unsubtle insinuations, the ever-present belligerence, passed Mama by. Whatever insult George hurled at us he hid under a smile.

'Little girl like you shouldn't be driving a big car like that Daimler. Mate of mine knows a bloke that'd give your mum a good price for that car. Isn't that so, Jan?'

Then he'd smile at her, and look into her eyes. And she'd smile back.

The Fuchses next door grew ever more dubious about us. 'That man, Juliana, some sort of worker, is he?'

'Mama's boyfriend. A carpenter.'

'Seems to like a drop now and then.'

'Does he? Hadn't noticed.'

'Is everything all right, Juliana?'

'Fine, just fine.'

Of all the things George hated about me, the way I spoke English – in that manner peculiar to the de Veres and The Avenue – irritated him the most. I observed him over a few nights. Half a bottle of beer was all it took to turn him into a bastard spoiling for a fight. Thursday nights, his payday, were the worst. That was when plans for the weekend were hatched. Dancing on Friday. The races on Saturday. A day out with the Thirty-Niners, perhaps, on Sunday.

'You gunna drive us to Leggett's, Julie?'

'No.'

'I should dob you in to the cops. You're not old enough to drive.'

'Go on. You wouldn't have anyone to drive you around then. You can't drive, can you, George?'

He'd let this information slip one night and I used it as part of my world war against him.

'Never said I couldn't drive.'

'You were drunk at the time. Come on: tell us how you get from second gear to third gear.'

'You Dutch. Bloody smart-arses.'

'I think,' said Mama, 'you are not using nice words, George.'

'It's that Julie's fault. Go on, give us a couple of quid, Julie. That'd see me and your mum right for dancing and the races.'

Then Mama said unexpectedly, 'She's got a thousand pounds somewhere. Philly has to sign for it.'

'A thousand pounds! Near on two years' wages! Kid like that's got no right to a thousand pounds. She should be out working. That'd knock that Pommy accent out of her. Got a good mind to give her a hiding one of these days. Fancy car. Money. Never heard the like. Told me mates at Rosella and the Thirty-Niners and they all said the same thing. Knock some sense into that Julie, they said.'

I opened another bottle of beer and poured George a drink in one of Papa's crystal tumblers. I gave it to him, with a whisper. 'Lay one hand on me and I'll shoot you. I have my father's gun.'

'You gunna have a glass, Jan?' George asked blurrily.

Mama shook her head. She rarely drank. 'Just give him some money, please,' she begged.

I refused. Our funds were almost exhausted and the Dikkertjes had returned none of our three thousand pounds. The bankbook needed Philly's signature and Philly wasn't here.

Where are you, Philly?

My school results were barely good enough for me to be promoted to the next form. I had gone from top of the class to second from the bottom. On a school noticeboard Prince Henry's had placed an advertisement for holiday work. Next to this, the head had put up a note saying girls at her school were expected to study over Christmas. Yet girls with jobs were allowed to leave before the school year ended. I applied to the hospital's employment office and was offered a choice between cleaning floors and working in the diet kitchen. I chose the kitchen. Shifts began at six in the morning and three in the afternoon. My job, the chief dietician explained, was to prepare meal trays according to people's dietary needs. Some patients, for instance, were allowed salt and pepper; others, on salt-free diets, pepper only. 'You'll find this job easy,' she said. 'You can read English. The other women here can't. We've had to colour-code all the trays.'

It wasn't just English the other women had trouble with. Most of my new workmates couldn't read in any language. Some were recently arrived migrants. Others had been in Australia since the early 1950s. They had no real need for English. The ladies, as I came to think of them, had brought their culture with them to the new country, and they lived and worked among their own people. They had a simple aim: life, for their children, had to be better. Until I arrived one of the dieticians had to check every tray before it was sent out. After a few days they realised they could leave that task to me.

The ladies had a love of life, a sense of generosity and humour, and they valued me for the two things I had that they never would. I could read, and I spoke English in a way that didn't betray my migrant origins.

One fortnight, we'd work ten days and have four days off. The next fortnight, we'd do twelve on and two off. For the twelve-day fortnights I earned twenty-six pounds; for the others, thirteen pounds. I drove to work in the Daimler and parked on a back street. In the steamy atmosphere of the hospital diet kitchen, having a large car was regarded as fortuitous rather than suspicious. The ladies were addled with family dramas that could be solved only by the attendance of nearly everyone in the kitchen. And at a pinch, the Daimler could fit eight.

Living in Malvern, the other side of the Yarra River was a mystery to me. And driving the women to wherever they needed to go introduced me to other people's lives. I never entered their houses, or involved myself in their dramas. They didn't want that. Instead I stayed listening to the car radio while they went in. The men, invariably the cause of the drama indoors, would come out and inspect the Daimler.

When the domestic mayhem was solved the women shoved themselves back in the car without so much as a backwards glance. Long conversations on the way back to Prince Henry's dissected what had been done to whom. They didn't want my opinion. I just nodded and listened and drove. That was my role. The women marvelled at my ability to read at break-time. They had no interest in reading. Their lives were rich inside the novels of their daily lives.

Mama met me at Prince Henry's one afternoon as the shifts were about to change. We were catching a tram to the city. She was early. She came down the lift and entered our world of heat and steam. My workmates studied her, fascinated, taking in the cut of her dress, the matching shoes and handbag, the elegant gold chain at her neck, the diamond brooch in the lapel of her summer coat. The next week all the women turned up to work in matching shoes and handbags.

Shortly before Christmas I rang the Dikkertjes to tell them how much they owed us at compound interest.

'You're becoming hard like Lord Stolburg,' said Mr Dikkertje.

'Your mother would only spend it at the races,' said Mrs Dikkertje. 'We're doing you a favour not giving you your money back.'

'Mama and George,' I said, 'would probably like somewhere to have Christmas dinner.'

At this, Mr Dikkertje came back on the telephone. 'Oh, that depends on.'

'Good. I'll drive them to Blackburn at ten o'clock. I am sure you will all have a marvellous Christmas lunch together. I'll be working, unfortunately.'

Mama — mad, mad Mama — was excited by the idea of Christmas lunch at the Dikkertjes' and she got to work creating a smart summer frock. I volunteered to be rostered on all through Christmas and New Year. The pay was double.

On Christmas morning I took an hour off for the drive out to Blackburn. George wore a suit even more old-fashioned than usual and carried a bag of a dozen bottles of beer. Mama had a basket of presents. She held them up defiantly. 'I bought these,' she said, 'with my winnings.' George grimaced. To his chagrin, Mama had a talent for picking winners. She didn't bet according to the stars or any prevailing whim. No, she studied the form, applying herself as studiously to the art of gambling as she did to her stamps. If a horse had won twice in a row, she reasoned, it probably wouldn't win a third time. If, on the other hand, a horse had been rested for a month after two wins, the probability was that it might win. She hated any suggestion of cruelty to horses, and there were particular jockeys and trainers she never bet on.

Mama always brought a 'certain amount' to the races. She learnt to leave enough money behind so that we could eat. She did not want to know about *mortgage*. That was my responsibility. I was also responsible for Papa's funeral debts. Together, these soaked up the whole of my pay from Prince Henry's. I allowed myself ten shillings a fortnight for petrol and five shillings for incidentals. Mama thought we were managing. But we were getting desperate. We needed that thousand pounds in Papa's bankbook.

The Dikkertjes, meanwhile, had built a triple-fronted brick veneer. The houses around them were double fronted. For the trip to Blackburn, Mama and George sat together in the back seat of the Daimler, which took up almost the entire length of the

Dikkertjes' driveway. The Dikkertjes were fatter than ever; Mrs Dikkertje was pregnant.

'She's still driving that car,' Mrs Dikkertje screeched, 'even though she's much too young.'

'She's a bloody good driver,' George retorted.

The two of us looked at each other, surprised at this endorsement. George blushed.

'You will come in for a minute, Julie?' Mr Dikkertje said. 'We know you have to leave as soon as possible for your important work at the hospital.'

'Today,' said Mama, 'we will not argue.'

Mama pretended to be interested in the Christmas tree, which had been carefully positioned in the middle of a circle of armchairs. I wondered how everyone was going to talk to each other through the foliage. 'We didn't want to obscure the view,' Mrs Dikkertje explained, 'from our very expensive windows. I've got a new necklace. Father Christmas is bringing it to me. It's plastic, very snazzy. You should get rid of those diamond brooches, Jan. And that bluebird brooch you're wearing, Julie, so sentimental.'

'Papa gave Mama some lovely jewellery before the war,' I said. 'She was happy then.'

George let out a grunt. 'She should sell them sparklers. She doesn't need them. She's got the races and dancing and me.'

The hospital had sent as many patients home as possible. There were three of us in the diet kitchen: two to prepare the meal trays, and a cook to reheat turkey and vegetables cooked the day before. To save money I always tried to eat at work. But the constant smell of food suppressed my appetite. I wasn't able to take full advantage and was becoming thin.

One of the cooks had taught me how to make an omelette. I was eating my staple meal – omelette and salad – when I felt someone sit down beside me on the bench near the giant dishwashing machines.

'Hello, Jules,' Philly said, 'that looks good. Can I have some?' He too had lost weight. He looked older.

'I'll fix you an omelette.' And after a gulping silence, 'Did you go to the Netherlands? To Middelburg?'

He nodded. 'When they've finished rebuilding the city it will be beautiful. I'm sorry. So sorry. Give me a hug, dear girl.'

The ladies clapped.

Philly and I drove with the windows down all the way out to Blackburn. Mrs Dikkertje was shouting as we pulled up. 'Not true! It's not true!'

'It bloody is,' said George.

Mama was sobbing in the front garden. She didn't seem to recognise Philly.

'Julie,' Mrs Dikkertje said, 'you tell that stupid George these flowers are called fuck-sias, not foo-shee-ahs.'

'And them things,' said George, 'are bloody cotoneaster, not cotton-easter, you silly cow. Hello, young fella.'

Philly extended a hand, silently noting George's cauliflower ears and squashed, red-veined nose.

'Philip de Vere. Season's greetings to you, Mr and Mrs Dikkertje.'

The Dikkertjes gaped at him in utter, horrified bewilderment.

'Our name is not Dikkertje.'

'Beg your pardon. That's what Lord Stolburg called you. Ah, my mistake. Those flowers are *fuchsias*, by the by, and those branches with red berries are *cotoneaster*. The gentleman is quite right.'

'It's not true!' Mrs Dikkertje wailed. 'Get out, you, you poofter!'

Mama was cheerful again on the drive back to Malvern. 'Mrs Dikkertje gave me ten pounds, Juliana. So sad, Philly, about Jack. He had a coronary conclusion. That's what made him pass by. George, isn't Philly the handsomest boy?'

'Yeah, well, Jan, if you like that type. I'm more of a man's man meself. That Graham Kennedy on the television – he's my sort of bloke.'

'*Ach*, poor Philly,' said Mama, 'what a dreadful cough you have.'

13

Where the River Winds and Gum Trees Wave Tired Limbs

The night feels heavy with the possibility of rain. Frederick Munro's Goulburn mansion is lit up all the way from its bluestone footings to the decorative edging below the roofline. The lights are to celebrate my husband's sixtieth birthday. Pearl, Joanie and I are in the sitting room, with Pearl's wheelchair positioned in such a way that it won't bump into the antique furniture. All the other guests are gathered round the piano in the next room. Oscar has been most attentive, bringing us drinks and canapés.

Frederick explores some thrilling chords on the piano. The crowd falls silent. A soprano breaks into 'Happy Birthday'. Oscar and Frederick stand together in front of the piano, partly obscuring the photograph of Brigadier Michael Munro, ready to accept the toasts of their guests. '*To Oscar and Frederick.*'

Belatedly, a caterer's assistant presents the three of us with a tray loaded with glasses of Bollinger. 'This,' she says, 'is the birthday boy's favourite champagne.'

'Fancy that,' I reply. 'When Oscar and I celebrated his fifty-ninth in Vienna last year – we were there for Mahler's Third – I understood my husband didn't like champagne at all.'

The caterer's assistant blinks and walks away.

'Good for you, Jules,' says Joanie, grabbing an unopened bottle of Bollinger and shoving it in a side-pocket of Pearl's wheelchair. 'Let's go.' Tonight we have no trouble loading Pearl into the car, perhaps because we are all a little tipsy.

'A bottle of Bollinger,' I say, 'costs more now than a month of mortgage payments did in 1963.'

★

I had assumed the entire thousand pounds in Papa's bankbook would be ours once Philly returned home. But a hundred pounds on solicitors' fees here, another hundred pounds there, and before long less than half the original amount remained. Soon I would have to go back to school. Working only weekends in the diet kitchen, there was no way I could earn enough to cover the bills that lay scattered across my bedroom desk.

'Do you like this dress?' Mama asked, dancing in front of my dressing table, trying to catch every angle of her reflection in the mirror. 'I made it for Philly's birthday party. I hope you have something suitable, Juliana. With all your working there must be enough money to buy material so that I can make a dress for you.'

'We have bills to pay. Philly's party is outdoors. A skirt and blouse will do.'

'George thinks you should give me more money. He doesn't think it right for a sixteen year old to have control of the money.'

That did it. 'Here, Mama! These are the bills. This is a statement of my wages. This is how much we need to pay on the mortgage for the next year. Philly says the credit squeeze means there is no hope of us selling the house at a good profit and resettling in the Netherlands. This is what I can expect to earn if I work every weekend. Look at the figures, Mama, and tell me what you see.'

I threw my book of sums at her, expecting her to storm out. Included in my calculations were the amounts she and George demanded to indulge their passion for the 'sport of kings'. Mama made a modest profit from betting. George did not. We were supporting him when we could barely support ourselves.

Mama's pretty party dress spread wide on the floor as she bent down to pick up the book of sums. She leafed through it with the same fierce concentration she brought to her stamps, to the races. In the aftermath of Papa's death I had forgotten how clever she was.

'Juliana, how can this be? These figures suggest we cannot survive in this house for long.'

I wanted to berate her for lending money to the Dikkertjes, to George.

'You are too young,' Mama went on, 'to be worried about these matters. George says he can sell the Daimler for at least five hundred pounds. Let's do that.'

'The car is worth far more than that.'

'Then why don't we sell it?'

I had to think before answering. I was losing my easy facility with Dutch. 'If we sold the Daimler,' I said, 'nothing would be achieved. We need thousands not hundreds of pounds. If we keep the Daimler I keep something of my father, Jack Stolburg. I'm a Stolburg, Mama.'

I'm a Stolburg and even if the Nazis come and torture us we never cry.

Unexpectedly, tears leaked from my eyes. Mama was already gone.

Philly declared that his twenty-ninth birthday had to be celebrated in style. 'Next year when I'm thirty I'll be too old.' Arty and Griselda invited everyone Philly had ever known: friends from kindergarten, school, a handful from the medical profession. A cricket game was in full swing in the back garden when Mama and I arrived. Philly kissed us both three times. 'Learnt that in Amsterdam. The three times kiss of the Dutch.'

'Gawd, Philly, all that kissing must take up a lot of time,' said Arty.

'I love the way you've cut that skirt on the bias,' Morgana said to Mama. 'So flattering – and the length is just right for you.'

'The short fashions are not good if you are older,'

Mama replied in her halting English. 'Skirts must flatter the legs, not showing too much. And never put stress on the seams.'

She glanced at Morgana's dress pulled tight across her backside.

'I wish,' said Morgana, 'I could get you to make something for me.'

'You'd have to pay her,' I cut in.

An awkward silence thudded into the long grass. A cricket ball lobbed over our heads. Morgana touched the bluebird on the collar of my blouse. 'Lovely diamonds.'

'Jack gave her that brooch when she was a baby of two,' Mama said. 'Juliana was much spoiled. A naughty child. Always climbing on things. Jack called her monkey.'

'Bowl us a couple, Philly,' yelled Arty.

'You know I'm no good.'

'Aw, c'mon. Be a sport. You were in the cricket team at school.'

Philly got up out of his chair with a sigh. He stumbled towards the roughly mown strip, his lean body gathering pace. With a flurry of flailing arms he let the ball fly. The batsman swung. And missed. 'Not fair! Thought you said you weren't any good?'

Philly shrugged. He strolled back down the length of the garden and ran at the pitch again. This time the ball hit the batsman in the groin. 'Heck, Philly. I'm not wearing a box.'

Philly shrugged again. 'I much prefer the company of ladies,' he said, walking away.

In the weeks after the party Morgana brought over a heap of clothes that needed altering. At first

Mama charged too little. 'Two and sixpence,' she said, 'is not enough to let out a seam. Next time I am charging Morgana seven and six.' Soon Mama was making enough to supply her with the 'certain amount' she needed for the races.

Hart became a victim of the credit squeeze, going into liquidation, then bankruptcy. A bank wrote to us saying they had taken over the debt and our mortgage had to be paid in full within thirty days. There wasn't a bank in Australia willing to lend money to a sixteen-year-old schoolgirl and a woman earning a sporadic income as a dressmaker. 'You aren't,' laughed one bank manager, 'even citizens of this country.'

Philly and Uther promised to act as guarantors. Still we could not obtain finance. Philly told me to stop paying the mortgage. 'Wait,' he said, 'until the house is repossessed.' Instead I deposited my diet kitchen earnings into a school bank account. For the money to be withdrawn, my signature had to be countersigned by Philly. Then George began talking of his house in Armadale. 'You could move in with me, Jan. Julie could live with that poofter fella's family. The girl's sixteen, she can find a job and board somewhere. The only schooling worth having is the school of hard knocks.'

But Mama was adamant that I stay at school and remain with her. As for me, I was still hanging onto Papa's dream: that our house could be sold at a profit, that there would be enough money for us to return to the Netherlands.

Mama asked George to show us his house. But the roof, he said, was being repaired. Or a new stove was about to be fitted. The way he talked about it, though, it seemed substantial. 'There'd be a few little things we might need to do,' he said. 'And you'd have to sell that car.'

George took it upon himself to help Mama dispose of our other possessions. 'I've got mates in just about any field you can think of who'll give us a good price.' I was at school the day a mate of George's removed all our Persian carpets for ten pounds.

The following Saturday, while Mama and George were at the races, Philly and I piled the smallest and most valuable items – the porcelain, the silver, our paintings, bits of furniture – into the Daimler and ferried them across to Philly's cottage in East Prahran. Mama made no comment about any of this. Decisions to do with our future life seemed beyond her.

Repossession of the house happened quickly. Few people came to the inspection, and those who did declared the house too big, or too old-fashioned, requiring too much upkeep. The auction took place in an office in the city. The amount fetched did not cover the amount still owing. An eviction notice was hand-delivered the following day, giving us a week to vacate The Avenue. Mama and I packed our remaining belongings into a small removalist's truck. A few odds and ends went in the Daimler. The large pieces of oak furniture that had been in the Stolburg family since the seventeenth century were left behind.

Armadale had some charming streets. George's house was not in one of them. We weren't to know that. He hadn't told us the address until the morning of the move. It was then that we drove down a narrow

269

road of grim workers' cottages. The Daimler stretched across the front of two of them. Separating George's cottage from his neighbour's was a party wall. There were two bedrooms, a bathroom, a lounge and kitchen, and a toilet outside the back door.

'The girl can have the front room,' said George, jiggling the door key. 'You and me, Jan, we'll have the other bedroom.'

Mama took her time inspecting each room, careful not to touch the walls with her clothes, her handbag clasped tightly under one arm. The backyard was a small square of knee-length grass that George had unsuccessfully hacked at with a scythe. The scythe lay abandoned under a broken clothesline.

'No good youse looking like that,' said George. 'Here's a roof over your heads. That's more than that fancy bloke you were married to managed to do for you.'

'I will sleep with Juliana in the front room,' Mama said.

'Oh no you don't. I want what's coming to me. Not just on Saturday night, neither – anytime I want. Here's one to be going on with, you migrant bitch.' George's arm bent back, brushing the wall behind. All the old power of his boxing training came back to him. He smashed Mama across the face. Her head swung sideways. Her cheek coloured. He lifted a hand to hit me. I ran out to the backyard. Returned with the scythe.

'Juliana!' cried Mama. 'No!'

George raised his fist again. I heaved the scythe up high, gripping the handle with both hands.

George stared at the scythe. 'Well,' he said, panting, 'youse two have the front room then.'

He backed away up the little passage, leaving Mama and me free to shut the door to the front room and sit on the double bed we would have to share.

'We must unpack,' said Mama. I watched her closely, fearing she might retreat into her mind, as we tried to cram our life into that tiny space. 'Don't worry,' she said, through swollen lips. 'The Nazis did worse than this to me.'

I threw the scythe in the metal rubbish bin on the front veranda. Mama never slept with George again.

There was a third presence with us in that front room: the Singer sewing machine. Mama asked me to make a sign on a sheet of white cardboard and hang it in the window. *Dressmaking and Alterations.* The sewing machine folded down into a table. We'd sit on the bed and eat at that table, or study at it. Mama worked on her stamp collection there. It even had a mirror if we needed a dressing table. 'See how handy the Singer sewing machine is,' Mama would say.

Within days we realised we had swapped one mountain of debt for another. George did not own his house; he rented it. He was running two months behind and about to be evicted. I took care of the arrears at a real estate office on Chapel Street. After that Mama and I paid half the rent.

Mama's dressmaking didn't bring in enough money on its own. She returned to what she had been in the first place: a servant. In the mornings she cleaned for Toorak ladies. In the afternoons

and at night she sewed. She still went dancing on
Fridays and to the races on Saturdays. On Sundays
she attended to her stamps and wrote to Oma and
Opa. How far away they seemed. I saw one of those
letters:

*We are both well. We have had to move to a smaller
house. We will probably be back in the Netherlands by
Christmas.*

I knew by then we were never likely to return
home. The Cold War was deepening and events
were developing in a place called Vietnam. Mama
feared the time of the Nazis was coming again. We
had imprisoned ourselves in a hovel in an Armadale
backstreet with a violent, ignorant bastard whom
Papa wouldn't have employed in the most menial
of jobs. And we were sharing a bed. That was
the worst thing. 'No privacy,' we complained to
each other.

We learnt to ply George with beer. The pubs
would shut and he'd stagger home to a meal
manufactured from Rosella tins. Whether it was
peaches or whether it was baked beans and sausages
didn't seem to matter. And all the while we'd keep
topping up his beer, enduring his abuse of us as a
pair of deceiving migrant bitches who had airs and
graces above their station, until he was too drunk to
stand. Then we'd escort him to his linoleum-floored
bedroom.

On Sundays, while Mama busied herself with
her stamps in the bedroom, George 'painted' in the
lounge room. He copied cartoon characters from
newspapers onto the front of envelopes and coloured

them in with watercolours. Balloons sprouted out of their mouths: 'Hey postie, send this letter to Nance in Korumburra.' On Sunday evenings he prepared a roast dinner of lamb, potatoes, pumpkin and tinned Rosella peas. We had never seen pumpkin on a plate before. 'Pig food,' I'd say under my breath, remembering how Opa used to feed it to his prized animal. George liked his lamb 'done to perfection' – brown and black all over. The Sunday roast was the only meal we ate with him.

'You want some knocking about, you migrant bitch,' was his standard reply to anything I said. 'Girl like you should be working. Not bludging at school.'

'I have been working. All weekend while you were at the races.'

'Migrant bitch.'

He had Vera Lynn records he played over and over but he hated it when Mama and I sang along:

There'll be bluebirds over the white cliffs of Dover,
Tomorrow, just you wait and see.
There'll be love and laughter . . .

Some nights, after George had fallen into a deep, snoring sleep, Mama and I got in the Daimler and drove to wherever the fancy took us. We imagined another life for ourselves in Toorak's leafy streets. 'Dreaming is cheap,' Mama said. A spot in Kew, above the Yarra River, became our favourite place. The river wound below and gum trees waved tired limbs at us. Hidden behind leaves and branches were houses. 'One day,' Mama said, 'I would like to see more of Australia. The places where there aren't people. Just trees and animals.'

On one of those balmy evenings I said to her, 'Mama, I want to know about Uncle Justien.'

She said nothing for a minute. Maybe two. 'Understand I will never speak about the camps.'

'No, Mama.'

And then she took a deep breath. 'The Stolburgs hated the Nazis. Hated that the Netherlands was invaded by the Germans. Queen Wilhelmina thought the Dutch could remain neutral, like in the first war. Justien was as angry about it as Jack and Siegfried. But you know what, Juliana? The Stolburgs didn't think they would be affected – the German name, you see. And at first life did go on as it had before, except that we lived in a city that had been bombed. Many people moved out to other islands. Then one morning the Germans came through Middelburg with their trucks and guns. All able-bodied men had to report for work at the shipyards in Vlissingen.'

'Had the Germans started rounding up the Jews yet?'

'Not until the following year. You had to be registered if you were Jewish. Or if you were an artist or a gypsy. I didn't register. I went to their stupid Calvinist church every Sunday. I didn't think of myself as a Jew. And Jack and Justien didn't think they had to go to the shipyards. The Germans came for them in the middle of the night: four polite men in tailored uniforms. We are the sons of Count Siegfried, Justien told them. Didn't make any difference. Later, Jack and Justien and a big group of men escaped during a British bombing raid on the shipyards. Jack said the Dutch sang the national anthem when the British bombers were overhead. They kept singing even when the German machine guns mowed them down.'

And that, I was sure, was the end of Mama's story.

But she took another deep breath. 'Jack,' she said, 'heard about the round-up of Jews in Amsterdam. He sent me a message. Go into hiding, he said. At first I went to Oma and Opa. But I couldn't stay there – I'd have endangered the whole community. I don't know when Justien became a collaborator. I don't know what the Nazis promised him. I was living in the keep on Tholen when he came for me with his German friends. That's Spanish Jack's wife, he said. And he pointed at me. He didn't tell them I was a Jew. He probably thought I would be held captive until Jack gave himself up. But your papa knew that if he did that we would both be executed. As soon as the Nazis left Zeeland Siegfried disowned Justien. That was as good as signing his death warrant.'

Outside, a car disturbed the gravel of the parking lot we considered ours, by the river and the gum trees.

'Is that everything you wanted to know, Juliana?'

We were trapped inside the horrible little terrace. I was afraid to leave the Daimler at home in case George somehow managed to sell it. I was afraid to drive it to school because not only was I unlicensed but the car was now unregistered. And the drunken violent rages were getting worse. Working weekends at Prince Henry's gave us some money. Mama's cleaning, dressmaking and wins at the races gave us some more. One day she said, 'We have to break out of this prison.'

The lights were on at Philly's house in East Prahran. 'He has planted roses,' Mama said. We sat in the Daimler for the longest time. Mama held her handbag in front of her body with both hands.

'Are we doing the right thing, Juliana?'

'We have no choice.'

We got out of the car. Mama proceeded slowly up the path, touching the flowers and shrubs, as if this were a carefree summer's evening not a dismal winter's night. A boy, a few years older than me, opened the door. He leaned one hip against the door-frame and shook the hair out of his eyes. 'Yeah?'

'We were wondering if we could speak to Philly. We're friends from The Avenue.'

'Not home. Back at ten.'

'Can we wait for him?'

The boy raised his eyes to a streetlight on the opposite side of the road. He gestured for us to enter. Then he switched on the television and ignored us. Toppling stacks of records were strewn in all directions. Mama sat down delicately on the couch. She had to move a pile of dirty towels to make room for herself. She was still clutching her handbag in front of her. 'I think we should go now.'

I put a hand on her arm. We had decided on our course of action.

There was a key in the door. 'Hello, darling!'

The boy and I looked at each other.

'Juliana. Janna. How delightful!' said Philly.

He kissed us both three times. The boy's face tightened round the eyes. A red flush crept up his neck. 'Go out for a while, would you?' said Philly.

I had a speech prepared. Now it stuck in my throat.

'What's happened?' asked Philly.

It was Mama's turn to blush. 'We must leave George,' she said quietly.

Philly nodded, as though that was a given.

'We have brought all our jewellery,' she added.

A jumble of gems spilled from her handbag, flashing rainbows round the room, everything but the Japanese ring and the wedding ring that she wore on her fingers and the bluebird brooch in the Spanish trunk. These three items, we agreed, we would never part with. 'We thought,' said Mama, 'that if you, a man, were to take these things and sell them we might get a good price. There are also Jack's medals. George says they are worthless in this country. I am not so sure. I, I . . . I have no more English.'

'No,' said Philly.

My heart sank. He wasn't going to help us. If Philly wouldn't help us, who would?

'No. No, I won't let you do this. Let me think. Are you going home tonight?'

My voice croaked. 'Everything we have is in the Daimler.'

'Good. I have a spare bedroom.'

'We are not beggars,' I said. 'We can go to a hotel. The boy . . .'

'Time he left.' He smiled. He put an arm around each of us. 'We had better unload the Daimler.'

'We don't have much anymore,' I said.

Philly placed the Spanish trunk in the hallway and the sewing machine in the spare bedroom. 'Two single beds,' Mama whispered. 'We don't have to share.'

The boy came back in the early hours. We heard him arguing with Philly, then the soft squeaking of the bed. The four of us breakfasted together, the boy pale and red-eyed. He looked all about him as if drinking in the fine details of this place. Philly read a hospital report, making occasional notations with a red pen.

'See ya, Philly,' the boy said.

'Mm.'

I followed the boy to the door. 'Can I drive you somewhere?'

'Nuh.'

'Goodbye then.'

'Yeah. See ya.' He looked up and down the street, a scuffed suitcase slung over his back, then headed in the direction of Malvern Road.

The two weeks we stayed in Philly's cottage were like a holiday, Mama said. She gathered up his scattered heaps of clothes and put them away in cupboards. She filed his records alphabetically by composer. She polished the wooden floors and made the whole place gleam. I caught the tram to school every morning and returned in the afternoon to a warm, secure haven. I wished we could stay with Philly forever.

Instead he found us a two-bedroom flat in the next street and paid the first two months' rent. Morgana gave us armchairs and beds she said she no longer needed. We carefully distributed our scraps of furniture and our few porcelain pieces: the Meissen shepherdesses, some Dresden musicians. We bought the finest dining table we could afford – a yellow laminex-and-chrome affair – and stuck a cloth over the top and the silver salver in the middle. The de Vere family solicitors had the Daimler re-registered in Philly's name. A high-ranking police friend of Uther's arranged a licence for me.

Money had been spent on us, and favours called in. We owed the de Veres so much. Mama tried giving Morgana one of her diamond brooches. Morgana laughed. 'I never wear things like that. But you could take up this skirt for me.' From that moment on Mama did the sewing for all the members of Philly's family, and charged little. We had preserved a thin thread of honour.

The flat Philly found for us was on a broad and gracious street. We were on the ground floor and could hear the upstairs tenants arguing. But there was a patch of earth out front where Mama made a minuscule garden. In her bedroom window, facing the street, we put up our sign. *Dressmaking and Alterations*. Before long Mama's closet was filled with clothes needing to be altered. She was able to give up cleaning other people's houses. I hoped, at last, to concentrate on my schoolwork.

If there had been a righteous God instead of an erratic one, this new life might have provided Mama and me with a second chance. But I was tired. So tired. I leaned my head against the cool wall, just for a moment, I thought, and fell asleep in class. 'Do you think you could be bothered concentrating on British history for just five minutes, Juliana?' the teacher snapped. The class burst out laughing as I shook my head to clear the fog in my brain.

On weekends I took my books with me to Prince Henry's. My aim was to study whenever there was a spare moment. As often as not the books stayed unopened. As soon as I sat down my eyes closed. The ladies had to nudge me awake. I fell asleep behind the wheel of the Daimler, waiting for a stop light to turn green. A bleating horn woke me that day. After school I came home and lay on my bed, intending to rest for a few moments before tackling my schoolbooks. Invariably I'd wake an hour later from a deep sleep. Then at night a thumping in my chest wouldn't let me sleep.

We had a new PE teacher, Miss Stitt. Shitty-Stitt, we called her. Miss Stitt said the school was filled with fat, indolent slobs. The senior girls in particular infuriated her. At school assembly she pounded a fist into her own skinny thigh and declared, 'You will run around the oval once a week until you are fit.'

The first week I barely made it. My heart didn't stop hammering for the rest of that day. The next week, just before we were due to begin our lap, I asked Miss Stitt if I could see her.

'I had rheumatic fever when I was a child,' I said. 'Running makes me feel sick.'

'Sick? How? Nauseous?'

I stared at Miss Stitt's basin-cut hairdo. It seemed plastered to her head.

'Hammering in my chest,' I said.

'What nonsense. You need to get fit. All you senior girls are fat.'

I laughed out loud – I couldn't stop myself. I was one of the skinniest girls in the school.

'Right, Stolburg, that's it. Get running.'

I started to jog.

'Run, Stolburg.'

I ran. The school buildings disappeared from my vision. I saw palm trees quivering near Albert Park Lake, and golfers ambling behind balls.

'Run, Stolburg.'

The sky swam above me. I looked up, hoping for the high white clouds of Zeeland.

'Run! Run!'

I remembered how I'd run to Buitenrust once with Fritz and Hansje and Jankees and Otto, and we'd run all the way into an adventure in the minefield. Otto had died when his heart stopped beating.

I lay down on the grass. For the first time in weeks the hammering in my chest stopped. Shitty-Stitt was standing over me. 'Get up, Stolburg. Run.'

'Fuck you. You Nazi.'

I felt a foot kick me in the side as I slid towards a warm darkness. When I woke I was in Prince Henry's emergency department. A nurse in a nun-like headdress had a scowl on her face. 'Your heart is galloping. Why do you have this large bruise on your thigh?'

'Rheumatic fever,' I managed to spit out. 'Makes you bruise. Out of all proportion. That's one of its legacies.'

'Are you on a maintenance dose of penicillin?'

'Allergic to penicillin.'

'Nonsense. Healthy girl like you doesn't have an allergy to penicillin. I'll call a cardiologist just to make sure.'

'Please call Dr de Vere. He works here.'

A cardiologist listened to my heart. 'Erratic heartbeat. You have a heart murmur. You should be on medication for that. You say you've had rheumatic fever? We'll put you on a drip, slow down that erratic beat.'

'I'm allergic to penicillin.'

'Call me if she develops a rash.'

'Please call Dr Philip de Vere.'

In the days that followed, as I slept and woke and slept and woke, Philly was there whenever I looked up. From a faraway distance I saw his face become haggard. The circles under his eyes turned black as night. Once, I heard him shouting. 'You bloody idiot! If she told you she was allergic to penicillin, why didn't you perform a simple skin test?'

'Why are you so interested in this girl, Dr de Vere?'

'Incompetent bastard,' Philly muttered. His hand found mine as I tipped back into sleep.

Through a haze I smiled at the ladies from the diet kitchen who came laden with flowers and cards.

Mama didn't visit and Philly was vague when I asked him about this. 'She seems to be in denial.' He frowned. 'Odd reaction.'

After two weeks I was released with instructions to rest.

Rest. Rest as much as possible. Rest is the ultimate cure for the effects of rheumatic fever.

Philly was on duty so I caught a tram home. The Daimler was parked in the street. Mama's sign – *Dressmaking and Alterations* – hung untouched in the window. A customer was with her, a woman who had put on weight and needed to have all her skirts released at the seams.

'My daughter,' Mama said. 'She has been in hospital.'

The woman bid her goodbye. And Mama began shouting. The words passed over me. None of them made sense. I had disgraced her, shamed her, made a fool of her. Mama's last words were these: 'Make yourself useful. Do the vacuuming.'

Tired, so tired my bones felt disconnected, I dragged the vacuum cleaner out of the wardrobe and began stroking the floor. Mama's sewing was a hazardous business. Pins embedded themselves in the carpet; messy, thready fluff refused to be sucked up. I left the vacuum cleaner running for a moment while I moved a stool. I heard a sound. It came from behind. I looked out the window. Nothing. Then I heard another sound. Heard her fingernails scrape against the metal rod of the vacuum cleaner. Heard the motor suck air. Felt the motion of her arm as it swung from behind her body. Felt the rod collide with my skull. I went down on one knee to rid my ear of the ringing. And remembered. She had hit me over the right ear once before with a cast-iron frying pan. Then I spoke.

If you ever hit me again I will kill you.

I will kill you with the same gun Papa used to execute Justien.

Blood trickled out my ear. I could only half-see through my right eye. I tripped and swayed round the corner to Philly's house. 'I will kill her,' I said, slurring. 'Or she will kill me.'

I collapsed into an unconscious state and stayed there for days. When I came to I was living with Philly. I did not speak to or see Mama for a year. We didn't live together for ten years.

14

With the Gods

Pearl's new room is everything I promised her: luxurious, small and tinged with death. She has some questions.

'How long is the average stay?'

'Three and a half years.'

Oscar's eyes roll to the back of his head. 'Do you have to be so brutal, Juliana?'

'I like to know the stats,' says Pearl. 'Most people who are into horses want to know the stats. You boys can kiss me goodbye now. I'll see you when you get back from Luxemburg. I want a few words alone with Juliana.' She gives Oscar a tight squeeze before he goes. 'I can't believe I have a son of sixty.' Then she swings her wheelchair towards me in a businesslike fashion.

'I'll come straight to the point. Am I ever going to see you again, Juliana?'

'I don't know.'

'That's what I thought. I'll wish you all the best for the future, then.'

Dog is allowed to visit so long as he does not stay overnight. He leans against Pearl's legs, watching, as our car pulls away. Joanie drives slowly down Auburn Street, Goulburn's main thoroughfare, where the drought has sent deep cracks through many of the town's elegant stone façades. Rain has peppered the land. There are hopeful spikes of grass. But without stock or crops, the farms seem hollow. Driving up the Federal Highway we see puddles of water in the vast expanse of Lake George. 'Don't be fooled,' says Joanie. 'That lake is full of mirages.'

At the airport in Canberra we tell her not to park. 'Drive on, drive on,' we say, and she glides away from us with a perfunctory wave. We are efficient at checking in luggage, waving our passports, negotiating security checks. I have trained myself not to start whenever Frederick uses his surname.

*

Philly visited Mama regularly during the year I didn't see her. Sometimes he visited her three times a week. Through Philly, I learnt of each new boyfriend. 'She has things so arranged,' he explained, 'that they must take her dancing, to the races and out for dinner at least once a week.' Some of the boyfriends were married, a romantic situation Mama had come to prefer. One of them was especially keen on racing and gave her a guest ticket for the members' area. There, her elegant appearance, her expensive jewellery, attracted more men.

'She's quite happy without me, then.'

'She worries you might forget Dutch,' said Philly. 'Otherwise she seems . . . adjusted.'

To say I didn't see Mama that year is not the technical truth. Sometimes I spied her from a distance: doing her shopping, boarding a tram, coming out of the hairdresser's. She had found a new hairdresser in Prahran who set her curls every Friday morning, enabling her to make a stunning appearance at Leggett's Ballroom that evening. Early on a Saturday she had a comb-up in preparation for her afternoon at the races. And every three months she dyed her hair to disguise the encroaching grey.

'She's comfortable with rituals,' Philly said.

Philly had returned from Cambridge with a love of English music and an admiration for the writings of Yukio Mishima. I read Mishima's *Forbidden Colours* with Elgar's cello concerto playing in the background. The sixties were the time of Joan Sutherland and Luciano Pavarotti, of Rudolf Nureyev dancing or doing almost anything. We were indifferent to The Beatles and The Rolling Stones. Philly expressed a mild interest in Bob Dylan because one of his lovers liked folk music. When that affair ended, so did Philly's interest in protest songs.

Philly's friends did not regard me with any special curiosity when they visited. 'Not getting on with Mama,' was how Philly introduced his new housemate.

I accompanied him to operas at the Princess Theatre. He'd walk through the entrance with me trailing after him, up and up, until we were with the gods. We sat so high up that Philly's head brushed the ceiling. We absorbed the grandeur of the chandeliers, the acres of decadent gilt. Mama went with Philly to operettas.

'Do you realise,' he said, 'that she saw *Die Fledermaus* with Julius Patzak in Vienna before the war?'

'Did she?' I affected boredom at anything to do with my mother.

Philly allowed me to work at Prince Henry's in school holidays and every third weekend during term. I was back to performing near the top of the class. He ensured I didn't tire myself out, making me lie in bed for half an hour and drink a glass of milk before starting on homework. He fussed over my school uniform, insisting my shirts be ironed and starched. He combed my hair into pigtails. And he reminded me constantly to be careful. 'It doesn't do for a schoolgirl to be living with a man twice her age, even if he is a poofter. The world wouldn't understand.'

'Mama understands,' I said.

'Your mother might not be able to explain to someone in authority quite what our relationship is.'

Quite what our relationship was wasn't clear to me.

One hot February day, when even the shadows seemed diminished, we were released from school the moment the mercury inched above a hundred degrees. I walked in the front door of Philly's cottage and threw my horrid straw hat down the passage. It landed near the Spanish trunk. I heard a record player in Philly's bedroom – Maria Callas as Tosca – and entered without knocking. A young man was bent over the bed. Philly was behind him. They were naked and the way the sweat shone on their hairy legs struck me as beautiful.

'Go away, Juliana!' Philly shouted. 'Can't you see I'm fucking someone?'

Oh, I thought, backing out, so that's how they do it.

When the young man left, Philly barged into my room. I was reading Mishima's *Confessions of a Mask*.

'Knock in future, will you?'

'You too.'

We glared at each other and collapsed laughing.

I thought about that scene in Philly's bedroom over the next few days. I had arrived home early that afternoon, but not that early.

Mama and I were bound to meet eventually. We lived almost round the corner from each other. I was driving along High Street when I saw her standing at a tram-stop in the rain.

'Want a lift?'

She hopped in casually. 'You are taking good care of the Daimler,' she said, looking around.

'I can still smell Papa's cigars when I clean the upholstery.'

She nodded. 'The leather needs looking after. *Ach*, this Australian sun. Everything dries out. You had better come to dinner on Sunday night. Bring Philly.'

'Mama,' I said, 'where's the Japanese ring?'

'Mrs Dikkertje borrowed it. Just for a week. I made her a red evening dress. Mr Dikkertje has a new job, something important, in the city, and they want to impress everyone at the company dinner-dance. It is good to see migrants become successful.' Mama frowned, and touched her bare left hand. 'My hand feels strange without Françoise's ring.'

'Please make sure you get it back, Mama. Some day I would like to have that ring.'

Sunday came around and Philly raided Uther's wine cellar. He bought a large box of chocolates to give to Mama. We dressed with care, Philly in sports trousers and a jacket he'd found in England, and me in white stockings, court shoes and my good going-out dress: a maroon A-line frock that ended above the knee. The bluebird brooch and the watch Papa gave me when I was little were still my only pieces of jewellery.

Unbeknownst to us, Mama had invited the Dikkertjes. They'd swapped their Volkswagen for a Holden, completing their transformation into real Australians. They had even managed to produce a round little boy.

'We thought our boy could call your mother Nanna,' said Mrs Dikkertje, the Japanese ring on her finger.

'Nanna! Nanna!' the fat bundle echoed.

'Please return that ring to Mama,' I said. 'It is a family heirloom.'

'Oh, that depends on,' Mr Dikkertje interrupted. He opened Philly's bottle of Grange '51 and proceeded to pour it into champagne flutes.

'I really think that wine ought to breathe a little,' Philly said. 'And – perhaps different glasses?'

'Ah,' said Mr Dikkertje, 'this Australian wine. Breathing does nothing for it. The wine you want to drink is French or German.'

Philly poured his wine from the champagne glass into a wine glass. I held out my palm until Mrs Dikkertje removed the ring. I put it back in its accustomed place, on my mother's hand, and Mama gave a little sigh. 'Look, Juliana,' she said, 'how my stamp collection has grown.' She brought out two new albums. 'These New Guinea bird ones will never be worth much. But the colours – so pretty.'

'You should put that silly bluebird brooch with those stamps,' Mrs Dikkertje giggled. 'So old-fashioned. So sentimental.'

'*Zo*, you are still a doctor?' Mr Dikkertje asked Philly.

'Yes,' said Philly, 'still looking after lunatics.'

The silences multiplied. Mama tried to fill them. 'The horses were all against me yesterday. Every horse I bet on was walking backwards.'

Mrs Dikkertje turned the subject around. 'Jan tells us, Julie, that you are living with Dr de Vere?'

'I am Juliana's guardian,' said Philly, 'according to her father's will.'

We watched Mr and Mrs Dikkertje tear a roast chicken limb from limb, feeding titbits to their open-mouthed child. When they were done Mrs Dikkertje said, 'We have brought the dessert. Black Forest cake. I am eating for two, you know. We are hearing the patter-pitter of little feet again.'

Philly stifled a laugh with a mouthful of cherry and cream.

'I think,' I said, 'you mean pitter-patter.'

'Oh, you are always correcting me, Julie. Just because you learnt to speak like you're something English. At least we are citizens of this country. Real Aussies. We have a Holden.'

Philly stood up. 'We must go. Juliana has schoolwork and I have an early start.'

We walked home, holding hands, the way we often did, not noticing the car cruising slowly along behind us. Then the car sped up and we saw the Dikkertjes' piggy faces.

'Bugger,' said Philly. 'Bugger. Bugger.'

The Dikkertjes rang the high school headmistress next morning to tell her I was living with a homosexual man. They rang Prince Henry's to report that Dr de Vere had a schoolgirl living with him. The hospital board was not interested. The school authorities were a different matter. A Victorian Education Department official came to see Mama. He found that whatever knowledge of English she might have possessed had deserted her. She showed him a bedroom where I supposedly slept. The de Vere family solicitors gave the headmistress a copy of Papa's will.

'Do you reside with this guardian, this Dr Philip de Vere, or with your mother?' the headmistress asked.

'My mother, of course,' I said.

'I'll be glad when you leave this school, Stolburg. You're a loner. An odd one.' She shuffled the papers on her desk. 'Whatever all this is about, you'll be gone in a few months. Make sure you get good results in the end-of-year exams.'

Mama came to Philly's house a few days later. 'This place could be tidier,' she said, lifting a pile of our clothes up off a chair. 'Well. This homo business the Dikkertjes are so worried about – I don't care about that. Juliana can't get pregnant. Is that not so?'

'It would be difficult,' Philly replied.

'And Juliana and I cannot live together,' Mama said. 'That is not the business of anyone else. If you give me a key I will make sure this house is kept nice.'

'I don't think,' Philly said when she left, 'your mama quite understands the nature of homosexuality.'

The usual rewards for conforming behaviour – being a prefect, house captain, form captain – never came my way at school. I hadn't made friends. Didn't develop schoolgirl crushes on teachers. My reports all said the same thing. *Inclined to be a loner.* On the last day of my school career the other girls rushed from staff room to staff room, leaving cards or presents for their favourite teachers. I drove off in Papa's Daimler without a backward glance.

I'd seldom attended school functions, but I made an exception, right at the end, for speech night at the Melbourne Town Hall. The headmistress called out my name from the rostrum and I went up to receive the book token that went with being school dux. Philly and Mama were sitting close to the front, and when I returned to sit next to them they both had tears in their eyes. 'You didn't tell me about this,' Philly whispered.

'Not that big a deal.'

The school choir sang 'You'll Never Walk Alone'.

'Bullshit,' hissed Mama. Her English was by now as proficient as it was ever going to be.

While the rest of the school swamped the auditorium and sipped orange cordial, we three slipped out onto Swanston Street, Philly's arms entwined between Mama's and mine.

I won places at Victoria's two universities. But the only financial assistance either of them offered was a Commonwealth scholarship or a teaching bursary. The bursary was generous enough but I had no wish to be a teacher. Without telling Philly I sat the public service exams, hundreds of us crowding into the government offices opposite the state parliament buildings. Before we began, we were told we might have to wait two years before being offered a position. Upon hearing this, some people walked out.

I enjoyed the day, a day of intelligence, mathematics and general knowledge tests. One of these tests I knew quite well. It was a psychological profile Philly used on his patients. *How often do you play sport? Tick the appropriate box. Two to four times a week? Less than once a week? Never?*

The examiners were looking for team spirit. I ticked *two to four times a week* and hoped they wouldn't want to know which sports. At the end of the day they asked if any of us were competent in other languages. I put up my hand.

A group of us were invited into another room. Once inside, we were put through language-based exams. My knowledge of Dutch got me through the German paper. Six years of Latin helped me guess most of the answers in the Spanish and Italian papers. Working in the diet kitchen, I had picked up a few Greek phrases. I was not examined in Dutch, my first language. When I queried the supervisor about this he said there was no need; I had topped the state matriculation results in that language.

One by one the other candidates were asked to leave.

'Sit outside,' the supervisor said to me.

For half an hour, I sat. When the supervisor returned he asked if I was prepared to come back the next day to a different place: Victoria Barracks on St Kilda Road.

'On a Sunday?'

'Australia is at war in Vietnam,' the supervisor replied. 'The Cong don't take Sundays off.'

The following day I was interviewed by men who did not introduce themselves. They wore civilian clothes but I could tell from their short hair and upright bearing they were soldiers.

'You have a talent for languages,' one of them said. 'Your score on the intelligence tests is above average. You're a loner. Self-sufficient. Your personality profile is a good fit for our purposes. Do you think you could learn an Asian language?'

'I am part-Japanese.'

The silence in the room was so intense I thought I heard dust motes colliding.

'How do you feel about the war in Vietnam?'

'The way I see it, the north invaded the south. I am not sure about Australia's involvement but I think the war may be justified.'

The men, as one, whoever they were, settled back in their chairs.

'How do you think you'd like working here at the barracks?'

'I like the old buildings.'

'Your psychological profile tells us you can be discreet. That's the sort of person we're looking for. Someone we can trust with sensitive material.'

Philly was horrified when I repeated the gist of the interview back to him. 'You didn't say that about Vietnam? Tell me you didn't!'

'I did say that. I need a job. A real job. Not a kitchen job.'

'You won a university place!'

'I need to support myself and my mother. The Department of Army will pay me while I go to university part-time.'

'What will you study? What faculty?'

'I'm going to study psychology and sociology. Living with a psychiatrist, I surely have a head start.'

'Dear God,' said Philly. 'What have I done? Am I going to come under their scrutiny? Do they know you live with a homosexual? And what are they doing recruiting an eighteen-year-old girl with a history of rheumatic fever?'

'I passed the medical. My heart wasn't murmuring. I didn't mention the rheumatic fever and they didn't ask.'

I did not tell Philly that his life had already been scrutinised, that my new masters knew I had been living in his house for nearly three years. I did not tell him that for the sake of my career, and his, I had been advised to find my own accommodation.

Becoming a public servant had a major benefit: Mama and I could more easily become Australian citizens. I did not want to give up my Dutch citizenship but to be an Australian public servant, I had to. And being an Australian citizen meant Mama could claim a widow's pension. Up till then she hadn't been eligible for any assistance. The formalities took place in the same office building where I'd sat the public service exams. Mama liked the parchment paper and the picture of Queen Elizabeth II on our naturalisation documents. She received her first pension cheque for sixteen dollars three weeks later.

★

The uniformed young men and women marching about with machine guns have transformed Amsterdam's Schiphol International Airport into a scary place. As well as the guns they have automatic pistols on their hips and, judging by the bulges near their boots, some form of weapon tucked into their socks. Oscar and Frederick are oblivious to these youngsters. But I have spent a lifetime specialising in, among other things, the psychology of those who should or should not be allowed to bear arms in defence of their own or someone else's country. I cannot help wondering how many bystanders, in the event of a shootout, might get caught in the crossfire.

'*Zo*, Skippy,' the man inspecting my passport says. He gives it a vicious stamp.

Nederlands geboren. Zo, je komt terug . . .

Dutch-born. So, you're back . . .

He says this as if I've been gone minutes.

'*U ben bedankt*,' I say to the man.

Oscar grins and Frederick looks puzzled as we head to the hotel taxi-bus. 'You haven't seen her in Dutch,' Oscar explains. 'She said to that guy: *you are thanked*. That's high Dutch. She could have said, informally, *dank je wel.*'

'I didn't know,' says Frederick to Oscar, 'that you understood Dutch. You never said.'

In our years in Europe, Oscar and I often flew to Amsterdam to go to the Concertgebouw and the museums. We found there was only one place to stay, *Oud-Zuid*, Old South, a neighbourhood of tall Edwardian houses roughly bordered by the Rijksmuseum, the Van Gogh Museum and the Vondelpark; far, far away from the red-light district and smelly canals favoured by the tourists. Our hotel is gay-friendly and directly behind the Concertgebouw. Tonight we are seeing the *Four Last Songs* of Richard Strauss.

'The irony of the songs is that they can only be sung by a voice in full possession of youthful vigour, yet they are all too often performed by singers past their prime.'

Not for the first time, Frederick has echoed something Philly once said.

★

Heeding the advice of my masters at the Department of Army, I moved into a place of my own. Kia Ora was a pre-war block of flats on St Kilda Road, and every day I walked through the double glass doors I breathed in the building's solidity, its permanence. My flat was on the second floor and had views to the park. It also had a second bedroom, for Philly. He kept his cottage in East Prahran, maintaining a pretence that he lived there. Really he lived with me at Kia Ora. The other tenants – gentlewomen who had run through their money but liked to keep up appearances – took no notice of our domestic arrangements. For entertaining guests, Philly and I set up a dining table in the wide entrance hall. Our friends thought that avant-garde.

Mama still went dancing and to the races. Occasionally she contacted the Dikkertjes in the hope they might return the money they owed her. Years of sewing were finally catching up with her and she complained of failing eyesight and constant backache. By the end of the 1960s we had saved up enough money for her to visit Oma and Opa. She cried for days after she returned to Australia. But she was steadfast. 'Europe is finished. I am never going back.'

Briefly, she'd met up with my aunt in The Hague. 'Not only has Katrien taken all the titles held by Siegfried,' she laughed, 'but she's revived a few that haven't been used for centuries. Never has a lady-in-waiting had so many titles.' Katrien was also deriving income from some of the family properties in Zeeland.

'What about Buitenrust?' I asked.

Mama shrugged.

Her beloved Opa died soon after. Mama was pleased to have seen him one last time and heartbroken to miss the funeral. In accordance with Jewish custom, he was buried within twenty-four hours of his death. Mama continued to write to Oma as regularly as ever, but the letters back from Flanders became more and more sporadic.

I was an odd one among the women working at 'Army'. The other women were overwhelmingly consigned to the typing pool and clerical duties, whereas I had officer equivalence and officers' mess privileges and time off to attend university. At the age of twenty I had my own office. A male soldier-cum-secretary sat outside, filtering those seeking access to me. Whenever I encountered other women – in the toilets, or walking between offices – they enthused over their flat-sharing arrangements, their marriages, engagements, babies. I earned enough money to live in my own flat and drove a big and fancy car (although the Daimler *was* getting old). I didn't have a boyfriend and wasn't interested in babies. The few vacancies that came up in my office were clerical ones and I was inundated with male applicants every time. Women did not wish to work for me.

I was part of a shadowy unit that shared intelligence with NATO – specifically the NATO cataloguing system, a vast database that was in the process of being computerised. My job required not only discretion but the ability to think logically, dispassionately. My first boss, a veteran of the occupation forces in Japan and Korea, drilled into me that an army marches on its stomach and its spare parts. 'If a guy can't fix a gun that's jammed, if he can't find the part to fix it, he's a dead man.'

Philly worried that our relationship was preventing me from meeting 'marriageable' men. I worried that our relationship was getting in the way of him finding a man he could love and spend his life with.

'All the men I meet are boring or married,' I said.

'All the men I meet are keen to experience a homosexual encounter,' Philly said. 'Other than that they are boring or married.'

On the day Brigadier Michael Munro was due to report to Victoria Barracks – opposite the Shrine of Remembrance, that odd construction Mama had once thought might be some pagan temple – the barracks hummed with excitement. Michael Munro was the youngest brigadier in the Australian army, a two-tour Vietnam veteran, handsome and unmarried. I looked up from my paperwork marked 'eyes only', sensing movement by the door. He was standing against the door-frame, one hand touching the lintel. His dark hair was within a breath of being too long to be considered of regulation length. His uniform had been altered by a tailor to flare less at the hips, emphasising his broad shoulders. The material was not too unforgivably tight around the crotch.

'I'm Michael Munro. If you are Miss Juliana Stolburg, I am your new master.'

'Sir,' I said, extending my hand.

'Call me Michael. May I sit? I like your office. Sparse. None of that feminine clutter. Yet . . .' He paused. 'This room could only be occupied by a woman. How fascinating. I've been reading your file. Impressive. I've put you in for promotion. I know you've been acting second–in–command. I am going to make that permanent. You'll be the equivalent of a major. How old are you, Miss Stolburg?'

'Twenty-two, sir.'

'Not bad.'

An unfamiliar noise in the passage: a child.

'Come here, rascal,' the handsome brigadier said. 'This boy who looks so agonisingly like me is my brother. Say hello to Miss Stolburg. The wretch sings in the St Paul's choir, if you please. So long as his voice doesn't break he's on a full scholarship at Trinity College. My parents had to pay full fees for me – not bright enough, and I certainly can't sing. Can I, Freddy?'

Frederick Munro, aged eleven, had a pubescent beauty that ought to have been captured by an artist. Black curls circled an oval face. He had knowing, disturbing eyes. Freddy shook my hand politely. But he wasn't interested in me. He worshipped his brother, couldn't take his eyes off him. They left my office and I watched from the window as they crossed St Kilda Road, bypassed the Shrine and headed for the Botanic Gardens. The little boy copied the way his older brother walked. It involved an exaggerated rolling of his slim hips.

By late afternoon my promotion had been made official. It was a different Michael Munro who returned to the barracks that afternoon.

Businesslike.

'Bring me up to speed on these projects.'

Ruthless.

'You've spent enough time on that. There are more urgent matters.'

Deadly.

'Cut that man loose. Put him on the ground. Either it will be the making of him or he will break — then he's no longer a concern of ours.'

Charming.

'Would you like to have a drink in the mess with me after work? I am quite safe around women.'

'I live nearby,' I replied. 'Perhaps you would like to come home with me? Have a drink there, sir?'

'Do I get to ride in that fabulous car I've heard about?'

'I walk to work. The Daimler is parked in the garage.'

'Give me the address. I'll be there once I've read a few more reports.'

Mama was at home with Philly. He was binding her thumb. 'The needle went through it,' she wailed. 'I tried ringing you but they said you were in conference and couldn't take calls. I am getting too old for sewing.'

She sobbed on Philly's shoulder. The doorbell rang. Mama straightened herself up. 'I must go. You have visitors.'

Philly looked at me. Usually we rang each other if there were to be guests.

'Mama,' I said, 'I'll take you home later. Wipe your eyes. I want you to meet this man, both of you.'

I expected Michael to have changed into civilian clothes. He was still in uniform. The soft lights of the sitting room made the red brigadier's braid on his lapels and around his cap stand out crimson. His brown eyes fastened on Philly. Philly blushed beneath the man's scrutiny.

'I'm Michael,' he said, holding a hand out to Philly, ignoring Mama.

'Dr Philip de Vere,' I interrupted. 'And this is my mother, Janna Stolburg.'

Michael Munro shook hands with Mama. His eyes stayed fixed on Philly.

Relax, Philly, be charming, urbane. Don't let him see how much you want him. Don't give him that power over you.

Mama and I left the men alone while we prepared drinks and nibbles. 'I don't like that Michael,' Mama said. 'He has a hard look.'

'He's been to Vietnam, Mama.'

'Bah. Your papa was in the war for five years. He never looked like that.'

We sat down to dinner at the table in the entrance hall. 'I love Tosca,' Michael Munro said. He had taken Philly's position at the head of the table. 'Don't tell the chaps at work I'm into opera, Miss Stolburg. Don't want them knowing I'm a poof.'

'Really don't approve of that word,' said Philly.

Michael tapped Philly's hand with the back of a spoon. He entertained us with stories of his war, with tales from Nui Dat, where the Australian taskforce was based. 'Guys had it in for this cook, a national serviceman. Poor bloke. He listened to the classical music station. Hated the rock channel. The camp stoves work on kerosene. One night the men put petrol in the stove instead of kero. Cook lit the stove and the kitchen tent blew up. Fellows were diving for cover all over Nui Dat. They thought the Cong had finally managed to drop a bomb on us.'

'What about the cook?' asked Philly.

'He was in hospital in Saigon for a couple of months. Knew who did it. Refused to dob them in. They sent him back to Nui Dat afterwards. I listed him as wounded in action. That'll help him later on – pensions and stuff. Hey, Stolburg, is your mother okay? Does she blab?'

'I am a graduate of the University of Dachau,' Mama said.

Michael didn't stay the night. I heard them shushing each other, the sound of a shower; noises I had heard for years. Philly slept in next morning. Usually he was at the hospital by seven. I brought him a cup of tea and a biscuit.

'Open the bloody window, Jules. Two men ejaculating – dear God. I think we might need new bed linen.' He looked exhausted. 'Didn't sleep a wink. Michael left about three, I think.' He yawned.

'Happy?'

'Mm. Do you know Munro means *peak*? Michael Munro is the apex. He is the one.'

I kissed Philly goodbye and walked to work, confident I had brought two people together.

'Stolburg! In here!'

Michael Munro had taken possession of his new desk the way he took possession of everything in his life. The only thing disrupting the desk's surface was a paper knife.

'Sit! Dr Philip de Vere has rung this office three times this morning. Do you have an explanation for that? It is not yet 0900 hours. You're late, by the way. I begin the working day at 0800.'

'I suppose Philly wanted to speak to you.'

'Why?'

'Surely?'

'Last night did not happen. Do you understand? I like to fuck men. I do not want to be involved in their lives.'

'But when you meet Philly's family . . .'

Michael Munro strode around the desk and sat in front of me, legs spread wide. 'Do you really think I want to meet Philip's family? Or that I want him to meet mine? Good God, woman, I wouldn't let a man like that anywhere near my brother.'

'Philly is not interested in young boys. Not even ones as pretty as your Freddy.'

'You may tell de Vere I will call on him from time to time. Dismissed.'

Half an hour later he was in my office. 'From now on,' he said, 'I want you to be ready at twenty-four hours notice. Keep a bag packed at all times. Philip and your mother cannot know the details of your journeys. Impress upon them that they must be discreet.'

'Philly. Philip is known to everyone as Philly.'

'Stupid name for a man.'

I didn't tell Philly the things Michael had said. They didn't make sense to me. 'Michael won't answer my calls,' Philly said that night. 'He used me as he would a prostitute.' I held my friend while he wept. I wished I'd never introduced him to Michael Munro. I believed that was the end of the matter. Philly would not allow himself to be abused.

15

History's a Bitch

Oscar and Frederick are raking over the performance of Strauss's *Four Last Songs* at a restaurant not far from the Concertgebouw. We discovered this place years ago. The food is unexceptional: variations on fish and chips. But the fish is the freshest in the Netherlands, the potatoes come in big floury chunks and the view down to the street below is unique. We eat and watch members of the orchestra ride off on bikes, instruments strapped to their backs. Oscar's favourite is the elderly gentleman hunched over the handlebars of his ancient bicycle, body doubled over beneath his double bass.

★

'I like to watch the people go by,' was the first reason Mama gave for not wanting to move in with me. Another flat, larger than mine, had become vacant in Kia Ora. 'Besides,' she added, feebly, 'I will be too far away from everything I know.'

We both knew the real reason. She was afraid of living with me.

'We'll share everything,' I said. 'Fifty–fifty. Flatmates.'

'Whoever is there for breakfast is there for breakfast,' she said, coming round to the idea.

Philly had another idea. He found a block of four flats on Toorak Road. Instead of renting, he proposed we buy the two on the top floor. That settled it. 'Whenever I get sick of Juliana,' Mama said excitedly, 'I can visit Philly. I will look after both flats. *Ach*, I will be so busy I won't have time to see what's happening on Toorak Road.'

To help with the deposit, she sold her Hitler stamps at auction. 'I always knew,' Mama said, 'that Hitler would be worth something one day.' Thirteen years after Papa's death I had finally acquired a piece of paper called a *mortgage*.

Michael Munro was transferred to Canberra. The Department of Army, along with the air force and navy, had been replaced by the Department of Defence. I inherited Michael's old job. Whenever he was in Melbourne he contacted Philly. If Philly made himself unavailable, Michael pursued him, convincing him that this time things would be different. Each time it ended in Philly's tears.

After a posting in the United States, Michael

brought back a new term – *gay* – and a new situation: *coming out of the closet*. He told us what they meant over dinner at one of South Yarra's many bistros. Other officers tended not to wear uniform outside work hours to avoid confrontation with people opposed to the war in Vietnam. Not Michael. Michael Munro was rarely out of uniform. It was as if he sought aggravation.

'*Zo*,' said Mama, 'this being gay and coming out of closets, what difference is it going to make?'

'It will lead to acceptance,' said Michael.

'*Ach*. You have to accept yourself first.'

★

Frederick is leaning against the door-frame, a hand touching the lintel. 'Tell us again why we're approaching your Middelburg sideways?'

Your brother used to stand like that, owning any and every room.

'Juliana likes to approach everything sideways,' says Oscar. 'All those years of being a spook.'

'I was never a spook,' I say. 'I dealt with sensitive matters from time to time.'

'Such as?'

'I don't recall.'

I long to return to Middelburg. I woke last night and thought I heard Nehalennia, the goddess of the sea, calling me.

The highlight of our three days in Amsterdam is a performance of Mahler's Fifth, with the Latvian Mariss Jansons conducting. To Frederick's irritation Oscar and I have booked seats on the podium, facing the conductor, almost within the body of the orchestra. The orchestral experience of these seats, we assure Frederick, is incomparable. In the quarter of an hour beforehand I soak up the names immortalised in gold leaf below the balcony. Among them is Gustav Mahler, whose conducting of his own works was said to be the most electrifying ever heard at the Concertgebouw.

Mariss Jansons is a slight man, physically unremarkable. He walks past our seats and with a quick bow to the audience takes his place facing the orchestra. He holds up his arms until there is total silence, and then he seems to grow, to become Mahler. With a nod he summons the opening trumpet call. His baton does not appear until the beginning of the funeral march. He exercises utter control of the orchestra: with his eyes, with a lift of the chin, with the whole of his body. There are no histrionics and no expansive gestures.

Mahler is supposed to have said of the Fifth: *I wish I could conduct the first performance fifty years after my death!* He died before the First World War, having written an elegy for a dead Europe.

At the conclusion of the performance Jansons pauses. He appears to be gathering strength, ready to accept a standing ovation. He turns around and looks at the audience, lowering his head to his knees to accept their adulation. Then he lifts his head back up and walks off past us. Emotionally shattered. Suit drenched with perspiration. The ovation goes on and on but the maestro does not return. Eventually the orchestra deserts the stage.

It is time we left, too.

I am content to see the palace at Het Loo through Oscar and Frederick's eyes, wandering behind them as they flit from room to room. They have no interest in Queen Wilhelmina's study. 'Such an ordinary desk!' They are more taken with Prince Hendrik's. 'Those antlers. Grotesque!' Since my last visit, a photograph – a gift from Katrien – has been placed on the desk. It is a picture of Prince Hendrik, Kaiser Wilhelm and my grandfather standing before the castle at Doorn. 'That's Siegfried,' I say to an empty room. Oscar and Frederick have moved on to the next.

We spend half a day at the Kröller-Müller, a private art gallery in the middle of a nearby forest. Helene Kröller-Müller, the daughter of German industrialists, was among the first collectors to buy the paintings of Vincent Van Gogh. The forest is a surprise to Oscar and Frederick. They see a place of beauty, a wild oasis in the heart of the Netherlands they had no idea existed. I see a battlefield where the Resistance and the Germans fought desperate battles. I see a place of misery where the citizens of Arnhem, driven away after the failed Allied offensive of 1944, tried to survive the starvation winter, the *Hongerwinter*, that followed. I see the beginning of the end of Walcheren. Had the Allies been successful at Arnhem, our island would not have needed to be sunk.

'We must go on to Luxemburg tomorrow,' Frederick reminds us that evening.

I have developed an inexplicable reluctance to see Luxemburg again. Oscar, the one who did not want to go back, is now eager to return. 'I wonder,' he says, 'if *the voice* is still up to his tricks in the cathedral. You'll be interested in this boy's voice, Frederick. All of Luxemburg was entranced by him.'

On the morning of our train trip from Arnhem to Luxemburg, I wake to a flooding period. It is the sort of event that cannot be staunched by tampons. Bulky pads are required. Before we get as far as Maastricht I have exhausted my supply.

'I must leave this train,' I say. 'There's something I have to do in Maastricht.'

'What?'

'Something I need to get.'

'Can't you get whatever it is in Luxemburg?' says Frederick. 'Not far now.'

'We will all stay with Jules,' Oscar overrules him. There is a softness in Oscar's eyes. 'Frederick, you and Jules go for a bite of lunch. I'll fetch what Juliana needs.'

Over an appalling cup of coffee at the railway station café, Frederick mutters to me, 'I don't understand you two.'

'Oscar has to find a pharmacist for me.'

'Some pills? You should have said so.'

Oscar returns with an enormous paper bag under his arm.

'Biggest pills I've ever seen,' says Frederick, and then, as I disappear into the toilets, I hear him say, 'Oh.'

Maastricht is another place Oscar and I know well. We came here often for concerts. We'd spend hours climbing the old town's hilly battlements. Before the next train leaves there is time to see the church of St Servaas, where there are gruesome relics that date back to Charlemagne's reign. I have been inside many times. I tell the men to go ahead. I rest in the courtyard beside a gigantic bell surrounded by flowerbeds. It was one of the few bells not taken by the Germans, spared on account of its decorative Hohenzollern eagles. In the peace of the ancient courtyard, the sun on my back, I feel a heaviness, a lethargy. The end is not far off.

Oscar appears next to me, and takes my hand. 'You're pale as a sheet. I thought all that business was over for you, Jules.'

'Menopause refusing to end nicely, that's all.'

'Anything to be concerned about?'

'Nothing I can't deal with.'

The event has ceased by the time we have travelled through Liege. Clervaux. Ettelbruck. Mersch. Then the city of Luxemburg. As we exit the station an old acquaintance recognises us. 'Jules! Oscar! How lovely to see you. Back for another posting?'

'Just visiting. Unfinished business. This is Frederick Munro. Oscar's partner.'

'Oh. Good luck, all.'

We are booked in at the Mercure Hotel, opposite the station.

'Madam Stolburg, ah, how nice to see you again. And Monsieur Oscar . . .'

'A single room for me, please. A double room for the gentlemen.'

'But of course, Madam.'

Once we're inside the lift Frederick ticks me off for being so blunt. 'Being blunt,' says Oscar, 'was the best way to circumvent gossip in Luxemburg, we always found.'

'If you two are so enamoured of all things Luxemburg,' Frederick says, 'I can't imagine why you ever left here. Or each other.'

'Temper, temper. Shall we take this boy to the cathedral, Jules? Or shall we punish him and go by ourselves?'

The rooms have bathrooms joined back to back. Frederick is singing while he showers: 'O Mio Babbino Caro', Oh My Beloved Father, a soprano's song and an odd choice for a man. His voice retains the clarity that made him an outstanding chorister at St Paul's nearly forty years ago. But it is devoid of the talent that might have turned him into a great tenor.

Two years after I met Michael Munro, the boy's voice broke. 'We're waiting to see if Freddy will be a tenor,' Michael said. 'We might have to wait as long as four years. My parents are desperate for him to have an operatic voice.'

Michael never mentioned his brother again. The boy did not have a voice, after all.

Oscar's voice has joined Frederick's. Their singing becomes something else and I close the door.

On the bridge over the Petrusse valley, Frederick hoists himself high on a wall. The slopes below us are covered in orange and blue flowers. At the bottom of the gorge a dreamlike city winds in tandem with the riverbed, ancient houses scattered along its banks. 'I didn't realise,' says Frederick, 'that Luxemburg would be like this.'

Across the other side of the bridge we follow the sound of the bells to Our Lady of Luxemburg cathedral. Although Oscar and I left six months ago, conversations resume as though we were in church last weekend.

'Who is the beautiful man?' someone asks.

'Oscar's partner.'

'Ah.'

The grand duke and his duchess take their seats in the balcony. A courtier hisses in my ear. 'Lady Juliana, Monsieur would be pleased if you would attend him.'

'I am not dressed formally,' I say. 'I am visiting Lux. I no longer work here.'

'Even so.'

With an encouraging wink from Oscar, I climb up to the balcony. The grand duke gives me the three times kiss. 'Sit by me. What have you been doing, Juliana Stolburg? What title have you decided to adopt?'

'Nothing much. Remembering. No title.'

The grand duchess leans over her husband. 'Juliana,' she says, 'who is that beautiful man next to your husband?'

'His partner.'

She is Cuban by birth and inclined to hiss.

The organ sounds the processional and the priests, acolytes, choirboys and choirgirls march in behind the bishop. The congregation rises. A collective sigh travels round the church as *the voice* sings the opening notes of the Kyrie. Oscar and I tried to hear this boy as often as possible. His antics as much as his voice enthralled us. His hair has grown. It reaches down

317

to his waist. The black fall is parted in the middle. Diamonds glint in the lobe of each ear. His eyes, as he sings, cast a spell.

See how gorgeous I am.

I could have any of you, man or woman, if I chose.

His lazy, effortless talent is infuriating, beguiling. When the old bishop croaks on a note the boy covers for him. *The voice* — somewhere between a boy soprano and an alto — soars over the congregation, drowning and absorbing all.

The grand duchess whispers, 'We have discovered his name is Valentin.' At that moment *the voice* casts his liquid eyes on her. '*Diablo,*' she mutters. The boy's face has a triangular, feline quality.

I glance down at Oscar. He is looking all around him, taking in the scene. He has heard *the voice* many times, and while admiring the boy's talent he is otherwise unaffected. Frederick, I see, has inched forward in his seat, slightly hunched over. I have seen him sit like that before, concentrating, listening to voices at the Sydney Opera House.

Don't allow their eyes to meet.

But I am begging an absent God. Slowly, as if drawn by a magnet out of hell, Frederick's eyes rise and he stares at Valentin. The boy stumbles, falls silent for a moment, resumes singing. At first Oscar is unaware. Then he casts an anguished look up at me.

★

'History's a bitch who keeps repeating herself,' Philly said when he came back from a holiday with Michael

Munro. They had gone to Bali, travelling separately, staying in different hotels. Philly waited for Michael all one night and the whole of the next day. 'He came, we made love, and now I've got some bloody thing he picked up from fucking a rent boy. I'm done with him, Juliana. He's a predator.'

A month later Michael rang Philly to say he was getting married. The girl was the daughter of a colonel. Michael told Philly he did not love the girl but marriage would be good for his career prospects. He wanted to rise to become a full general, and he thought the senior ranks were prejudiced against him because of rumours about his sexuality. I was working among the senior ranks by then. I knew they despised his hypocrisy, not his sexuality.

Philly played the funeral march from Wagner's *Götterdämmerung* over and over until the record was scratched.

★

Oscar and I walk back to the hotel, just the two of us. 'Frederick,' he explains, 'wants to speak to *the voice*, find out if he is a music student, if he is having voice coaching. He won't be back tonight.' The man walking by my side in the fading spring light has to be coaxed across the cracks in the pavement. He might as well be blind.

I am waiting in the hotel lobby when Frederick comes in at dawn. He starts when he sees me. He looks all of the fifty-one years he has been allowed to live on this earth.

'Follow me, please,' I say.

He sits opposite me in a plush booth in the dining room and waits obediently for coffee to be brought out. Waiters are setting tables ready for breakfast.

'Why are you up so early, Juliana?' His tone is light, unconcerned.

'I was waiting for you.'

'How melodramatic. This is none of your business.'

'No? I will not allow you to destroy Oscar.'

'Oscar knows I need space sometimes.' He looks about: at the ceiling, the tops of the windows, through the doorway out to the lobby. 'I should probably go to him.'

'He's sleeping. Finally. He was devastated when you didn't come back last night.'

'I was talking to *the voice*. Time got away.' Frederick rises. 'I think I will go upstairs.'

'Sit down.'

'For God's sake, Juliana.'

'A great friend of mine was hurt by your brother.'

'By *Michael*?'

Now I have his attention.

'I have no idea what you're talking about.'

'You and I met once,' I say. 'You were a child. Eleven, I think. I was twenty-two. Surely your brother mentioned Philly?'

'Philly?' Frederick's face crinkles. 'Do you mean Philip, the psychiatrist? He was a friend of Michael's. Nothing more.'

'More than that. Much more.'

Frederick blushes.

'Bad luck for your parents,' I say. 'Two sons, both gay. Michael was my master for a while. I introduced him to Philly. I kick myself every day for that. Do you know what Michael did?'

Frederick's head shakes. 'Michael's been dead thirty years. He was my hero. Can't you let it be?'

'I won't let you do to Oscar what your brother did to Philly. This morning Oscar and I are going to Vianden, to the castle in the clouds where my ancestors came from. Join us. There is something I want you to see. Tomorrow Oscar will accompany me to Middelburg and you can do whatever you want to do with *the voice*. Sort out whatever it is you have to in Luxemburg. Then come to us at Buitenrust.'

I fling a scrap of paper at him with the address on it.

Rage makes his nostrils flare.

'I do not want to go with you to this bloody castle. Or to your Middelburg. I have an appointment with the director of the Philharmonie. I'm tired and I want to go to bed.'

'That boy, *the voice*, is eighteen at most. I am not surprised you're tired. Sore too, probably. You're over fifty, Frederick. Still a beauty, but that will fade.'

The train is ready to pull away. At the last second Frederick leaps aboard. We see him walking along the corridor, searching for our compartment. 'To Vianden, as commanded,' he says. He has not seen Oscar since the previous evening. All the way to Vianden they do not speak, just gaze out the window at different parts of the scenery.

Vianden is shrouded in clouds. Frederick looks at the picturesque river that drawls through town. Buildings hug the water, reminiscent of a time when the river, not the road, was the main traffic artery. 'Well, where is this bloody castle?'

Oscar, with a gentle smile, points heavenwards. The clouds part obligingly. Frederick cranes his head right back to take in the great heft of the castle as it looms above the little town. 'Oh,' he says. 'Shit.'

'That's what I said the first time Juliana brought me here.'

The castle is a kilometre up in the air. It is possible to reach the gates by driving up the steep and winding road. But walking is more interesting. We are too early for any of the cafés clinging to the route. Halfway up we come to a twelfth-century church: a simple, Catholic place of worship. Inside is a statue, supposedly an early Stolburg duke. Before the altar is the crypt of a woman. A sculpture – the woman's likeness – lies on top of the crypt, feet pointing at the altar. The woman's features have worn away. Her name was Juliana Stolburg. She died some five hundred years ago.

The orange and purple flowers I have with me are not for this Juliana, my namesake, but for my grandfather Siegfried, who lies in the crypt beneath her sarcophagus. I have never brought him flowers before. This is a farewell of sorts. I may not pass this way again.

The castle is treacherous. Some of the more

perilous staircases have been blocked off. Tourists are not allowed to wander at will but must follow the signposts. In one of the armouries is an object most fascinating and horrible, a chastity belt, with a spike that was inserted into the vagina. If by some remote chance its wearer managed to have sex and conceive while her lord was away at the crusades, any child descending the vagina would have its skull pierced. A DNA test has been performed since Oscar and

I were last here and on a small square of paper are the results. Menstrual blood, faeces, calcium and foetal tissue were found. Frederick looks as if he might throw up.

My favourite part of the castle is a colonnaded open-air walkway. The surrounding countryside, all the way to Germany, makes for a majestic sight. This castle was besieged many times but proved impregnable. Time, ultimately, defeated the fortress. After several centuries it was abandoned in favour of more modern palaces.

From the edge of the walkway is a sheer drop. There are no security guards or cameras up here. I climb a narrow staircase, through a narrow doorway and onto the highest battlement. My feet dangle on a loose stone no wider than a house brick, a kilometre of nothingness below.

'Papa used to call me monkey,' I say to Frederick, who has followed me. 'No fear of heights.'

He looks down and shakes his head, as if to free himself of the dizzying depths.

'Was Michael a spy?'

'Yes.'

'Were you?'

Lunch, at a restaurant in town, is uncomfortable. Oscar and I have dined here before and recommend the trout to Frederick. When the fish arrives it tastes like sawdust.

Oscar does not notice the ruin that is Wallonia as our train speeds through Belgium. At Brussels he organises our luggage like an automaton. As my heart begins its beat – *Walcheren! Walcheren!* – the dead man beside me sees and feels nothing. I point out various landmarks. He sees only the inconsequential: how fat the sheep are; a pear orchard. 'I didn't know pears grew here,' he says.

The train commences its long and thrilling entry into Middelburg, the city gradually unfurling alongside the great canal. 'Buitenrust,' I say to the driver at the taxi rank. He deposits us at the gates. 'This place is a wreck. No one here.'

'Look,' I say to Oscar, 'those are the gatehouses. We lived in that one, and Siegfried and Françoise in the one opposite.'

Oscar smiles at me.

We enter the manor house, where even a dead man cannot fail to admire the inherent grandeur, despite the curtainless windows, the peeling paintwork. The house has been thoroughly cleaned. Without the scatterings of bird shit and plaster dandruff, the bones of the building are revealed. We amble from room to room, our feet echoing behind us. Oscar says nothing until we reach the top-floor room I slept in last time, where the sunlight streams in from two sides. 'This is lovely,' he says.

He does not reproach me for creating a sort of nest on this floor, when the kitchen and only working bathroom are four storeys below. 'I would have chosen this room, too,' he says. The power has been connected since my last visit. There are tea bags, a jar of coffee and that is all. I am reluctant to leave Oscar alone. Obediently, like an aged dog, he walks beside me to the supermarket. He does not offer any suggestions as to what we might eat. On the walk home he insists on carrying everything. Someone has left a box of fresh vegetables for us in the kitchen.

'The farmer,' I explain, 'who has been looking after this place.'

'Nice of him.'

That night Oscar lies on his back next to me, not sleeping. Towards dawn I am woken by a sound above. Oscar has found the trapdoor and is standing on top of the tower, clutching the railing, a soft wind ruffling his hair. His tall shape in front of the rising sun reminds me so much of Philly that my heart contracts.

He turns to me. 'You were talking in your sleep. *Philly*, you were saying, *Philly*.'

'Come away from the railing. I'm not sure it's safe.'

He points to the German bunkers. 'How could your mother stand those excrescences?'

'She couldn't. Being made to live in the gatehouse must have been like being tortured all over again.'

'Don't worry,' Oscar says, 'I won't jump. I heard rain in the night. If I were to hit the ground my body would bounce and leave me crippled but not dead.'

'Frederick will come to you. I am sure of it.'

He pulls me to his chest and holds me. The wind whistles around us.

'You've said so little about this island in all the years we've been married. Tell me about Philly and your mother. Complete the last chapter. It's always been Philly, hasn't it?'

16

Dinosaur

On Toorak Road the double brick of our 1930s building kept out street noises. Large windows framed a bustling panorama folding and unfolding in the 'village' below. Mama found it funny that we lived in a ghetto called Toorak Village. 'So silly,' she said, 'all this English decoration on the buildings, when most of the people living here are Jews.' She set up the Singer sewing machine in front of the French windows of the living room. On the balcony and in the stairwell she created pot-plant gardens. She shopped in Toorak Village for our two households, complaining that the Austrians who ran the patisserie were making her fat with their delicious cakes. She sewed clothes for herself so that she was decently dressed for the races and for dancing. But she no longer sewed for a living. She had time to read and to work on her stamp collection.

'I am happy,' she said one day.

One of our first big purchases was a Dutch bookcase at an antiques auction in Richmond. Philly scoffed at the green curtains behind glass, which hid the books.

'How bourgeois,' he said. 'Remove them at once.'

Mama demurred. 'Calvinists keep their books behind curtains.'

'Siegfried didn't,' I reminded her.

'*Ach*, Siegfried was different.'

The curtains remained, concealing Mama's complete collection of Émile Zola's works. She still had boyfriends who sometimes stayed for breakfast. They were discouraged from intruding on our lives. From time to time, she fussed that, at twenty-seven, I didn't have a boyfriend. 'You and Philly . . . *Ach zo.*'

I was involved in a project that required me to fly to Canberra every week. Sometimes up and back the same day. Other times I stayed overnight. Mama was proud of me doing something so glamorous as flying to the capital of Australia for my job and told the downstairs neighbours I was part of something 'top secret'. The project was classified but mundane, in truth, involving the logistics of moving the Australian taskforce's equipment from Vietnam to Singapore rather than shipping it back home. When I had to go to Singapore for a month, Mama was beside herself. 'I won't tell anyone,' she promised. She waved from the balcony as a car with a defence-force flag picked me up to take me to Laverton airbase. 'That's my daughter!' she shouted to one of her cronies across the road. 'She's going to Singapore. Top secret!'

Philly was offered a six-month research position at Harvard. We encouraged him to go. 'Please God, he will meet someone else other than that Michael,' Mama said.

'I thought you didn't believe in God.'

'*Ach*, there are so many Jews in Toorak mentioning God; now and then doesn't hurt.'

In nine years at Defence I'd had no more than a few days off. I applied for leave over Christmas and all of January so that Mama and I could finally see something of Australia. Mama, true to character, relished the planning, the buying of maps, the calculating of distances. In her forays into Toorak Village she asked everyone she knew what sights we ought to see. Every night I returned home to a newly amended must-see list.

The Daimler was at last showing its age, with rust spots at the bottom of the doors. The suspension was no longer smooth and the steering was getting heavier and heavier. But I couldn't bear the thought of retiring it just yet. Papa's Daimler, I decided, deserved a motoring holiday as much as we did.

Philly left for the United States in early December. I drove him to Tullamarine Airport. As we parted, he said to me, 'Michael has a US posting. Perhaps, finally . . .'

'Michael has a wife,' I said.

'That's going to be all over soon.'

As he loped away to board his aeroplane, I noticed that his fine blond hair had become thinner and carried the first streaks of grey. He was forty. He looked older. A copy of Mishima's *Confessions of a Mask* peeped out from under one arm.

On Christmas Eve we rose early and packed the Daimler, heading out of Melbourne along the Hume Highway. Mama was in raptures when we stopped for coffee at a roadside lay-by and saw kangaroos. We ate a Christmas dinner of cold chicken and salad in a caravan park at Narrandera. Our caravan was the furthest away from the others. We turned our backs on the other campers and pretended we were alone in the middle of genuine, Australian bush. The previous evening we'd been corrected for mispronouncing the name of this place, putting the emphasis on the wrong syllable. Over the following few weeks we mispronounced and misunderstood nearly every town we came across. Narrabri. Gunnedah. Goondiwindi. Murwillumbah . . . All of them would defeat us.

Mama had never been to Canberra. We visited the building where a bushy-browed Labor prime minister now ruled. We drove past Yarralumla, the place where governors-general spoke on behalf of the English Queen. At Russell Offices a guard recognised me and saluted. In reality, I think he was saluting Papa's Daimler, but he made Mama happy.

I took her to lunch in the officers' mess. As I was collecting our drinks the general who was my direct boss asked me who the beautiful woman was.

'That's my mother. Would you like to meet her?

Her English is erratic and she's obsessed with racing.'

The general came over to our table. 'I am a friend of your daughter's.'

Mama eyed his uniform. 'I think you must be her boss?'

'We work together.'

The general had been in the Netherlands during the war. 'I was at Operation Market Garden in Arnhem,' he said.

'My husband and Prince Bernhard told Churchill and Eisenhower it was madness to go into the Netherlands then.'

'A terrible failure. Terrible. I'm honoured to meet you, ma'am. I have to go back to work now. See you after the holidays, Juliana.'

'Did you hear that, Juliana? He called me ma'am.'

On the way to Sydney we stopped in Goulburn for afternoon tea at the Paragon Café. In the cool green park opposite, children splashed in the fountain and wide-canopied trees blanketed the area in shade. The tropical colours of northern New South Wales took us by surprise. We gorged ourselves on mangoes and avocadoes. We celebrated my twenty-eighth birthday with a counter lunch at a pub in Casino. 'This is the real Australia,' Mama said. On the wall of the ladies' lounge were Hans Heysen prints. A group of bikies were behaving badly in the front bar.

'*Ach*, remember Jack's motorbike, Juliana? We had some fun on that, didn't we?'

'Papa looked so handsome,' I said, 'in his leather coat. Remember, Mama, how he always wore that leather pilot's helmet and that long coat?'

'And goggles! Remember the goggles?' Mama laughed. '*Ach, lieve Jack.*'

'I loved the sidecar.'

She laughed again. 'You never really had a pram. You had the sidecar, Siegfried's horses and Papa's boat. *Aapje.* A monkey. That was you.'

Outside Southport, on a two-lane highway, from a distance that seemed miles and miles away, I saw a lone motorbike coming towards us in our lane. To avoid him I swerved into his lane at the same time as he must have realised he'd drifted. We both made the wrong decision. In the seconds before impact I was able to swing the Daimler around, but not far enough. Never far enough.

The motorcyclist and I were physically unscathed. Mama was killed instantly.

★

'Lady Juliana!' A man is waving frantically at us. 'I have found something,' he says. It is the friendly farmer who has been looking after Buitenrust. I introduce him to Oscar. The farmer apologises for his poor grasp of English, then with only the hint of an accent tells us that while he was removing some overgrown bushes he discovered a coffin. 'I wanted to tell the Lady first,' he says, 'before calling the police.'

The farmer takes us to a spot near his boundary. The bushes were suckering, he explains, causing a nuisance on his land. The coffin is partly sticking out.

The wood has rotted in the damp soil. In one corner I see a metallic glint. I reach for the shovel; it reveals a plaque, made of lead, of the rising sun.

'This is the body of my grandmother,' I say. 'Françoise Stolburg. Papa intended this to be a temporary burial place.'

★

In the police car on the way to Southport Hospital one of the police officers asked me how much I earned. I told him.

'Jeez,' he said.

At the hospital I was interviewed by an inspector. I explained about the motorbike rider being in the wrong lane to start off with.

'He's denying he was ever in your lane. He says you were in his lane all along. I'm inclined to believe you, not him. You wouldn't have swerved a heavy car like that unless you had to. Your Daimler's a write-off, by the way.'

'I killed my mother. Nothing else matters.'

'They told you she's dead, did they?'

'I could see that for myself.'

'Right. Right. The bloke that brought you in reckons you're a hotshot in Defence. Is there someone you want me to ring? Family? Boss?'

'No.'

'Well, you get some shut-eye and I'll look in on you in the morning.'

A nurse brought me Mama's valuables: her wedding ring, a necklace, her handbag. The ring had a speck of blood on it. The band, I noticed, had become thin in one place.

I couldn't call Philly. The hospital didn't allow international calls. I couldn't ring Oma in the Netherlands to tell her Mama was dead. I needed to hear the sound of my first language. Dutch. I rang the Dikkertjes.

'Oh, how tragic. Of course we will help. Is there a spare key to the flat? With the neighbours downstairs? Very sensible. We will organise a funeral. Don't worry, we are Jan's oldest friends. Trust us.'

When a nurse arrived with a tray of pills I grabbed at them.

*

The discovery of Françoise's grave has given Oscar purpose. The police and my lawyer arrive together, followed by a Middelburg council official. There is a long discussion about where the rotting casket should be taken. A group of burly men try lifting it out of the ground but it is held fast by mud. Eventually a crane is brought onto Buitenrust land. With a sucking sound the coffin is hoisted onto a ramp and into a hearse. The dirt is quickly shovelled back into the hole.

Oscar is almost cheerful, suggesting we eat at a restaurant in the Heerengracht, not far from my parents' and grandparents' homes.

'You're strangely calm,' he says to me. 'I'd have thought finding Françoise like that would upset you terribly.'

'Françoise died in 1953.'

★

I woke from my narcotics–fuelled sleep positive that the Dikkertjes had ransacked our flat on Toorak Road. Berating myself for my insanity in ringing them, I packed my few belongings into a paper bag, walked out of the hospital and caught a taxi to Coolangatta Airport.

'What happened to you?' the taxi driver asked.

'Nothing. Why?'

'There's blood coming out of your ear. And your right eye is filled with blood. Here. Look in the mirror.'

I was as he described.

'Must have hit my head.'

'Think you should see a doctor?'

The next flight to Melbourne was leaving later that day. I waited. The vision in my right eye flickered. I rang Mr and Mrs Dikkertje asking them to pick me up from Tullamarine. Mr Dikkertje answered.

If you say that depends on I will kill you.

When I arrived in Melbourne they were nowhere to be seen. I stood out the front of the terminal, wondering what had possessed me to call them. Just as I was about to climb into a taxi they drove up. Mrs Dikkertje poured herself out of the vehicle.

'Look, Julie, we have a new car. Do you like it?'

'My mother has just died.'

I got into the taxi.

The flat on Toorak Road was hideously empty. The dripping of the kitchen tap echoed through every room. I saw Mama's shadow in the mirror above the settee. I heard Mama's and Philly's voices, they were arriving home together; then I realised the voices came from the street. The Singer sewing machine in front of the French windows had a new, insistent rhythm.

You killed her. You killed her.

I got through to the pub in Oma's village in Flanders and asked someone to fetch the old lady, saying I would ring back in ten minutes. The years had not improved my Yiddish–Flemish. It took a long while to make Oma understand I was ringing from Australia.

'Juliana?' she said. 'Juliana?'

'*Moeder is dood. Moeder is dood.*'

'*Got! Got!*'

Then the phone cut out.

My head was spinning. I had to call Philly. Before I could lift the receiver the phone rang.

'Can you come, Jules? Please. I need you. Can you come to America?'

'Philly,' I mumbled.

'He's left me. Michael's left me. It's all over for good this time. I don't think I can bear it. Please come, Jules.'

I could hear the funeral march from *Götterdämmerung* playing in the background.

'Philly, you don't understand, something's happened to Mama. I'll come when I can.'

And then the phone cut out again.

I fell asleep on the settee. When I came to, the armrest was covered in blood. The front of my shirt was also bloody. At first I thought it was Mama's but in the shower blood flowed from my ear. I turned the water to cold and stood under it until I felt less groggy.

I had a funeral to arrange. I called Philly's parents. Morgana answered. Her voice sounded distant. Flat.

'Juliana. I thought you were in Queensland.'

'It's Mama . . .'

'Philly is dead, Juliana. Our beautiful boy has committed suicide. Uther and I are flying to Boston to bring back his body.'

★

It is the middle of the night and Oscar is standing in front of the window, wearing only his underpants, his thin body outlined by the moon.

'I am sure Frederick will come back.'

'I don't think I could bear it if he doesn't.'

Oscar lets me lead him back to bed, where he cries himself to sleep.

The wonder of the clouds that dance above this island, the breathlessness of the light, will be with me until the end of days. Oscar's head is on my chest. I wonder if he can feel my irregular heartbeat. Perhaps it's these stairs, climbing up and down four flights, that causes my heart to jump. Perhaps it's the legacy of rheumatic fever finally catching up with me.

Sunlight through the windows, from east and south, casts shadows on the wooden floor. Oscar stirs.

'I smell bacon and eggs.'

I smell them, too, rising four floors. We dress quickly and creep downstairs.

'Hello, you two.'

It's Frederick, in the kitchen, cooking.

'Thought I'd surprise you. Great house, Juliana. Must be forty rooms. All empty. How are you going to fill them all?'

Don't, Oscar, let him see how desperate you were for his return.

Don't give him that power over you.

'How did you get here so early?' asks Oscar, casually.

'Hired a car. Can't think why you two are so mad about trains.'

'When did you leave Luxemburg?'

'Midnight. Belgium is best seen by dark. Middelburg's a bit trickier; no cars allowed in the middle of the city. When I got to your castle, Juliana, I walked around the back and there was this box of marvellous eggs and bacon and the freshest bread. You've obviously got the locals well trained. And *the voice*, before you ask, did not translate beyond the cathedral. Just another young man singing too far ahead of himself. That voice will have disappeared by the time he's thirty.'

'Well,' says Oscar, 'fancy that. We've had our share of excitement, too, you know. The body of Juliana's grandmother turned up in the grounds.'

★

Mama was buried next to Papa at Springvale Cemetery on a blazing January day. A crowd gathered at the graveside. I'd rung everybody in her address book, people who had met her through the races, through ballroom dancing, lives she had touched in a small way. I asked the rabbi from the Great Synagogue in Toorak to officiate at the lowering of the coffin. Most of the people there were surprised when he mentioned that she had been in Dachau. To the end she maintained her resolve to never speak of her experiences.

The Dikkertjes did not attend the funeral. There was no one from Philly's family; they had all gone to America.

I went back to our flat and began packing. Not that I knew where I was going. I just knew I had to leave Toorak Road. I didn't speak to anyone at work about the accident – or Philly's death. I caught meaningful looks sometimes. I began to behave oddly, even to myself: misplacing my attention in meetings, distracted by black shapes skulking at the corners of my vision. A few weeks after Mama's death I stood to speak at a conference. A blinding headache stole my words. I couldn't read the black words typed on white pages. And then, nothing. Later, in hospital, I could not remember anything beyond that act of standing and preparing my mouth to speak.

'You have a subdural haematoma. You probably hit your head on the driver's side window when your car crashed. We'll have to operate to relieve the pressure.'

Go ahead. Bore a hole in my skull. Hope I die before I wake.

During the operation they found scar tissue. 'You must have fractured your skull,' said the neurologist, 'perhaps when you were very young. There is a weakness there. The anaesthetist became quite concerned about your heart murmur while you were under.'

'My heart has murmured since I was a child.'

'Well, you'll be all right now. Cheerio.'

Cheerio. With half the hair on my head missing, I resumed packing. The last room I entered was Mama's. Her ballroom dancing dresses sprang from the cupboard, as if she was about to step into them.

Can you zip me up?

The little cupboard in the dressing table where she kept her precious things was locked. The key rattled awkwardly. When the door flew open the cupboard was empty. The Dikkertjes had taken Mama's stamp albums and jewellery. Then I saw something, at the back, a tiny glint. Sapphires and diamonds. Mrs Dikkertje had never liked the bluebird brooch. I laughed and then I cried.

Mama had already sold the valuable Hitler stamps and those she hadn't were pretty but worthless. I regretted the loss of her diamond brooches. They had been a constant reminder to Mama that she was happy once, before the war. The ring given to Françoise by the Meiji emperor did not have great monetary value; it was the story that was priceless. The Dikkertjes would not have known that story. I rang the police. They searched the house in Blackburn. Nothing was ever found.

In his will Philly left me everything he owned. I had not realised he was a wealthy man. His family challenged the will. I didn't contest. Morgana sent me Philly's copy of Mishima's *Confessions of a Mask*.

Inside the back cover was a yellow fare chit from the Massachusetts Bay Transportation Authority. The only sentence underlined in the whole book is this:

You're nothing but a creature, non-human and somehow strangely pathetic.

The yellow chit has never faded.

Towards the end of that year, 1975, the Labor government was dismissed from office and a government of a different persuasion took its place. This momentous event passed me by; I had relocated to Canberra and become the ultimate public servant, able to be trusted with great secrets.

That same year, three years after the Americans and her allies departed, the government of South Vietnam fell. Secrecy and rumour surrounded the final moments of one of the last Australians to die there. An eyewitness reported that a man was standing on the wing of a plane loaded with orphans, waiting to take off for Australia. Something attracted his attention. There was shouting from the crew. The man remained on the wing, facing a sniper whom the eyewitness thought might have been a woman. Slowly Brigadier Michael Munro stretched out his arms as if welcoming death. There were two shots from a powerful pistol. His body slid from the wing as the plane carrying the orphans took off.

As a final homage to Philly's love for this man, I made sure that Michael's family believed he died a hero.

That awful year was also the last time I visited Singapore. I thought it best to dispose of Papa's gun. I pulled it apart and tossed the pieces into the sea off Penang, keeping only a small circle with the initials J.S.

★

Oscar and Frederick are returning to Australia by a circuitous route taking in Vienna, Salzburg and Paris. We eat our final meal together at a card table in the ballroom at Buitenrust and get drunk on expensive champagne. I wear a black dress and the black pearl suite. Black on black. The bluebird is pinned to my shoulder.

Oscar puts on *Die tote Stadt* and my favourite aria: *My sighs, my tears*. Frederick asks me about the pearls. I tell him everything I remember, all the legends ascribed to this treasure wrested from the sea.

'You're a dinosaur, Juliana, nibbling on the lawn of history.'

'Quite right,' I say. 'The last dinosaur.'

Next morning I watch from the tower as they pack Frederick's hire car. From a distance Oscar is so much like Philly. Dear, dead Philly. As they turn into the road skirting Middelburg, the men wave as one and don't look back.

Shadows envelop Buitenrust and tendrils of dew bless my bare feet as I walk through the park. The farmer has planted a tree over the spot where Françoise lay sleeping for so long. Her son Justien still sleeps there, wrapped in the soil of Walcheren. A bullet is lodged in his heart and one in his skull.

The sky is azure but grey clouds are scudding.

'The weather never stands still in the land of the sea,' I hear myself say.

Suddenly I long for the hard blue light of Australia.

Acknowledgements

I am grateful to Peter Rose for his initial reading of this novel. At all times Peter gave generous advice and was available when I needed someone to talk to. My agent, Mary Cunnane, guided this project when it was little more than disconnected episodes. Thank you, Mary.

Rod Morrison, the Picador publisher, was not only brave enough to provide a home for this work – but to say, 'You have to rewrite this, Elisabeth, and it will take as long as it takes.'

In a late reading, Christopher Menz pointed out a crucial deficiency in the manuscript. Thank you, Christopher, for your friendship and support throughout.

Christian Ryan was a brilliant and meticulous editor. *Met hartelijk dank.*

Finally, Rob, for everything.